HANDBAGS
AND
HOMICIDE

HANDBAGS
AND
HOMICIDE

DOROTHY HOWELL

KENSINGTON BOOKS
http://www.kensingtonbooks.com

KENSINGTON BOOKS are published by

Kensington Publishing Corp.
850 Third Avenue
New York, NY 10022

All Kensington titles, imprints, and distributed lines are available at special quantity discounts for bulk purchases for sales promotion, premiums, fund-raising, educational, or institutional use.

Special book excerpts or customized printings can also be created to fit specific needs. For details, write or phone the office of the Kensington Special Sales Manager: Attn. Special Sales Department. Kensington Publishing Corp., 850 Third Avenue, New York, NY 10022. Phone: 1-800-221-2647.

Kensington and the K logo Reg. U.S. Pat. & TM Off.

Library of Congress Card Catalogue Number: 2008924424
ISBN-13: 978-0-7582-2374-6
ISBN-10: 0-7582-2374-9

First Printing: July 2008
10 9 8 7 6 5 4 3 2 1

Printed in the United States of America

To David, Stacy, Judy, and Seth.

Acknowledgments

The author is extremely grateful for the wit, wisdom, knowledge, and emotional support of many people. They are: David Howell, Judith Howell, Stacy Howell, Seth Branstetter, Martha Cooper, Candace Craven, Lynn Gardner, Diana Killian, Tanya Stowe, and William F. Wu, Ph.D. Many thanks to Evan Marshall of the Evan Marshall Agency, and to John Scognamiglio and the talented team at Kensington Publishing for all their hard work.

CHAPTER 1

"I'd die for that purse," Marcie said.

"I'd kill for it," I replied.

Thus, the difference between me and my best friend, Marcie Hanover.

We were at the Beverly Center, L.A.'s mecca for expensive handbags, and we'd come to worship at the altar of Gucci, Prada, Fendi, and other high-end gods.

Calling Marcie and me appreciative of designer purses wouldn't do our neuroses justice. To say that we were obsessive, compulsive, crazed white twenty-somethings might be more accurate.

We'd long ago faced the truth: we're handbag whores.

Marcie glanced at her wristwatch. "Guess you'd better go, huh?"

I looked at my own watch. It matched the Dooney & Bourke barrel bag I was carrying.

Nearly two o'clock. Time to go to my "other" job.

With great reluctance we left the Kate Spade display and the black hobo purse for which Marcie had been ready to die and I'd been willing to kill. The November, Sunday afternoon crowd carried us through the mall toward the escalator to the parking garage, and I had every intention of actually leaving. Then, I swear, light suddenly beamed down from

above, and really, I swear, angels began to sing, and Marcie and I were frozen in humble reverence.

The Louis Vuitton store.

I gasped and she made that little mewling sound that I
suspected—ugh, gross—she only made during sex, and we
both rushed to the display windows.

Louis Vuitton. Now, this was a company. These people
knew how to make bags. They knew their accessories.
From key chains to steamer trunks, they had it all. Handbag heaven, no doubt about it.

Then I spotted it. A gorgeous organizer at center stage
in the display window.

My stomach knotted and my heart raced. It took everything I had not to lick the glass.

"I'm getting that," I declared.

"It's nearly seven hundred dollars."

"I'm getting it."

"But what about buying Christmas gifts?" Marcie
asked.

"Screw Christmas."

"And your New Year's resolution? You took that second job so you could pay off your credit cards."

I hate it when other people make good sense.

"I'm getting that bag," I said again, mentally etching
the conviction into the lining of my brain.

"You're going to be late," Marcie said, glancing at her
watch again. "You know what happens if you're late."

I was glued to that window. "Yeah, in a minute. . . ."

"Now, Haley," Marcie said with a fierceness you
wouldn't expect from a petite, blue-eyed blonde. "Step
away from the handbags. Now."

She tugged on my arm, breaking the spell.

"Thanks for talking me down," I told her.

You can't find a friend like Marcie just anywhere.

"See you," she called, as I walked away.

I found my Honda in the crowded parking lot and

headed north on the 101 freeway, visions of the Louis Vuitton organizer dancing behind my eyes.

I had to get it. I had to. And I could manage it. I could.

Just a week ago I'd taken a second job at a department store for extra money. I wanted to go all out for Christmas this year, I'd told myself, really do it up right, give everyone a fabulous gift. I wanted some things for myself, too of course.

And there was that slight miscalculation I'd made in my checking account.

So with my evenings and weekends free, I'd taken a part-time, Christmas-help job as a salesclerk at Holt's Department Store. It was a midrange store that carried clothing and shoes for the whole family, housewares, kitchen items, and small electronics.

Holt's wasn't my first choice. I'd applied at all the upscale stores—the ones that carried designer handbags, where I could avail myself of a sizable employee discount—but none of them had offered me a job. So I ended up at Holt's.

Holt's motto was "Of Course You Can," the *you* being the customer, unfortunately. As a salesclerk, I had to provide top-quality service at all times, to assist customers in every way possible, to go the extra mile for them, and do it all with a big of-course-you-can smile on my face.

All of this for about seven bucks an hour.

Yeah, right.

Holt's had policies and procedures in place to handle any situation, and these had been reviewed in depth during my orientation, or at least that's what someone told me later. I drifted off during orientation.

I took the off-ramp and whipped around a couple of slow-moving cars to get into the Holt's parking lot, then cut off an SUV and grabbed a choice space near the door.

I sat in my car for a moment looking up at the blue neon sign that spelled out HOLT'S in cursive. I'd been here five

days now and, so far, my journey to The Dark Side of retail wasn't great.

Not that I think I'm all-that, or anything. But, jeez,
come on. Seven bucks an hour to fold merchandise, stock
shelves, and actually wait on customers? And smile at the
same time?

Maybe I wouldn't feel this way if I didn't already have a
real job. Again, not to sound bigheaded, but it's with the
most prestigious law firm in Los Angeles, with sumptuous
offices located on three floors of the best building in Century City.

So you might think that I, Haley Randolph, with my
long, coltlike legs, shampoo-commercial-thick dark hair,
and my fifty percent beauty-queen genes, have superior
skills of some sort to be sought after by such a highly re-
garded firm. I don't. So then you might believe it was simply destiny, serendipity, or good mojo that got me the job.
Nope. It's that I'm a heck of a partier and know how to
pick a great club.

I woke up one Sunday afternoon about four months ago
with a business card clutched in my hand from some guy
named Kirk Keegan. An attorney at a law firm on Wilshire.

I shot up in bed. An attorney? What had I done last
night?

I didn't remember a car accident, or being in jail—I'd remember that, wouldn't I? But I didn't remember this guy
either, so could I really trust my memory?

He called later that afternoon and I stood horrified at
the sight of his name on my caller ID.

Was he calling to warn me that the police were on their
way to arrest me and that I should make a break for the
border, take a room on the second floor of the Motel
Marta in Cabo under the name Juanita Rivas? Attorneys
do that, don't they?

Damn, I should have paid better attention in Spanish
class.

I'm not big on suspense, so I answered the phone. Kirk Keegan's voice came through smooth and mellow, despite the background noise.

"We met at the club last night," he said.

We did?

"Yes," I said, because I definitely remembered going to a club. Otherwise, I was clueless.

"I was impressed with you," Kirk said.

And why wouldn't he be? I was carrying a beaded BJ bag and had on the sweet little black dress I'd just bought at Banana Republic.

"So I wondered if you're interested in Pike Warner?" Kirk asked.

Pike Warner . . . Pike Warner . . . was that the new handbag line from DKNY?

"Well, sure," I told him.

"Be there first thing Monday morning. I'll phone in a recommendation," Kirk said. "Human Resources is on fourteen. You still have my card, don't you? With the address?"

I looked down at the bent, dog-eared business card I'd spent the night with. Pike Warner was the law firm he worked for. Kirk Keegan was offering me a job there?

I didn't know the first thing about working at a law firm. My knowledge of the law itself didn't extend much past the consequences of exceeding the speed limit, and then only if you got caught, of course. I'd be completely lost. Totally out of my element.

"Sure," I said. "I'll be there."

"Good. Keep me posted. Let me know how it goes," Kirk said.

The next morning I called in sick at the real estate company where I worked, using the touch-of-the-stomach-flu excuse, a favorite of mine, and drove to the impressive office building in Century City.

The HR lady had only recently arrived on Earth from another planet, obviously, because she took one look at my job history—lifeguard, file clerk, receptionist, and two weeks at a pet store—and decided I might fit in nicely in the accounting department. When I announced I was pursuing my B.A., which really meant that the semester after high school I'd enrolled in community college, taken two classes, one of which was PE, she immediately scheduled me for the all-important Pike Warner employment evaluation. A test to see if I actually had any math skills, something the finance department seemed interested in.

Go figure.

I passed the test, receiving, oddly enough, the exact score as the guy sitting next to me, and was brought on board Pike Warner and made part of the Accounts Payable unit.

They gave me a huge salary—well, huge by my standards—and my credit card balances had gone up proportionally. Christmas was on the horizon. Gucci had come out with a new tote. And there was that troubling miscalculation I'd made in my checking account.

So here I was, sitting in my car, staring at the Holt's sign, shoppers streaming into the store like picnic ants on a sugar high, who expected to be catered to, waited on, and indulged by a minimum-wage grunt wearing an of-course-you-can smile.

Though Thanksgiving was coming up, the store wasn't decorated for Christmas yet, like most stores were. Something about a Holt's tradition, I vaguely recalled from a lucid moment during orientation. But the store was busy. Shoppers filled the aisles, talking loud, letting their children run through the racks of clothes.

Just inside the entry, Julie something-or-other sat at a table inviting customers to complete a credit card application and handing out half-pound boxes of candy for those who did.

Julie was nineteen—five whole years younger than me—small, cute, and bubbly, the perfect person to sell credit, or so I was told. I'd asked for the job myself—you got to sit down and look out the window—but was turned down. Apparently, my of-course-you-can smile needs some work.

The lines at the checkout were long, since only three of the eight registers were open. I made my way to the rear of the store, off the sales floor and into the area that housed our customer service booth, which handled all returns, exchanges, and accompanying complaints, the restrooms, the employee break room, and offices. Working in the customer service booth was a crappy job. It took a special kind of person to handle it.

Just as well that my of-course-you-can smile was subpar, I'd decided on my second day there.

I went through the swinging door marked EMPLOYEES ONLY to the break room. There were tables and chairs, a microwave, refrigerator, vending machines, and posters plastered all over the walls about job safety, our rights as employees, the current Holt's marketing plan, and a teaser about the store's upcoming surprise Christmas merchandise extravaganza.

Rita was in the break room too, standing by the time clock and looking at her watch.

Rita hates me. But that's okay. I hated her first.

Rita was in her late thirties, only slightly taller than she was wide, and had worked at Holt's, apparently, since sometime before the invention of the cash register. She always wore stretch pants and knit tops with farm animals on them. The Dooney & Bourke handbag I carried—not counting the matching watch—cost more than all the clothing in Rita's closet combined.

"I was just about to put your name on the board," she told me, voicing her approval yet sounding excited at the prospect.

Rita was the cashiers' supervisor. Holt's hierarchy of supervision had many levels. Store manager, assistant store manager, area manager, department manager, department lead, and at the very bottom rung of the ladder, minimum-wage peons like me. All the supervisors were designated by a number and they were forever being paged to a certain department, which also had a number. One-one to four-six. Two-three to seven-five.

It was at this point during orientation that my eyes had glazed over.

Rita was also the time clock monitor. If an employee was late coming in for a shift, Rita wrote the person's name on the white board by the fridge. Yeah, just like fourth grade. If you got your name on the board five times in one month, you got fired.

That I remember from orientation.

"And hello to you too, Rita," I said, as I punched my time card with a full eight seconds to spare.

"You've already had two lates," Rita said, as if my tardiness was some sort of personal insult.

"Thanks for keeping track of it for me," I told her. "I'll let you know when I need an update again."

"I ought to tell Richard about this," she said.

Richard was the assistant store manager. And, believe me, there was a reason the letters *a-s-s* were in his job title.

"Tell him what, Rita? That I was on time for work again today?" I asked, giving her my screw-you smile. That one I've got down cold.

I put my purse in my locker and hung my employee name badge around my neck. I'd asked for a name badge that had "Sue" on it, in case someone I knew caught me working in the store and I could claim to be my own identical-twin cousin or something, but apparently that was against company policy. Not that I'm ashamed to work a second job, or a job at Holt's. But come on, I work for Pike Warner.

"You're in ILA tonight," Rita said, looking at the schedule on the wall, as if I couldn't read it myself. She sneered at me and left the break room.

I gave her a minute, then headed out to the sales floor trying to remember what ILA was. They probably covered that in orientation. From the corner of my eye I saw Rita glaring at me from inside the customer service booth, so I strode across the sales floor as if I actually knew which department I was supposed to work in tonight.

Holt's was a one-story. It was big, but since it didn't have "mart" in the title, it wasn't big enough to get lost in. Or hide from your supervisor.

"You. Excuse me. You. Over here."

Thinking it was a customer calling me, I kept walking.

"Holly? Holly!"

I recognized the voice. It was Evelyn in Intimates—

Damn. Intimates department. The "I" in ILA.

I hate that department.

I love intimates—which means "lingerie" in retail-speak—but Holt's employees, at least the Christmas employees, didn't get to while away the time picking out panties or trying on bras, which takes all of the fun out of lingerie.

Evelyn wound her way through the racks. She was fortyish, neat, trim, and could pass for a junior high English teacher. Her idea of a midlife crisis would probably be switching to hoop earrings.

She took an exhausted breath. "Holly, if you don't mind, could you please—"

"It's Haley," I told her.

Evelyn froze and color flashed across her cheeks. "Oh. Oh dear. I'm so sorry. I thought—"

"It's okay," I said because now I was feeling sorry for her. "What do you need me to do?"

"If you don't mind, could you please recover this area?" she asked.

"Recover" is department store lingo for cleaning up after swarming hordes of customers.

Evelyn looked at the clipboard in her hand and gave me an apologetic half smile. "You get a break tonight, but no lunch."

That's because Richard did the employee work schedules and cut everybody's shift fifteen minutes short just to screw us out of a break.

"I'll be back later to check on you," Evelyn promised.

The department was a mess. Bras were falling off hangers, bikinis, thongs, and granny panties were all mixed together on the display tables, someone had strewn two dozen packs of panty hose on the floor.

Oh well. *That's what I'm here for*, I reminded myself. To work. Make extra money for Christmas. Buy that Gucci tote and the Louis Vuitton organizer. And do something about that concerning miscalculation in my checking account.

I started straightening the panty hose, keeping my head down to avoid eye contact with customers, listening to babies cry and the mind-numbing music on the PA system. Every so often a voice would break in, paging one of the store supervisors to Customer Service, the telephone, or to a register.

A momentary lapse caused me to glimpse a customer at the bra racks. I dropped to my knees behind the panty hose.

"Excuse me?"

Too late. She'd seen me.

I duck-walked around the end of the display, but I wasn't quick enough.

"Excuse me!"

She was twenty, maybe, wearing jeans and a low-cut T-shirt, and waving a bra at me.

I got to my feet. "Can I help you?"

I tried for my of-course-you-can smile but couldn't quite pull it off.

"This department is a mess! Totally! I can't find anything!"

"Would you like to complete a comment card?" I asked.

"No!" She shook the bra at me again. "I want this bra! In beige!"

I took it from her. Only a 32-B. How sad. I might have felt sorry for her if she wasn't being such a bitch.

I spent a few minutes looking at the style, then examining the tag.

"We're out of these," I told her.

She huffed loudly. "Could you at least go look?"

"Sure."

I took the bra, left the department, walked down the aisle past a couple of customers—whom I avoided—and through the double doors to the stockroom.

I loved the stockroom. It was absolutely huge. Towering shelves stuffed with crisp, new merchandise. A different section for each department. There were naked mannequins, signs, fixtures, and lots of racks and carts for moving merchandise. It was quiet back here too. The replenishment team worked early in the morning restocking all the merchandise in the store, and the truck team only showed up when there was merchandise to be unloaded. Almost no one came back here at night.

Just inside the door was Domestics, a rainbow of bedspreads, towels, and sheets. And a comfy place to sit too.

I pulled two king-size Laura Ashley bed-in-a-bag sets off the shelf, sat down, and stretched out my legs. Nice. I leaned back and closed my eyes, letting thoughts of that Louis Vuitton organizer fill my head. I would get it. I just had to figure out how.

After a while I got up, put the bed sets on the shelf, and went back to the lingerie department. The customer was still there, still fuming.

"We're out," I told her.

"Fine!" She stomped away.

I love this job.

I went to the bra racks and, yes, they were a mess. Totally. I spent a few minutes straightening them, then headed for the stockroom. There were racks of bras back there. I'd seen delivery trucks at the loading dock every day I'd been there, bringing tons of merchandise for the Christmas shopping season.

I wound my way through Domestics, past Housewares, and up the metal and concrete stairs to the second floor. A conveyor belt ran alongside the stairs for large items, along with an overhead conveyor for hanging items, and I was tempted to hop on and take the easy way up. But it was early in my employment with Holt's. No reason to do all the fun stuff right away.

The lighting was harsh and it was chilly as I wound my way through the shelves of merchandise to the far back corner of the stockroom where the intimate apparel was located.

There was Richard, the assistant store manager. I'd heard him being paged on the store PA over and over tonight. No wonder he hadn't answered.

Richard was facedown on the floor. Dead.

CHAPTER 2

Yes, Richard was dead. I knew that because I never missed an episode of *CSI: Crime Scene Investigation.* Follow the evidence, they said. And immediately I saw a huge pool of blood under his face and a big yucky-looking indentation in the side of his head.

If I'd liked Richard in the least, I would probably have felt bad about that.

I decided I'd better let someone know about this so I retraced my steps to the stairs beside the conveyer belt and picked up the wall phone. I'd always wanted to make an announcement over the PA. But what should I say? I didn't know the Holt's numeric code for finding a dead body, and simply announcing "cleanup in the stockroom" didn't seem quite right either.

Then a little stab of concern zapped me.

What if everyone thought *I'd* killed Richard? After all, I'd made a snide comment or two about him to other Holt's employees, which he deserved, of course, but still. And here I was, alone in the stockroom with his dead body, no one else around, no one to vouch for me.

Maybe I'd go get someone. Tell them we needed more bras in intimates. Get them to come up here and let them find Richard. Let them handle the police, the questions. Let them be the suspect.

Sounded like a good plan.

Hmm. Where was Rita?

I headed down the steps. When I went through the double doors onto the sales floor I spotted Evelyn waiting in Intimates.

"Where have you been?" she asked. "I've been looking for you everywhere—"

"I found a dead body in the stockroom."

Evelyn froze. "You—what?"

"It's Richard. He's in women's lingerie."

Her mouth formed a little O. "He's in women's lingerie?"

"Intimates," I said, gesturing toward the double doors. "Upstairs."

"And he's . . ."

"Dead."

I guess it finally sank in because Evelyn flipped out.

"Oh my God! Call 9-1-1! We've got to clear the store! Get these people out of here! Now, before—"

"Shh!" I grabbed Evelyn's flailing arms. "Keep your voice down. We need to keep this quiet."

"But—" Evelyn's eyes got huge and her gaze darted up and down the aisle. "Craig . . . where's Craig?"

Leave it to Evelyn to worry about reporting to her supervisor, at a time like this.

"We'll find Craig," I told her. "But we don't want to start a panic and have customers stampeding over each other. It's better to keep it between you and me for now."

Evelyn's eyes focused on me. "Yes, yes, I suppose."

"Come on," I said. "Let's go phone the police. And try to stay calm."

We went to the suite of offices in the rear of the store. I'd never been back there before. Evelyn had a desk in a room shared by all the supervisors. Only the store manager got a private office. I found a phone book in the bottom drawer.

"Just call 9-1-1," she said, getting all wild-eyed again.

"It's not an emergency. Richard's dead. He's not going anywhere."

"But—"

"Look," I said, "do you really want police cars, fire trucks, and paramedics rolling up to the front of the store, lights flashing and sirens blaring?"

"Well . . . I don't know."

"Go find me the phone number for the store manager," I told her. "We should call her too."

Evelyn dug through the desk drawer, seemingly thankful for something to do, while I made the call. I asked the officer who answered to kindly come to the rear of the store and we'd meet him there. Then I got the store manager's phone number from Evelyn and broke the news to her. Next, I paged Todd, the on-duty Loss Prevention guy.

Rita came into the office and Evelyn rushed to her.

"Oh my God. It's Richard. He's dead," she declared, then flung her arm toward me. "Haley found him—upstairs. She says he's in lingerie."

Rita turned a cool gaze to me. "That's sick."

The phone rang. It was Todd, the LP guy.

"You need to come to the office," I told him. "We have a . . . situation."

"I'm on break," he said.

I looked down at the receiver, then put it to my ear again. "Listen, Todd, something's happened. You have to come to—"

"Hello? I said I'm on break."

"Fine."

I slammed the phone down. The loss prevention division of Holt's was separate from the store's chain of command. They worked with store management, but didn't answer to them.

I turned to Evelyn. "How do I get hold of the LP supervisor?"

She tapped her fingers frantically against her forehead. "Oh, uh, that number is here somewhere," she said and started rifling through the desk drawers again.

"We need to block the stockroom entrances," I said, visions of *CSI* flashing in my head. There were two ways to get into the stockroom from inside the store, an entrance near the customer service booth and another near the intimates department.

"Rita, get another area manager and you two stand at the doors," I said. "Don't let anyone in. The police are on their way."

She glared at me for a minute with even more disdain than usual.

"I don't believe what you said about Richard," she told me, then huffed out of the office.

Evelyn came up with the phone number for the loss prevention supervisor and I called it. Voice mail came on so all I could do was leave a message.

At that point, I couldn't think of anything else to do except wait for the police and Los Angeles County's version of Gil Grissom and the gang to show up. I turned to Evelyn. She was straightening up one of the desks; I guess she wanted things to look tidy when the detectives showed up.

"Let's go open the doors to the loading dock," I said to her.

I figured Rita would have stationed herself at the customer service booth entrance to the stockroom, so I went the other way to the double doors near Intimates. Craig Matthews stood guard, alerted to the situation by Rita, I guessed. Craig was Evelyn's supervisor, the area manager for ILA, Intimates, Loungewear, and Accessories.

Craig was nearing his fifties, and everything about him was pretty much average. He looked confused, troubled, and I wondered what Rita had told him when she'd asked him to serve guard duty at the stockroom doors.

"Craig, isn't it just awful?" Evelyn declared, twisting

her fingers together. "I mean, for Haley to find Richard . . . like that."

Craig looked at me. "It's true?" he asked, his bushy brows drawn together.

Jeez, like I wouldn't know a dead body when I saw one?

"Yeah, it's true," I said. "We're going to let the police in."

"Evelyn, you stay here," Craig told her, and pushed into the stockroom ahead of me.

I heard the sirens when we wound our way to the loading dock, and was a little annoyed. I'd distinctly told the guy on the phone not to blast their sirens. Why don't people do as instructed?

The two big roll-up doors were the only way into the stockroom, other than through the store, and luckily Craig knew how to open them. He hit a couple of switches. A light over the door flashed yellow and a loud beeping noise sounded, like one of those big trucks when it backed up. The doors rolled open, making all sorts of racket.

Outside, I saw a black-and-white police car and an ambulance approach, their red and blue lights flashing in the darkness. A plain Crown Victoria followed. Uniforms swarmed inside and Craig directed them to the stairs that led up to the second floor of the stockroom. Two men in suits ambled in. They introduced themselves as Detectives Shuman and Madison.

Shuman was the younger of the two, kind of handsome in a discount-outlet sort of way. Madison had thinning gray hair and a round belly that made him look like he was about seven months along.

"Who found the body?" Detective Madison asked.

"She did," Craig said, gesturing to me.

Shuman pulled a notepad from his jacket pocket, asked my name, and wrote it down.

"Did you hear anything?" Detective Madison asked.

"Like what?"

He looked at me like I was dumber than dirt.

"Footsteps? Breathing? Another person nearby? The murderer, maybe?"

The murderer might have been up there when I found Richard?

Oh, crap.

What if he'd seen me? Wanted to silence me? What if he'd attacked me? In *Holt's*?

No way was I dying in a midrange retail store. I'd have dragged myself to an Abercrombie & Fitch—somehow.

"Ma'am?" Detective Madison asked, making the word sound more like "dumb-ass."

Both detectives were staring at me now. So was Craig.

"I didn't hear anything. Or see anything," I told them.

"We'll talk to you later," Madison said, looking disgusted.

The two detectives headed up the staircase, Craig walking in front, explaining the layout of the second-floor stockroom where Richard's body lay.

I stood there watching them go, feeling a little miffed, for some reason. I didn't really want to go upstairs and see Richard's body again, but I mean, jeez, I was the one who found him.

I left the stockroom through the double doors and saw that a uniformed officer had taken up guard duty in place of Evelyn. A few customers took note of him as they went past, pointing and bending their heads together to whisper.

Evelyn rushed up to me from the bra racks. "What's going on back there?"

She still looked rattled and I wondered why she just didn't go home.

"The detectives are upstairs," I told her, wondering suddenly why I didn't go home. If finding a dead body wasn't a good reason to leave work, what was?

"This whole thing is just so . . . sordid," Evelyn declared, pursing her lips distastefully.

"I'm not feeling so good. I think I'll go home."

That snapped her out of her stupor. "Oh, well, aren't you scheduled to work until closing?"

I guess the look I gave her—which was certainly not my of-course-you-can smile—jarred her.

"I could go ask Craig if you can take a break," she offered and waved at the stockroom doors.

"I'm taking a break, Evelyn," I told her. "If Craig has a problem with that, tell him to come see me."

"Well . . ." Evelyn twisted her fingers together.

"Besides, the police will want to talk to me. You don't want that happening out here on the sales floor, do you?"

More finger twisting. "Well . . ."

I doubted the detectives would be interested in hearing me say yet another time that I didn't know anything, but you never knew. Besides, if I stayed in the break room instead of going home, I'd still be on the clock.

Evelyn drew in a big breath. "Yes, yes, you're right. Probably. You should go to the break room . . . for a while. I'm—I'm sure—pretty sure—Craig will be all right with that."

"Whatever," I said and walked away.

At the customer service booth I saw that another uniformed policeman stood guard by the stockroom door, and that Rita was huddled in the back of the booth whispering furiously with the two girls who worked there. Rita threw me a look as I walked into the break room.

No one was there, which suited me okay since the whole thing with Richard's death had begun to irk me, for some reason. I decided I needed a boost. I eyed the vending machines.

If you couldn't indulge yourself after finding a dead body at your crappy second job, when could you? I got a ten from my purse, fed it into the machine, and started pushing buttons.

About thirty minutes later as I sat at the break room table catching up on my celeb news in *People* magazine and snacking on the array of chocolates I'd gotten from the vending machines, the door swung open and a man walked in. I'd never seen him before so I knew he wasn't store management, and from the look of him I doubted he was a cop.

Tall, light brown hair, thirtyish, dressed in jeans and an emerald-green polo shirt. Kind of handsome.

"Haley Randolph?" he asked, extending his hand. "I'm Ty Cameron."

I shook his hand and a jab of heat shot up my arm. Or maybe it was the three packages of M&M's, the Snickers bar, and the two Reese's Cups I'd just finished off.

"I came as soon as I got word," Ty said, nodding in the direction of the stockroom.

Now I knew who he was. The loss prevention phone number I'd called was just voice mail. This had to be the guy in charge.

"It's about damn time," I told him. Jeez, how much chocolate had I eaten? Even I could hear how wound up I was.

He studied me for a moment, then said, "I apologize."

"I called that idiot Todd, the LP guy on duty, but he wouldn't come help. He was on break. You ought to fire his sorry ass," I told him.

"Okay."

The break room door swung open and in walked Craig and the two detectives. Introductions were made and the men conversed quietly on the other side of the room, as if I weren't there flipping through *People*. Ty was doing a lot of murmuring so I figured the cops were chewing him a new one over the store's lax security.

Finally Detective Madison turned to me, the other men fanning out around him, all staring down at me.

"So, let me get this straight," he said, sounding really annoyed. "You were alone when you found the body and no one else was around."

"It's pretty complicated but I think you've got it right," I told him.

I need to lay off the sugar.

He didn't seem troubled by my testy attitude. Guess he was used to it.

"You were working near the stockroom doors, right?" Detective Madison asked. "Back there in the women's underwear section? Right?"

"That's right."

"And you didn't see anybody go into the stockroom?"

"No, I didn't," I said. Unless, of course, someone had gone in while I was crouched behind the panty hose display hiding from that bra customer.

I didn't see any need to mention that.

"So you saw nobody go in," Detective Madison said. "See anyone come out?"

"No."

"And when you found the body, you didn't see anyone in the stockroom? Anywhere?"

"I told you I didn't see or hear anybody in the stockroom," I said.

"So it was just you? Back there alone? That whole big stockroom and no one else was around?"

"Yeah, that's what I'm . . . telling . . . you. . . ."

My voice trailed off because even I heard the guilt coming through.

Both detectives looked ready to slap the cuffs on me. Ty looked suspicious and Craig appeared relieved that the killer had been found so quickly.

We all stayed like that for a minute or so, me trying to

look innocent—a lot harder to pull off than an of-course-you-can smile—and all the men glaring down at me.

Then Detective Madison turned to Ty. "Let's get the security tapes from the stockroom, have a look at them. You can point out who's who on the tape."

I froze.

There were security cameras in the stockroom? The police were going to look at the tape? Along with store personnel?

And they'd see me lounging on the king-size Laura Ashley bed-in-a-bag sets when I was supposed to be working?

Oh, crap.

Chapter 3

Would they fire me?

The idea hit me as I swung across a couple of lanes of the 405 freeway, cutting off two other drivers on my way to work the next morning.

I'd left Holt's last night before my shift ended, a crime only marginally less severe than murder, in the eyes of the store's management.

And if that weren't reason to let me go, seeing me lounging on the Laura Ashley bed-in-a-bag sets in the stockroom on the security tape would do it. The company was kind of nutty about expecting employees to actually work when they were on the clock.

They'd fire me. Probably. I mean, I'd fire me, if I saw me lying around on bed sets instead of working.

Or, maybe, I could beat them to the punch.

Red taillights flashed in front of me. I hit the brakes and ran right up to the bumper of the pickup in front of me to make sure none of the cars in the other lanes could cut in front of me. Traffic slowed to a crawl.

Maybe I'd sue them first. Post-traumatic stress, or something. Yeah, that might work. After all, I'd discovered a dead body in their store. I could sue them.

I was feeling a little excited now.

I could claim mental anguish or extreme emotional distress. Maybe even diminished capacity because just this morning I'd run a brand-new pair of Liz Claiborne panty hose while thinking about what had happened last night. Yeah, okay, I was really thinking about that rather good-looking Ty Cameron, but nobody needed to know that.

I worked for Pike Warner, the most powerful law firm in Los Angeles, maybe even the whole West Coast. No one in their right mind would go up against the legal big guns at Pike Warner. Holt's would cave. They'd be crazy not to.

The more I thought about it, the better I liked the idea. In fact, I was pretty sure I was feeling post-traumatically stressed at this very moment.

Or maybe it was just the traffic.

I swooped in front of a Beemer and hit the Santa Monica Boulevard off-ramp, and by the time I crept along with traffic until I reached the Pike Warner employee parking structure, I'd decided to talk to Kirk Keegan about my situation.

When Kirk had phoned my apartment four months ago and offered to recommend me for a job, I'd thought he was doing it to get into my pants. But, sadly, that proved untrue.

Kirk was an associate, looking to make partner in record time. He was really good looking and very ambitious. We'd had drinks after work a few times and seen each other around the office occasionally, but nothing romantic ever developed between us. Darn it. Seems Kirk Keegan was just a nice guy.

I parked and headed into the building along with all the other upwardly mobile, well-dressed employees. That's one of the things I liked about working for Pike Warner. The clothes and incredible accessories. Armani, Dolce & Gabbana, Rolex. And absolutely everyone could tell the difference between a Prada and a Gucci handbag with only a casual glance.

What I also liked was that I didn't need an of-course-you-can smile at Pike Warner. In fact, smiling was frowned upon.

The staid, reserved corporate environment at Pike Warner had been hard for me to get used to. Actually, it went against my grain. In the four months I'd worked there I'd only heard the F-word once—and I'm the one who said it.

The law offices took up three floors of the building. Accounting, Human Resources, Document Retention—which was really the file room—and some of the consultants worked "down on fourteen," as everyone referred to it.

Never mind that we were in one of the most prestigious buildings in one of the biggest cities in the world; in the realm of Pike Warner, support staff were "down on fourteen" as if we were troglodytes, toiling away in the bowels of the earth.

Associates were simply "on fifteen," and the founding partners, Pike and Warner, two old geezers I wouldn't recognize if I backed over them in the parking garage, were "up on sixteen."

At Pike Warner, everyone aspired to be "up on sixteen," and by 9:02 a.m. on my first day of employment, I knew there wasn't anything any employee wouldn't do to scratch, claw, or sleep their way up to sixteen.

When the elevator opened onto the fourteenth floor and I stepped out with the crowd, I spotted Kirk Keegan standing in the hallway, briefcase in hand and looking sharp in Armani.

Perfect. Just the man I wanted to talk to today. Was this a good sign, or what?

"Hey, Kirk, how are you—"

"Good morning, Haley. Sorry, I've got to run," he said and rushed into the elevator before the doors closed.

Huh. Well, okay. This was still a good sign. At least I knew he was here today. I'd hook up with him later.

The magnificent view of Los Angeles stretching to the

ocean was visible through the big windows on my right as I walked down the corridor and into the accounting department.

I don't know how people who do not sit at a desk with a telephone all day, every day, ever manage their personal lives. How do they schedule their pedicures and make plans for the weekend? To say nothing of where they get their pens, pencils, and sticky notes.

As always, a few kiss-asses were already in the accounting department, seated at their desks and actually working. They glanced up at me, then averted their gazes quickly as I walked past and into the accounts payable section.

I stopped short. A uniformed security guard stood at a desk in the corner. My desk. Everyone in the room turned and looked at me.

"Miss Randolph?"

And there was a cardboard box sitting in the center of my desk, filled with—was that my personal belongings?

"Miss Randolph?"

The voice of Mrs. Drexler, the head of the accounting department, finally registered. She stood in the doorway of her private office, staring at me expectantly.

"Could I see you for a moment, please?" she called.

Everyone was watching me now and I got a sick feeling in the pit of my stomach. Like the one you get when you walk into a room carrying a Burberry handbag and realize the occasion called for a Fendi.

I followed Mrs. Drexler into her office and she closed the door, not that it mattered since the walls were all glass, allowing everyone in the department to see what was going on.

"Please, sit down, Miss Randolph," she said, lowering herself into her desk chair.

Mrs. Drexler was immaculately groomed. If Barbie had a stepmother, she would look just like Mrs. Drexler.

She waited until I dropped into the chair in front of her

desk, then laced her fingers and placed them just so on a file folder on her desktop.

"Miss Randolph, over the weekend we conducted a routine audit of the accounts payable unit," she said.

An audit? They did that?

Oh. Okay. Then this couldn't be something bad. I did my work perfectly, just as I'd been trained. I filled out my forms legibly in black ink, stapled at the required forty-five-degree angle. I'd never had one of my payment requests rejected by the girls in Cashiering.

I was getting a promotion. Sure, that's what it was. That's why my desk had been emptied and a security guard was standing by because now I was too important to do those things myself, and certainly couldn't move through the building without a proper escort.

I'd get a raise too. My heart jumped. I could get that Louis Vuitton organizer—which I'd desperately need in my new, more responsible job. I could take care of that disconcerting miscalculation in my checkbook and I could *quit my job at Holt's.*

I nearly sprang out of the chair and threw my arms around Mrs. Drexler.

But there was something about the way her right eyebrow crept up that kept me from doing that.

Truthfully, I don't think Mrs. Drexler ever really liked me. She never seemed to appreciate my sense of humor, my witty rejoinders, or the clever repartee I engaged in on the rare occasion when I could coax another employee in the department into actually speaking aloud.

So I waited and Mrs. Drexler continued.

"The auditors found some . . . irregularities . . . in your work."

The sick feeling in my stomach wound into a knot. "What sort of—"

"An investigation is under way," she said, speaking very slowly.

"But I didn't do anything wrong," I said, hearing the desperation in my voice. "What did they find?"

Mrs. Drexler patted the file on her desktop and I saw my name on the tab. Oh God. My personnel folder.

The knot in my stomach hardened into a brick.

"I can't go into details until our investigation is complete," Mrs. Drexler explained.

"You have to tell me—"

"Miss Randolph, it would be in your best interest not to say anything more," she said, looking at me meaningfully.

"But—"

"As of this morning, you're being put on administrative leave."

"You're—you're firing me?"

"Administrative leave," Mrs. Drexler corrected. "Just until our investigation is complete and a determination has been made."

"How long will that take?" I asked, hearing the desperation in my voice.

"You'll be notified of the outcome."

No. No, this couldn't be happening. It just couldn't. There had to be some sort of mistake.

"Can I talk to your supervisor or the auditors, or somebody?" I pleaded. "I never did anything wrong. I followed all the guidelines and—"

"Security will escort you out," Mrs. Drexler said, sitting back and folding her hands.

I looked up to see the security guard standing in the doorway. I gulped and turned back to Mrs. Drexler.

"You'll let me know when everything is straightened out?" I asked, sounding hopeful and awfully pathetic.

She nodded solemnly. "Of course."

My knees wobbled as I rose from the chair. At the door, I turned back.

"Is that *paid* administrative leave?" I asked.

"No."

And so, my humiliation complete, I left her office.

In a gross departure from Pike Warner procedure, absolutely everyone in the room looked up from their work and stared at me. Me and my security escort, that is, as I made the long, embarrassing walk of shame.

I picked up the cardboard carton. Inside was my Universal Studios coffee mug, my bottle of hand lotion, a half pack of Juicy Fruit, and the potted ivy in the Wonder Woman planter my mom had sent me on my first day of work here.

Everyone stared as I left the department. Everyone stared in the corridor and in the elevator. Everyone stared as I crossed the lobby, their gazes jumping from the security guard to the cardboard box, then to me.

At the door, the guard stopped and I walked out alone. Everyone on the street stared. And in the parking garage.

I threw the box in my backseat and sped away, humiliation and outrage boiling inside me.

Irregularities in my work? An audit? An investigation? And I'd been placed on administrative leave?

And it was unpaid leave.

How was I going to live?

I broke out in a cold sweat.

How would I pay my rent? My utilities? My car payment? How would I manage Christmas and get that Louis Vuitton organizer? And how would I cover that astronomical error in my checking account?

Well, I would just get another job. The idea hit me like a bolt as I shot up the on-ramp onto the 405.

Sure. I had experience now. I'd worked for the biggest, most prestigious law firm in California, the West Coast—maybe even the world. I could get a job with another attorney in a snap. And I could demand a higher salary because now I had experience.

Except—

The knot in my stomach doubled.

Except what sort of reference and job history would I give? If I said I'd worked for Pike Warner—which I'd have to do if I wanted another job in accounts payable—they would call for a reference. And what would they be told? That I was on administrative leave for irregularities—investigation pending.

I'd never get a decent job. And that meant—

The horror of my realization caused me to bolt upright in the car seat. I swerved right, onto the shoulder. My front fender scraped the retaining wall before I hit the brakes and slid to a stop.

Cars whizzed past me on the left as I clutched the steering wheel, staring ahead at my doomed future.

I was going to have to work at Holt's—*forever.*

CHAPTER 4

Okay, I hadn't been fired. That was the good news. I still had a job at Pike Warner, technically. Administrative leave wasn't the same as being fired, was it? I mean, if they'd wanted to fire me, they would have, you know, fired me. Right?

I shot across two lanes of traffic and headed down the off-ramp toward Pico Boulevard.

Sure. Of course. They could have fired me but they didn't. And that meant everything was still all right.

Except that I didn't have my Pike Warner income I'd grown accustomed to. I didn't know how I'd pay my rent or utilities, get everyone a fabulous Christmas present, or buy myself that Louis Vuitton organizer—plus I now had a huge dent in my front fender from where I'd swerved off the freeway a few minutes ago.

I followed traffic into the mall parking lot, swung into a space, and cut the engine. Could I sue Pike Warner for the damage to my car? I certainly wouldn't have hit that retaining wall if it hadn't been for them. Maybe I could make that a condition of accepting my job back. Wouldn't that just set Mrs. Drexler back on her well-pumiced heels?

I let that little fantasy play out in my head for a moment, and that made me think of Kirk Keegan. I fished my cell phone out of my purse and checked it again. Nothing.

He still hadn't called, and I was sure he'd heard the news by now. Gossip swept the three floors at Pike Warner quicker than a walk down the runway at Fashion Week. Last month when a secretary on sixteen showed up at work with a Birkin bag, we'd known it down on fourteen before the elevator doors closed behind her.

Kirk was probably getting all the details, the actual facts, not just the gossip, I decided, as I left my car. He would call me any minute now with the latest. I headed for the mall.

Yes, I know that hardly more than an hour ago I'd been humiliated by Mrs. Drexler and lost my *good* job, but that's no reason not to go to the mall. Besides, where else was I going at this hour of the morning? All of my friends were at work, and while I could phone them with my devastating news, this sort of thing was better shared in person. Over drinks. Jell-O shooters and a beer chaser, at least. So first things first.

I love the smell of the purse department in the morning. The scent of leather and rich fabrics. The faint aroma of glass cleaner wafting from the display cases.

I stood there gazing at the handbags artfully arranged in the case, drew in a deep breath, and let it out slowly. Yes, this was definitely where I needed to be right now.

A salesclerk approached. She looked like a mannequin—but not in a good way.

"Can I help you?" she asked from the other side of the display case.

No. No, I didn't need any help, and I certainly didn't need a new handbag. I was just here to take in the sights, the sounds, the smells. To rejuvenate myself after my difficult morning.

But, then, that's no reason not to keep up with the latest fashions.

"What's new?" I asked, waving my hand over the display case.

Mannequin gazed over my left shoulder with that

empty, glazed look in her eye. Obviously, she wasn't paying any attention to me. Couldn't she see I was on the edge here? I could snap at any moment.

"We just got in a shipment," she mumbled.

I froze. A new shipment? The latest bags? Just arrived?

"Where?" I asked, rising on tiptoes, my gaze darting around the department.

"Over there," the clerk said, and wagged her fingers at the other side of the display case.

I rushed to the other side and stopped in my tracks.

The almost-impossible-to-find, so-hot-it-smoked, Notorious bag—in red leather!

"Oh my God," I gasped. "It's gorgeous."

I gripped the display case with both hands to steady myself. I was feeling a little dizzy. Mannequin finally strolled over, took the bag from the case, and plopped it down. I scooped it up immediately, giving it the respect it deserved. My hands closed over the fine leather, and my heart raced faster.

Another woman appeared at my side and I drew away slightly, protecting the purse in my arms, fearing a kidnap attempt. Then I realized she was another clerk.

"Don't you love that bag!" she declared.

"I just saw this in *Elle* magazine," I said, and eased my death grip a little. "I can't believe you have one."

She glanced left and right, then leaned closer and whispered, "Drew Barrymore's personal shopper was just here. She bought five of these for her closest friends. This is the last one."

"I'll take it!"

Mannequin, seeing a sales commission flash in front of her face, suddenly came to life, wrapped the Notorious purse, and shoved it into a shopping bag, as I handed over my credit card.

I hated that she was getting the commission off my sale, but really, I can't fight everybody's battles, can I?

My stomach had that warm, gooey feeling as I looped the shopping bag over my arm and headed out of the store. Then it hit me.

Why had I done that? Why had I spent five hundred dollars on a purse—at a time like this?

I was in shock. Yes, that's what it was. I was still in shock over what had happened this morning at Pike Warner. I had to *do* something—other than buy a new bag, that is.

I pulled out my cell phone to call Kirk Keegan. He was my one true friend at Pike Warner. Aside from him, I didn't really know anyone else well at the firm. Except that guy Jack Bishop, who worked for one of the consultants. He was way hot. So hot, in fact, that I'm sure he screamed his own name in bed.

Kirk came on the line sounding a bit rushed. Kirk was always rushed. I blurted out my irregularities-investigation-pending news. He hadn't heard and that left me slightly annoyed. Word of my ordeal hadn't made it up to fifteen yet? How could that be? I mean, wasn't I important?

"When did this happen?" he asked.

I envisioned him taking notes. "This morning. Mrs. Drexler called me into her office. There's this whole investigation thing going on."

"That's normal," he said.

"I swear, Kirk, I never did anything wrong."

"Then you don't have anything to worry about," he said.

Oh. Yeah. Okay, that sounded good. And it made sense. I hadn't done anything wrong, so Mrs. Drexler and her team of investigators—I deserve a team, surely—would realize that.

Immediately I pictured how grand I'd look on my triumphant return to Pike Warner, strolling into the office carrying the new, so-hot-it's-cool, friend-of-Drew, Notorious handbag, in red leather, no less. I wouldn't bother taking the new bag to Holt's. No one there knew a thing about designer purses, and what was the point of carrying one if other people wouldn't be jealous?

I felt myself relax a bit.

"So you think everything will be all right?" I asked.

"I don't see why not."

Still, I couldn't let it go. "I think I should call Mrs. Drexler or her supervisor, or somebody," I said.

"I wouldn't push it," Kirk advised. "Nothing you say will make any difference right now. Not until they've completed the investigation."

Yes, that was true.

"I'll check around, see what I can find out," he promised.

I heaved a sigh of relief, grateful that he would go to all this effort for me when we hadn't even had sex.

"Just sit tight," he said. "Enjoy a few days off."

"You think that's all it will be?" I asked. "A few days?"

"Relax, will you? I'll be in touch," he said, and hung up.

Whew! Well, okay, that was good news. So good, in fact, that I just might be up to seeing my mom now.

My family home was in La Cañada Flintridge, a town set against the San Gabriel Mountains near Pasadena. It was only about twenty minutes from downtown L.A. but pretends to be a small town with tree-lined streets, a farmers' market, croquet tournaments, and a soapbox derby. All this in a place where homes and spacious estates are worth more than some Third World countries.

Our big Spanish-style house was left to my mom by her grandmother, along with a trust fund. Mom was a former beauty queen—really—and wore the crown of Miss California long before she married my dad.

He was an aerospace engineer doing top secret work for the government, which sounds more exciting than it really is. When I was growing up, for sometimes weeks on end, Dad would leave on Monday morning to work at some secret location only to return on Friday evening and not be able to tell any of us where he'd been or what he'd been doing.

I drove up the winding road and parked in the circular driveway. Juanita, the housekeeper who'd worked for us as long as I could remember, opened the door, rolled her eyes—which should have been my cue to run—and waved me toward the patio out back.

In keeping with her former beauty queen persona, Mom had on Gucci sunglasses, Jimmy Choo slides, capris, and was working the phone big time. Her day planner was open on the umbrella table beside the pool. That could only mean one thing. I started to make a break for the door, but she spotted me.

"Hi, sweetie." She mouthed the word at me, then went back to her conversation.

For as long as I could remember Mom has jumped from one project to the next, doing whatever struck her fancy. Everything from event planning, to marathon running, to competitive sand castle sculpting.

Mom's idea of a new project wasn't like everyone else's. No need to get in there and do the grunt work herself. Not my mom. As befitting a former beauty queen, she hired someone to do it. Personal trainer for the marathon. Private coach for the sand castles. A staff of six to handle the details of the event planning.

I was her project for a while. As her firstborn daughter I was expected to follow in her footsteps down the runway. But only fifty percent of my genes carried her beauty queen markers.

I endured years of tap, ballet, modeling, singing, and piano lessons, with my mom coaching me at every turn.

Honestly, I wasn't very good at any of it. My mom finally gave up when, at age nine, I tried twirling fire batons in the den and set the curtains on fire.

Luckily for everyone, my little sister came along a few years after me, a genetic duplicate of my mom. And she even liked all that stuff. Right now she was attending UCLA and doing some modeling on the side.

My brother got his share of Mom's beauty queen looks and an extra helping of Dad's brains. He graduated from the Air Force Academy a few years ago and was now flying F-16s in the Middle East.

After a few "fines, yeses, goods, and perfects" Mom hung up the phone.

"Great news," she declared, pushing her sunglasses up into her hair. "Everything's set for this Saturday."

Note, she hasn't asked why I'm here in the middle of the day and not at work.

"Saturday?" I asked, though I knew I shouldn't.

"The charity fund-raiser," Mom said and picked up her day planner.

"Which charity?"

She pursed her lips distastefully. "Something about sick people, I think."

Why had I come here? Why had I thought I'd get a little sympathy or support? It just went to show that I was still in shock. Yes, that was it. Despite Kirk Keegan's encouragement, I wasn't really over what happened.

"Yeah, okay, Mom, I've got to go now," I told her.

"One o'clock sharp," she called, flipping a page in her day planner. "Don't be late."

"For what?"

"You're helping me at the event," Mom said. "I explained my new business to you. Don't you recall?"

"Oh yeah. Sure."

I didn't really remember, but this was easier.

"See you Saturday," she called and picked up the phone again.

I headed back to my car. I desperately needed to get my friends together tonight. And I knew just the place, I decided, pulling my cell phone from my purse. As soon as everyone got off work at five, I'd have them meet me at—

"Oh, crap. . . ."

My shoulders slumped and I shoved my phone into my purse again.

I had to work at Holt's tonight.

I hate that job.

Would I make it two for two today? I wondered as I pulled into a parking space outside the Holt's store. Would I go inside only to be told—yet again today—that I'd lost my job? I mean, really, how seriously would Holt's management take it after they spotted me on the stockroom surveillance tape lounging on the Laura Ashley bed-in-a-bag sets? I mean, come on, I couldn't be the only employee who ever did that.

I got out of my car, relieved that I didn't see Rita outside the store holding up a "Haley, You're Fired" banner, and headed inside. It was a long, slow walk. I couldn't stop wondering how, suddenly, a crappy second job at a crappy department store, had turned into a good thing. What had happened to my life?

Bad as it was, it was temporary, I reminded myself. Kirk Keegan would call any minute now, give me the news that the investigation was speeding to a conclusion and I could return to Pike Warner. I'd just have to tough it out.

I amused myself with thoughts of that Louis Vuitton organizer, and that lasted until I walked into the employee break room. Several people were already there, some eating at the tables, others lined up next to the time clock waiting for a few more minutes of their lives to tick away before they punched in. Nobody was wearing an of-course-you-can smile. They all stared at me, then glanced away.

Oh God—just like this morning when I'd walked into the accounts payable unit at Pike Warner.

Louis Vuitton organizer . . . Louis Vuitton organizer . . . Louis Vuitton organizer. . . .

Mentally, I pushed aside all other thoughts and brought that organizer into the center of my being—which wasn't that hard, really—as I put my purse in my locker and donned my name badge.

Two of the employees rushed up, crowding around me.

"Holy shit, girlfriend, I heard what went down last night," Bella said.

Bella was tall, black, and about my age. Girlfriend had style, especially her hair. Tonight it looked like a water sprinkler. She was saving for beauty school. Bella hated everything about working at Holt's, so we hit it off right away.

"Is it true?" Sandy asked.

Sandy—I could only guess that her mom was a big *Grease* fan—was white and about twenty years old. She had reddish hair that she usually wore in a ponytail. Strands were always coming loose, hanging around her face, so she looked like a kindergarten teacher on a Friday afternoon. Sandy had a boyfriend. He was a tattoo artist. They met on the Internet.

I nodded. "Richard's dead. Murdered."

"I heard you found him—in women's lingerie?" Sandy said.

"Oh yeah," I said.

"So it's true?" Sandy asked, her eyes wide.

"I knew he was a sick bastard," Bella declared.

"Gross!" Sandy said, then shook her head. "You really had to see Richard *like that*?"

"I'd gouge my own eyes out," Bella swore, "if *I'd* seen Richard wearing women's lingerie."

They thought I'd found Richard actually wearing lingerie? Gross, all right.

"Everybody's all twisted up about Richard," Bella reported. "I heard two people quit already. And heads are rolling."

"Todd, the LP guy? He got fired," Sandy said.

Good, I thought. Todd deserved to be fired, yet I was mildly surprised to hear it, even though I'd mentioned it to that really cute Ty Cameron last night. How unlike anything with a corporate structure to move so quickly. But since Ty was head of Loss Prevention, I guess he could do what he wanted.

"And you know what else I heard?" Sandy said, drawing herself up.

I knew the most juicy bit of news was coming. I eased closer.

I love talking smack about people.

"The actual owner of the Holt's chain of stores is here today," Sandy said.

"The owner?" I echoed. I didn't know Holt's had an owner. I wonder if they covered that in orientation.

Bella leaned in even closer. "And do you know who's *not* here today?"

No, wait. I was wrong. *This* was the juiciest piece of gossip.

Bella looked back and forth between us; then her eyes widened and her nostrils flared a little and she said, "Glenna Webb."

"I hate that bitch," Sandy said.

I hated her too. Glenna Webb was the area manager of women's clothing. We'd had a couple of run-ins already.

"So what's the deal with her not being here today?" I asked.

Bella rolled her eyes. "Glenna was *doing* Richard."

"He's married," Sandy said. "And so is she."

I gasped. Oh God, this was good stuff.

"He used to watch her on the store surveillance cameras," Bella said. "I was in the security office once and saw him doing it. Now, that's *sick*."

"Maybe things will get better around here, now that Richard's gone," Sandy said.

"Don't count on it," Bella told her.

They went back to their table and I got in line at the time clock. I hung back, making it a point, as always, to be the last to clock in—I offset this by being the first to clock out—and took a look at the daily work schedule clamped to a clipboard, hanging on the wall.

I could tell this was one of Richard's schedules because it made no sense. There was no rhyme or reason to it, just the product of a sick mind, it seemed to me. Richard made up the work schedule for the entire store and he plugged employee names into date and time slots to suit his own whim.

No one could ever predict what day or hours they might be working, even after they requested to work only at specific times. And if Richard scheduled you to work and you couldn't, then it was up to you to find someone to cover your shift.

Crappy, huh?

I saw that I was assigned to the shoe department tonight. My spirits lifted. I loved working in the shoe department because the shelves were really high and it was easy to pretend you couldn't see the customers. Also, there was a stockroom right there at the department, and even if they didn't have bed-in-a-bag sets to lounge on, you could stay back there a long time, pretending to find shoes for the customers.

The door to the break room opened and Jeanette Avery, the store manager, walked in. She was easily in her fifties and might have been a nice-looking woman if it weren't for the hideous outfits she always wore. I could see at a quick glance that it was a suit sold here at Holt's. She always wore Holt's clothing. It must have been in her contract; otherwise no one in their right mind would be caught in a Holt's outfit.

She started talking to the ten of us who'd just clocked in and I moved to a strategic location at the rear of the group so she couldn't see me if I yawned, as she broke the news that Richard had been found dead in the stockroom last night. I guess management was taking it pretty seriously, what with this personal address from the store manager, plus a visit from the owner. There was probably a lawsuit in this somewhere—see how I truly belonged at Pike Warner?—and I decided to mention it to Kirk Keegan when he called.

While Jeanette Avery yammered on about Richard's death, I took a look at the employee work schedule again. About two weeks' worth of daily schedules were on the clipboard. I flipped back to yesterday, the day of Richard's murder, and saw my name near the bottom of the page. Richard's name was at the top, of course. Rita was listed too, along with Evelyn and that girl Julie, who sat at the front door handing out credit applications. Glenna Webb was there also. Lots of other people were too, of course, but I didn't recognize their names. I'd only worked here a few days and, so far, I'd done a pretty good job of blocking out most everyone and everything.

The crowd began to move toward the door and I realized Jeanette had finished speaking. I turned to go, then saw Rita across the room, glaring at me. I glared right back, of course, and left the break room.

I didn't get far. Jeanette Avery stepped in front of me. For a couple of heart-stopping seconds I thought she was going to tell me I was fired, but she didn't.

"I wanted to tell you personally that I'm sorry for what you went through last night," Jeanette said in a low voice.

She shuddered and I got the idea she was really upset about it.

It didn't seem like the best time to tell her I thought Richard was a prick or that most everyone in the store—including me—was actually glad he was dead. So I said what my mom had taught me to say in these situations.

"Thank you for your concern," I told her.

Jeanette seemed satisfied with my response. She drew a little breath and straightened her shoulders.

"The store owner is here today," she said. "He would like to speak with you."

The store owner wanted to talk to me? Personally? I wondered if I was getting some sort of award. I deserved one. I mean, I had kept the store employees calm last night, got the police here without causing a major scene that could have frightened the store patrons into a full-blown panic. I probably saved the company millions in lawsuits.

"He's in my office," Jeanette said, gesturing down the hallway.

I turned, saw an Armani suit and silk tie, and had a Pike Warner flashback. A gorgeous suit with a European cut and—oh, wow. *Oh, wow.* Ty Cameron was wearing it. Loss Prevention must pay better than I thought. And oh my God, he looked handsome.

"Hey, Ty," I called and gave him a little finger wave.

He nodded his head but didn't smile.

"Go ahead," Jeanette said, urgently. "He's very busy today."

"Go where?" I asked.

She pinched her lips together and bobbed her brows toward Ty. "Go talk to the store owner."

"But that's not—"

I looked at Ty and a really big knot hardened in my stomach. My palms started to sweat.

"That's Ty Cameron," I said to Jeanette. "He's the—"

"Store owner," Jeanette said through tight lips.

"But I thought . . . isn't he the . . ."

Oh God.

I turned to Ty. He stood in the doorway of Jeanette's private office waiting for me, and holding a videocassette in his hand.

Oh, crap.

CHAPTER 5

The first thing I did was check the desk. No personnel file with my name on the tab. A good sign, but I couldn't let down my guard.

"Please, have a seat," Ty said, gesturing to the chair in front of the desk.

The office was small, dimly lit, and furnished with a gray metal desk and black chairs. Everything was cluttered with stacks of folders and papers, and the walls had the same posters as the break room, notices about employee rights and wages, the store's sales target, the teaser about the secret Christmas merchandise.

It was a little disconcerting that store management had to be constantly reminded of these things.

I sat down. Ty circled behind the desk. He looked at me for a moment, then gripped the videocassette with both hands.

"About last night . . ." he said.

Oh God. He's going to fire me.

Ty looked at me for another moment, then sat down in the chair and placed the videocassette in the center of the desk.

He'd watched the stockroom surveillance tape and seen me sitting on the Laura Ashley bed-in-a-bag sets. And now he was going to fire me.

"I was shocked by what happened last night," Ty said in a concerned voice. He looked at me, then squared off the cassette and folded his hands.

I forced myself to sit still in the chair, but my mind raced.

If I lost this job, what sort of employment was left to me? Fast food? Doing nails?

"Everyone was stunned," Ty said, inching his hands closer to the cassette.

How was I going to live? Move in with my parents?

Oh God, no. There had to be something I could do.

Maybe I should offer to have sex with him. My spirits lifted a little—more than a little, really. He was awfully good looking, especially in that Armani suit. And I hadn't had sex in a while. The desk was kind of small, but if I braced my feet against the chair—

Oh my God, what was I thinking? I couldn't have sex with Ty Cameron to keep my job—I could under other circumstances, of course—but not for a job at Holt's. Jeez, what had I sunk to?

I straightened my shoulders and sat up a little higher in the chair. I'd already lost one job today—temporarily, of course—at the biggest, baddest law firm in the world. I'd faced Mrs. Drexler and walked away with my head held high. I wasn't going to buckle now.

"So," I said, staring right back at Ty, "what's happening with the investigation?"

His left eyebrow crept up a little and he sat up straighter, then pointed at the videocassette.

"The detectives watched the tape of the stockroom," he said, looking hard at me.

I refused to allow myself to flinch.

"And?" I asked.

He picked up the cassette, studied it for a moment, turned it over in his hands a couple of times, and laid it down again.

"I watched it too," he said.

I gritted my teeth and pushed my chin up.

"So, what was on it?" I asked. "Any leads in Richard's murder?"

The question hung between us for a long, excruciating moment while he stared at me and I stared right back.

"The images are black and white, and pretty grainy," he said.

"Did you recognize anyone?"

"I'm not familiar with every person who works here, so Craig Matthews looked at the tape, along with the detectives. He ID'd everyone," he said. Another moment passed painfully slow. "There was nothing useful," he finally said. "The cameras only cover the entrances to the stockroom, not the stockroom itself."

I nearly fell out of my chair.

"Oh well, too bad," I managed to say, as I stood up. "Look, I've got to get to work. I'm in shoes tonight and—"

"One more thing," Ty said, coming to his feet.

Oh, jeez, what now? If this guy was waiting to see my of-course-you-can smile, he could just—

"I wanted to thank you for keeping a cool head last night," Ty said. "You kept a lid on things, handled everything discreetly. I appreciate that."

"Oh. Well, you're welcome," I said and headed for the door.

"I took your advice," Ty said, moving around the desk. "I fired the LP guy on duty last night. We're going to have to shift some people around for a while to cover all the departments."

Great. Just what the employees needed. More changes.

I headed for the door but Ty jumped around me and opened it. He stood there looking down at me, and I couldn't help but notice how good he smelled. Or that my knees were shaking a bit and my heart seemed a little jumpy.

But maybe it was just my relief that I hadn't been fired.

"Thanks again," he said and gave me a little smile.

"No problem," I said and left the office.

"The detectives might want to talk with you again," Ty said. "They're coming by later."

"Yeah, okay, whatever," I said.

I walked away, stunned by my good luck. No one had seen me lying on the Laura Ashley bed-in-a-bag sets in the stockroom. The cameras didn't cover that area, or the film had been too grainy for my face to be recognized. Either way, I was off the hook. Thank God.

I decided my night needed a boost so I headed for the break room. Too bad you couldn't get beer from a vending machine. I settled for chocolate.

The break room smelled like one of those diet meals, and a girl was standing at the microwave gazing through the glass panel in the door. Somebody told me she'd lost twenty-five pounds. I have to say she looked great, but I still hate her, of course.

I ate my Snickers bar in silence, trying to come to terms with what had just happened. On the plus side, I still had my job at Holt's. And on the minus side, I still had my job at Holt's.

Why hadn't Kirk Keegan called me yet?

I decided to get my cell phone from my purse and check for messages. Who knows, maybe the Pike Warner investigation had already been completed and they were expecting me in the Accounts Payable unit tomorrow morning.

What a nice thought—almost as nice a thought as the memory of the red leather Notorious bag I'd bought this morning.

But as I dug through my purse, another thought came to me.

If Ty Cameron and the police detectives hadn't spotted anybody unusual on the stockroom surveillance tape, that meant Richard's murderer was an employee.

I was working with a murderer.

My hopes rose, as I thought it might be Rita. Or that bitch-face Glenna Webb. Cooler still, if it were both of them.

Whoever had killed Richard would be listed on the daily work schedule from yesterday. I remembered looking at it when I clocked in, so I went back to the clipboard hanging by the time clock and flipped the page. It wasn't there.

I looked at all the schedules, going back nearly two weeks. Yesterday's was gone.

Ty had said the police detectives would be in the store asking questions, but they weren't expected until later. Periodically, one of the managers would take the schedules from the clipboard and file them away somewhere, I guessed, but why would they take just one? Why not all of them?

I got a little chill as I left the break room and stopped at the customer service booth. Grace was at the counter, just finishing up with a customer. She was only about nineteen, just out of high school and taking some college classes.

"Hey, Grace, how's it going?" I asked, when her customer left.

"I'm freaked. Totally freaked," Grace said and shivered. "I heard that Richard was found in the stockroom—wearing women's panties."

Jeez, how do these crazy rumors get started?

"Can I see the work schedule?" I asked.

Lots of things are kept in the customer service booth, including a binder with another copy of the daily work schedule in case employees need to call in and ask what hours they're supposed to work. Grace laid it on the counter in front of me, then went to wait on another customer.

I flipped the page back to yesterday. The schedule was gone. All the others were there, but yesterday's had been removed.

Okay, now I was totally freaked.

Someone who worked in Holt's had murdered Richard. And someone was covering it up.

The shoe department at Holt's handled footwear for the whole family. There were rows and rows of tall shelves that were too close together for two strollers—or two large customers—to pass, and not nearly enough benches where customers could sit and try on shoes. The department was self-service but employees were on hand to hunt up a specific size or color in the stockroom and, of course, to clean up after thoughtless, inconsiderate people who tried on a dozen pairs of shoes and left the boxes and tissue paper on the floor.

Yes, I know I used to do the same thing, but that was different.

Tonight things were kind of slow in the store; I wondered if word of Richard's murder had gotten out and was keeping people away. A couple with three small kids was in the children's section, so I positioned myself at the opposite end of the department, near women's shoes. I usually hung out in that area anyway, so I could try things on when no one was looking.

Sophia, who was the department lead, walked up as I was looking at the pumps. She was a little powerhouse. Barely five feet tall, chunky, but in a muscular way. She was Hispanic. I couldn't guess her age, but I knew she had five kids.

"I heard you found Richard dead," Sophia said, then shook her head in disgust. "Bastard. Served him right."

I expected her to say something about Richard being found wearing women's lingerie, but she didn't. Thank goodness I didn't have to hear that again.

"Some of the other employees are kind of creeped out, knowing he got murdered right here in the stockroom," I said.

"Nobody should feel worried here in the store," Sophia said, "unless they're hurting other people, like he was."

"Richard was an ass, all right," I agreed.

"I've worked here a long time—a lot longer than Richard. Then he comes in here with his new ways, making changes, causing trouble," Sophia said. "Why should I pretend like I'm sorry he's dead? I'm not sorry. You ask me, I say he got what he deserved."

Sophia seemed deep in thought for a couple of minutes, then snapped out of it and waved her hand at the shoes.

"I've got paperwork in the stockroom. Come find me if it gets busy," she said, then disappeared through the door in the back wall of the department.

I looked at my watch. Hours to go before the store closed and I could leave. I needed to entertain myself somehow.

My thoughts flew to Kirk Keegan. He said I should give it a few days before expecting to hear anything from Pike Warner's investigation, but I didn't know if I could last that long. The clock was ticking, days were passing, and I wasn't getting paid my usual Pike Warner wage.

A customer wandered into the department, so I stooped down and pretended to straighten the boxes on the bottom shelf.

Mentally, I calculated what the loss of my Pike Warner income—even for a few days—meant in real-time dollars. It was a lot. Huge. It translated into the difference between a Dooney & Bourke and a Fendi bag.

I hoped Kirk got back to me soon.

Slowly, I rose and took a peek over the racks. No sign of the customer. Good. I turned and almost ran into her.

She'd sneaked up on me from behind. Was I losing my touch here?

I managed an of-course-you-can smile, by way of a greeting, and she gave me a weak smile in return. She looked good in Tommy Hilfiger jeans and a T-shirt, and carried a Chanel satchel.

"I love your bag," I blurted out.

"Thanks," she said, and I wondered what someone with her good taste was doing here in Holt's.

"Can I help you find a size?" I asked, thinking that I could hide out in the stockroom for an easy ten minutes, pretending to search.

She shook her head. "No, thanks."

We looked at each other for a few seconds and, I swear, I read her mind.

"The shoes are kind of crappy here," I said.

"Yeah. Kind of," she agreed. "Who's your buyer?"

"Probably the same person who orders the clothes," I said.

She laughed and I did too.

Okay, now I'm liking my job.

"I'm studying at the FIDM," she said.

"Cool," I said.

The Fashion Institute of Design and Merchandising in Los Angeles was world-renowned, so I knew she was serious about clothes and shoes—the important things in life.

"Holt's must be your don't-let-this-happen-to-your-store project," I said.

"You guessed it."

"We got in some boots that aren't too awful," I said. "Want to see them?"

"Sure."

I turned around and there stood Ty Cameron blocking the aisle. Oh God. Had he heard me talking crap about his store's shoes? I hoped not. *Oh, please, don't let it be so.*

"Could I see you for a minute?" Ty asked. "When you've shown this customer our boots?"

Damn it.

I walked two rows over to the boots and spent a really long time explaining every style to the customer—while wearing my of-course-you-can smile—then waited while she tried on two pairs and decided to buy one. I stretched it out as long as I could, thinking Ty would get bored and go away, but he didn't. He just stood there, watching. When the customer left, he walked over. I expected to get an earful about criticizing the store's merchandise—like it was my fault the shoes were awful—but he didn't say anything about it.

"Can you leave the department for a few minutes?" he asked.

I can *always* leave the department.

"The detectives are here," Ty said. "They'd like to talk to you again."

Detectives Shuman, the young one, and Madison, the old one, were in the office Richard had used when Ty and I got there. The file cabinet and desk drawers were open and everything looked sort of scattered, so I guessed they were looking for evidence.

I glanced at my wristwatch wondering if I could stretch this out until closing.

"Could I speak with you, Mr. Cameron?" Detective Madison asked, levering himself out of the desk chair.

Ty nodded and Detective Madison glared at me as the two of them left the office and closed the door. Detective Shuman moved away from the file cabinet and gestured at the chairs in front of Richard's desk.

"Want to sit down?" he asked, smiling. "I worked at Wal-Mart in college. Hard on the feet."

I sat down and he took the chair next to me. He had on a J.C. Penney, or maybe a Sears, sport coat, and a tie so awful it could have been purchased here at Holt's, but he pulled it off pretty well with the shirt he wore. Shuman might make a fun reclamation project.

We just sort of sat there for a while in silence, looking at each other, then diverting our eyes and gazing around the office, then doing the same thing all over again.

"I'm supposed to wait for Detective Madison," Shuman said after a while, and gave me an apologetic smile.

He seemed like a nice guy, probably the thinker of the two. I doubted Madison liked him very much.

"I don't know anything else to tell you guys," I said.

"I figured. But Detective Madison wanted to talk with you again."

Another silent moment dragged by.

"So, do you have any new clues?" I asked, just for something to say.

"Some," he told me.

"Like what?"

"I'm not supposed to say."

"Well, yeah, but can you tell me anyway?" I asked.

Shuman grinned, as if he thought I was cute.

"We found the murder weapon," he told me. "One of those carts that's used to move the merchandise around."

The store had two kinds of carts for moving things. One was a Z-rail, used for hanging items. I figured he was talking about a U-boat. It was a flat-bottomed hauler, about four feet long and a foot wide, with tall, removable bars on each end that gave it a U shape. Both were designed to navigate the narrow aisles. There were dozens of them all over the store and stockroom.

"Somebody pulled one of the metal bars off a U-boat and hit Richard with it?" I asked, feeling very Gill Grissom-ish. "A crime of opportunity."

Shuman studied the floor for a few minutes, then glanced back at the door before turning to me again.

"Look, Miss Randolph," he said in a low voice, "we found out about your job at the law firm."

I jumped. What? They know I'm on administrative leave from Pike Warner? They've been investigating—me?

"I don't think there's much to it," Shuman said, "but Madison thinks there's a connection."

"A connection?" I all but shrieked. "Between what?"

He motioned with his hand for me to calm down, and glanced at the door again.

"You got fired—"

"It's administrative leave."

"—and you work in accounts payable. Fraud is serious."

"Fraud? I didn't do anything fraudulent," I insisted.

"Then there's that overdraft on your checking account."

"It's tiny!"

"Plus all those credit cards you have."

"There aren't so many," I told him.

"You got a duplicate driver's license from the DMV. Madison thinks you're planning to disappear."

"My purse was stolen," I almost shouted.

"And Evelyn Croft? Your supervisor last night?" Shuman said. "She said you didn't seem upset when she saw you coming out of the stockroom after finding the body. Everybody agreed you were very calm."

"I'm good under pressure," I told him.

"So you see the connection?" he asked.

"No! I don't see any connection at all!"

"You have financial problems. You lost your job on the same day your boss here got murdered." Shuman shook his head. "Detective Madison thinks you're involved. He thinks Richard threatened to fire you and you killed him."

Oh my God. They're trying to pin Richard's murder on me. Me!

I was going to jail—way worse than getting fired.

I don't want to go to jail. I don't want my new BFF to be Large Marge. And jumpsuits make my butt look big—and orange is a terrible color on me—and do prisoners ever get to carry a purse?

Oh, crap.

CHAPTER 6

My apartment was in a sprawling complex in Santa Clarita, just off the freeway about thirty minutes from downtown L.A., unless there's traffic, of course, which there almost always was. Then the commute could take forever.

I liked my place. It was a new, upscale area where lots of younger people live. Great bars, restaurants, shops, and stores. When I first moved in I couldn't afford to do much with the apartment, but thanks to my job at Pike Warner—and my credit cards—I'd done the place up right. The very latest style, yet warm and inviting at the same time.

But right now, my living room seemed to be tilted a little. Then I realized it was me. And the Corona I'd worked my way through—it's always that last six-pack that gets you. I had help, of course.

My best friend, Marcie Hanover, sat on the other end of the sofa. I'd stopped on the way home and bought beer, cheese sticks, hot wings, and chips—everyone knows calories don't count when you're upset—and now we were in sweats, and had ditched the chilled mugs I'd brought out when she arrived. We were guzzling straight from the bottles.

"That Mrs. Drexler is a bitch," Marcie said.

"She's always been a bitch," I said, for probably the fifth time.

When I'd left Holt's tonight I'd phoned Marcie and she'd rushed over. I told her all about what had happened at Pike Warner. In fact, I'd told it several times now and, of course, the details kept growing and the story got worse, but that's just the way these things are done.

"And a fat cow too," I added, which wasn't true, but still . . .

"She's just jealous because you're prettier," Marcie said.

"And younger."

"How does she keep her job?" Marcie wondered, waving her bottle around.

"She must give one hell of a blow job," I said, then took another sip of beer. "Kirk Keegan is checking around. He'll let me know what's going on."

"I saw Kirk the other night," Marcie said.

She'd been with me at the club several months ago when I met Kirk. She hadn't been crazy about him, and even after he'd gotten me the great job at Pike Warner, Marcie still hadn't changed her opinion of him.

"You were working at Holt's," Marcie explained. "I went out with those girls from work, to that other girl's going-away party, at that place at City Walk."

"Oh yeah, right," I said and, somehow, knew exactly what she was talking about.

"Kirk was there."

"Who was he with?" I asked.

Marcie shrugged. "That dark-haired girl."

"Oh yeah. Her." I'd seen her around, but had never met her. She seemed sort of standoffish.

"I don't think it was a date, or anything. She only stayed a little while, then left."

I know Marcie added that last part because she knew I used to have a thing for Kirk. We'd gone out a couple of times, but it never turned into anything, and it still kind of bothered me, even though I always knew Kirk wasn't interested in a relationship with me. When we went to a club we always met there, and he never cared when I table-hopped or danced with other people. He did threaten to sue the club owner that night my purse was stolen, but I think that was just to show off.

"So I guess it's a good thing that you have that Holt's job," Marcie said.

"Oh my God . . ." I moaned, then told her that whole story.

"That's awful." Marcie shook her head. "Has *anything* good happened to you lately?"

I thought about it for a few seconds. "There's this really good-looking guy at the store."

I filled her in on Ty Cameron—but left out the part about the Laura Ashley bed-in-a-bag sets, the time he'd caught me talking crap about the store's shoes, the way I'd blasted him about firing Todd the LP guy the night of Richard's murder—which didn't leave much to talk about.

"He owns the store, or the chain of stores, or something," I said.

"He must be rich," Marcie said.

Rich is a relative term, according to my mom. As she says, there's money, then there's *money*.

"You should come by the store and look at him sometime," I suggested.

"Okay," Marcie said, then got up from the sofa. "I've got to go."

I glanced at the clock and saw that it was after midnight.

"Thanks for coming over," I said, and walked with her to the door.

"No problem." Marcie bumped into the table by the door and sent a stack of envelopes cascading onto the floor. Three days worth of mail. Unopened.

She picked them up and glanced at the return addresses.

I'd already seen them—mostly credit card companies, which was why I hadn't bothered to open them. I knew what they said.

Marcie looked hard at me, the way only a best friend can get away with.

"Are you okay with your money?" she asked.

"Yeah, sure," I said, taking the stack of mail from her. "Kirk said everything at Pike Warner will be straightened out in a couple of days. I'll be back to work by the end of the week."

"You could ask your parents for help," she suggested.

I'd rather dig out my left eye with a spoon.

"You know, there're lots of ways to make money these days. On the Internet, eBay. I'll think of something." Marcie studied me for a minute. "You need anything, you let me know."

"I will," I said. "Thanks."

"I'll come by the store and look at Ty," she said. "Are you working tomorrow?"

"I'm afraid so."

Marcie left and I glanced over the bills once more. Yep, credit card statements, plus one from the bank. My overdraft notice. Again.

I dumped them on the table, ignored the mess in the living room, and went to bed. Marcie was right. I needed more money. An option that Marcie, mercifully, hadn't mentioned sprang into my head.

I could work more hours at Holt's.

I woke the next morning with a headache and two very clear thoughts.

One, the only way to make real money on the Internet was with porn. Two, if Holt's found out about what was going on at Pike Warner, they'd fire me.

It was all too much to contemplate. The truth was I'd been through a lot. I didn't know whether or not I still had medical benefits, so I couldn't see a shrink, and that left only one way to heal.

I got dressed and went shopping.

The mall was quiet, mostly young mothers pushing baby strollers, older women with husbands standing outside dressing rooms holding their purses. This was a whole different side of shopping I hadn't seen before. No hustle and bustle, no crowds, no pushing and shoving.

I took a breath and strolled along, suddenly feeling comfortable here. No one around me knew I was on unpaid administrative leave, or that my checking account overdraft rivaled the national debt, or that I was the prime suspect in a murder investigation. To them, I was simply a woman of leisure. They probably thought I had a husband hard at work in some downtown high-rise, and I was wiling away the hours shopping for my next dinner party.

Oh my God. That sounded just like my mother.

I rushed into Banana Republic.

The salesclerks didn't pay much attention to me when I started yanking clothes off the rack—honestly, what sort of service was this?—and went into the dressing room. I tried on some DKNY jeans. They looked pretty hot, so I tried on a couple more pairs, plus the T-shirts I'd collected, and the two jackets. Everything looked great and actually fit comfortably, an alignment so rare in the fashion cosmos that I was obligated to buy them. I paid with my credit card and left the store with three shopping bags.

Wow, this was kind of cool. Not a bad way to spend a few days until Pike Warner called me back to work. That little naggie feeling crept over me again. I decided it wouldn't hurt to check on things. I pulled out my cell phone and called Kirk.

"I've already talked to people," he said, before I could even say anything. "Everything is moving along. Things are happening."

"Great," I said. I heard him rustling papers in the background. "How much longer before they'll let me come back?"

"I don't know."

"It will be this week, though, won't it? Before—"

"I told you not to worry," Kirk said.

"I'm not worried, it's just that—"

"I'll call you."

Kirk hung up and I stood there for a minute after I tucked my phone away. Okay, that went all right. Kirk had things moving and everything was working out. I didn't have anything to worry about. Well, I had plenty to worry about, but not my job at Pike Warner.

So that left me with shopping. It occurred to me that this was a golden opportunity to get all my Christmas shopping done. The stores weren't crowded, I wasn't pinched for time, I could shop leisurely and select a great gift for everyone. If I got started today, I could have everything finished before I went back to work at Pike Warner. So where to begin?

I looked up and down the long mall and spotted Macy's. They carried great handbags. It occurred to me that the green croc Betsey Johnson purse I'd seen in there last week would look great with my new DKNY jeans. So why not start out with a gift for myself?

I missed Pike Warner. At Pike Warner casual day meant wearing a suit without a lining. Nobody wore nice clothes at Holt's. Nobody carried a designer purse. I just didn't fit in here.

I stood at the time clock waiting along with a half dozen other employees, and glanced at my watch. I hadn't even punched in yet and already I was counting down the hours until I could leave.

The girl in front of me looked back. It was that girl Julie, the Holt's credit greeter who sat by the front door handing out credit applications.

"You're the one who found Richard, aren't you?" she asked quietly.

"Yep," I murmured. I passed the lanyard holding my name badge back and forth; I couldn't bring myself to put it on yet.

"Isn't it awful that he got murdered right here in the store?" she whispered. She gnawed on her fingernail. "My mom says I should quit. It's too dangerous here."

I got a little jolt of excitement. Maybe I could get her job. It was a cool job. All you did was sit at a table and hand out credit applications. You didn't have to actually wait on anybody.

"Several people have already quit," I told her, nodding wisely.

"Really?" Julie's eyes widened. "I liked Richard, kinda. I had no idea he was a perv."

I'd have to work on my of-course-you-can smile, though, which still kept morphing into a screw-you smile.

"Is it true that when you found him in the stockroom, he was wearing a thong?" Julie asked.

The time clock *thunked* as employees fed in their time cards and the line moved forward. I glanced at the work schedule on the clipboard and saw that I was assigned to the women's department tonight. Glenna Webb was on the schedule too. I wondered if she'd be here tonight, or if she was still too distraught by the death of her illicit lover.

As I headed down the aisle dodging two screaming kids, Evelyn Croft stepped out from behind mannequins dressed in workout clothes.

"Haley, do you mind—could you—that is—"

"I'm in women's tonight," I said.

She glanced around and nodded. "Yes. Yes, I know. But could I talk to you for just a quick minute?"

"Sure, Evelyn, take all the time you need."

She leaned closer. "Not here. In the office."

Okay, that's odd. But it kept me off the sales floor for a

few minutes, so I followed her to the back of the store. Rita was in the customer service booth when we walked past, and I saw her giving us the evil eye. I smiled and waved.

I'd been in this office the night of Richard's murder. The room seemed smaller this time, the light less harsh. Evelyn seemed just as upset now as she had been that night. She pushed the door closed quietly, then stood with her hand on the knob.

"What's up?" I asked, leaning back and bracing my hands against one of the desks.

"Those police detectives were here again last night," Evelyn said, still whispering. "They . . . they asked me about . . . what happened."

I figured the detectives had spoken with everyone working the night of Richard's murder, including Evelyn.

She pressed her lips together, then said, "They asked me about . . . you."

I straightened away from the desk, a little surprised. I'd wondered if Detective Shuman had told me the truth last night when he said he'd talked with Evelyn, and I'd considered that he'd made it up hoping to shock a confession out of me. Now I knew that he'd been telling the truth.

"I had to tell them what happened," Evelyn said, twisting her fingers together. "But they kept trying to make something different out of it. I'd say one thing and they would turn it around. I—I didn't mean to say anything bad about you, or implicate you in anything, but they wouldn't leave me alone."

"It's okay," I said.

I didn't know what it was about this woman that made me feel sorry for her all the time. She'd just told me that, thanks to her, the police thought I murdered Richard, and all I could do was try to make her feel better.

"The whole thing is silly," Evelyn declared, still wringing her hands. "I mean, you couldn't possibly have killed

Richard. And that other rumor going around that he was wearing pink panties and a Wonderbra—well, it's just ridiculous. Anyway, I wanted to let you know."

"Thanks for the heads-up," I said.

We walked out of the office together, and just as I got to the customer service booth, I realized I didn't have my name badge with me. I must have dropped it on the desk.

"I left my badge," I said to Evelyn, pointing back toward the office.

She nodded and kept walking and I went inside again.

I saw a personnel folder on the desk and my heart jumped. I looked closer and saw it wasn't mine, thank God. It was Sophia Garcia's.

I'd just worked with her in the shoe department last night and she seemed okay. Maybe she'd changed her mind about working here. Lots of people were skittish now, after Richard's death. Maybe Sophia was quitting.

I stole a quick glance at the door, then moved around the desk and flipped open the folder. On top of the stack of papers clipped inside was a Holt's employee action form. Sophia was being counseled for abusing the employee discount.

You could do that? That was probably something else they covered in orientation.

Attached to the form was a printout of the time, date, merchandise, sales price, and discount price of everything Sophia had purchased.

They kept records of that?

It didn't seem like so many things to me, but apparently Holt's didn't like it.

Or, at least, Richard hadn't liked it.

He'd stated on the form that Sophia was on notice and would lose her job if this continued. He'd signed the form the day of his murder. Sophia had signed it also, so that meant he'd actually talked to her about it.

Okay, I'm no James Bond, but wasn't this a motive for

murder? Sophia had worked here for years, she didn't like Richard, she had five kids, and couldn't afford to lose her job.

Hadn't the police seen Sophia's employee action form? If they had, surely they would have taken it for evidence. Hadn't they searched this office? Were they blind and incompetent?

Or had they stopped investigating when they got to me?

CHAPTER 7

So, Detective Shuman had told the truth when he said he'd talked to Evelyn Croft about me. Seems he'd also told the truth about investigating my credit cards and bank accounts, and contacting Pike Warner.

I didn't see how he could have found out anything from Pike Warner. First of all, they were lawyers. They wouldn't have said anything. And even if they had, how bad could it be? I mean, the worst thing I could have done there was use a wrong accounting code. Pike Warner had dozens of them, and they were mostly just alike, and really, anybody could have gotten them mixed up. I didn't handle any money, except to send an authorization to the girls in cashiering to disburse a check, and all of that had been decided long before I went to work there. Every invoice I received was from a company already approved by Pike Warner. I had a file cabinet with folders of vendors I was authorized to pay, up to a certain dollar amount. It was a no-brainer job.

And that certainly doesn't constitute fraud, as Shuman claimed, and it certainly wouldn't lead to Richard's murder. Even a detective should be able to see that an accounting error could be corrected.

All of these thoughts kept going around and around in my head as I worked in the women's clothing department, straightening racks of clothes. I wondered if I should talk to Detective Shuman about Richard writing up Sophia Garcia the day of his murder. I didn't want to get her into trouble. She had those five kids to take care of. She needed her job.

Badly enough to kill for it?

And what about Glenna Webb? Did the detectives know she'd been romantically involved with Richard? And that both Richard and Glenna were married?

Up until yesterday, I didn't know about Sophia or Glenna. It made me wonder who else at Holt's might have a motive to kill Richard.

It made me think that maybe I should do some investigating on my own.

The store was quiet again tonight. Only a few women were in the clothing department. No one seemed interested in trying on anything, except this one girl who seemed desperate to find any two articles of clothing that looked good together.

Not easy at Holt's.

She'd been at it for about fifteen minutes now, going through rack after rack with a kind of desperation that could only come from a last-minute occasion that requires clothing not already in your closet. She stopped suddenly, put her palm against her forehead, and heaved a heavy sigh.

Oh my God, she looked like she was going to cry.

I rushed over. "What's the occasion?"

She looked to be about twenty with a great figure. She could have found clothes anywhere.

She sniffed and drew in a big breath. "I've got a job interview with a really great company. Tomorrow."

"Tomorrow, huh?" I said, and got a great little adrenaline surge. "What sort of job?"

"Receptionist for a recording company down on Sunset."

My eyes bulged. "Oh my God, that's fabulous."

"Yeah, I know. And I need a fabulous outfit."

"Why on earth did you come *here*?" I asked, waving my arms toward the racks of clothing.

She waved her hands too. She was with me all the way.

"I had to. I don't have any money, so my grandma said she'd help me, and this is the only place she has a credit card, so she got me a gift card and charged it to her account," she said.

"Okay. Don't worry. We'll find something great." I turned in a circle, scanning all the racks of clothing. "You want to look businesslike, but cool. Edgy."

"Right."

"Follow me."

I made a sweep of the misses department, then crossed the aisle to Juniors, tossing clothes at her until she could hardly see over them, then loaded up my own arms. Somewhere between the black mini and the red cami, we introduced ourselves; it's impossible to go through something like this and not know each other's name.

We hit the dressing room and I flipped through everything, teaming tops with bottoms.

"Try these on, Jen," I told her. "I'm going for accessories."

I made another pass through the store, grabbing belts, scarves, costume jewelry, then pulled a half dozen pairs of shoes.

Oh, wow. I love this job.

Jen was at the triple-mirror outside the dressing room. We both studied her reflection.

"You can do better," I said. "Try another one."

On the fourth outfit, we knew we had it. I had her try on some of the jewelry I'd picked out, which really cinched the look, then handed her a pair of shoes.

"These look kind of slutty," she said.

"Yeah, I know. Aren't they great?"

"I love them."

While she changed back into her jeans, I went to the handbag section of the accessories department. I stiffened up, unable to move, unable to reach forward and pick up a single bag. I don't do well with nondesigner handbags. I think it's genetic. Once you've had designer, you can't go back.

But I forced myself. Jen needed a great bag for tomorrow and I had to find it for her. I gritted my teeth and plowed through the shelves until I came up with a beaded, black silk bucket. Perfect.

I felt a little wave of accomplishment. It had been tough, almost painful, but I'd managed.

Honestly, the things I do these days.

When I got back to the dressing room, she was frowning again.

"I can't afford all these things," she said. "My grandma's gift card is for a hundred dollars. I'll have to put some of them back."

I looked at the tags and did a quick calculation in my head.

"There's no way you're going to that interview tomorrow without this really cool outfit," I said. "Come on."

Bella was working one of the two registers that were open. I held back until she finished with her customer.

"This is Jen," I told her. "She's got a job interview tomorrow."

"Wearing clothes from here?" Bella grunted. "Where's she interviewing? Salvation Army?"

"Take a look," Jen said, holding up the wrap skirt.

A customer got in line behind Jen, but I ignored her.

Bella looked at each piece. "This is cool stuff. Where'd it come from?"

She pointed. "Haley picked it out for me."

"This outfit was *here*? In Holt's? All this time?" Bella rolled her eyes. "Jen, honey, you got yourself the only decent-looking outfit in the place. And you"—she pointed at me—"you the woman."

She rang everything up and it was more than the hundred-dollar gift card Jen's grandmother had given her.

Three people were in line now, waiting.

"She needs a discount," I told Bella in a low voice.

"Glenna Webb is supposed to approve all discounts," Bella said and huffed. "She's as tight as the ass she wishes she had. She don't give nobody a discount."

"Jen's interview is with a recording company on Sunset," I said.

"Screw the bitch," Bella said, and punched in Jen's discount.

I walked Jen to the door where she thanked me a dozen times and promised to come back and let me know how the interview went; then we hugged and she went on her way. I felt like a mom, or something, sending my kid out into the world. And I was really happy that I'd improved her chances of getting the job. The outfit was a killer, no doubt about it.

I turned back and saw Ty Cameron walking away from Bella's register. I got a little sick feeling in my stomach.

"What's up?" I asked Bella.

"He asked why I gave that girl a discount," she said as she scanned merchandise for the next woman in line.

"How'd he know?" I asked, stunned.

She bobbed her brows upward. "Security cameras. Everywhere."

"What else did he say?" I asked.

"Nothing."

Okay, that was odd. But oh well. All I cared was that I hadn't gotten Bella into trouble.

"I told him you'd found that customer a cool outfit," she said, swiping the customer's credit card. "He still didn't say anything."

That was sort of insulting. I'd located—and sold—probably the only cool outfit ever put together in the history of Holt's, and the owner hadn't said anything. Jeez, you'd think I'd get a plaque, or a certificate, or something.

I went back to the women's department and emptied out the dressing room Jen had used and put everything on hangers again. The outfits I'd put together looked really sharp. It was a shame to separate them, relegate the pieces to the depth of obscurity on the racks. A few minutes later I spotted Glenna Webb. She was the area manager for the women's clothing department.

Since she, obviously, didn't buy her clothes here at Holt's, Glenna dressed better than Jeanette Avery, the store manager. Suits, mostly, with sensible shoes. She took the dress-for-success mantra seriously.

Tonight she looked rough. She'd gone heavy on the makeup. I wondered if that was to cover her grief over losing Richard, her lover. It's hard to imagine Richard would arouse that sort of passion in anyone, so I wondered if something else was going on with Glenna.

I held up one of the outfits I'd selected for Jen. "I think this would look great on a mannequin in the juniors department—"

"We have *trained* personnel who do that," Glenna barked, and kept walking.

I hate this job.

But I was not going to let it get me down. Seven bucks an hour doesn't buy my self-esteem. I went back to work, returning the clothes Jen had tried on to the juniors department.

Sandy was working there tonight. She hurried over.

"Bella told me you put together a really hot outfit for a customer," she said, her eyes wide with amazement. "Can you help me find something? I've got a date tonight with this guy from my mom's office."

"Your mom, huh?" I asked, having a near-fatal flash-back to the one time I'd allowed my mom to set me up.

"I talked to him a couple of times. He seems nice," Sandy said.

Sandy was not lucky at love. Even though she was young and really cute, she was not the best judge of boyfriends. I say, it's one thing to *date* an asshole; it's another to *keep dating* one. Sandy didn't seem to understand that.

Then I remembered that Sandy already had a boyfriend. The tattoo artist she'd met on the Internet.

"What about your tat guy?" I asked.

Sandy frowned. "We broke up. He said I didn't under-stand his art and I had no soul."

"He *said* that?" I exclaimed. "Well, you're lucky to be rid of that guy."

"I miss him," she said, with a heavy sigh.

Jeez. . . .

"The guy from my mom's office invited me out to din-ner," Sandy said, as if she were really excited about it. "I hope he takes me to the Olive Garden."

The Olive Garden is where relationships go to die. I've never heard of a single Olive Garden first date that worked out.

But who was I to say anything? Maybe this guy would be the rare exception in Sandy's love life, the one who treated her well. I shouldn't judge.

I sorted through the clothes draped over my arm. "Take this . . . and this . . . and, yes—no—this. Team them with those red, beaded slides on the end cap. The slutty ones."

"Cool." Sandy took the clothes and hurried away.

After what seemed an eternity, the store closed. That didn't mean we could go home, however. All employees stayed a half hour after closing to "recover" the store, which meant refold and straighten the clothes, and make the place look as if no one had shopped there. This was the time of day when I worked really fast so I could be first in line at the time clock, but Glenna appeared at the last minute and told me to move some clothes around for the sale the next day.

I hate that bitch.

When I finally left the store, the parking lot was nearly deserted. The store had cut back on outdoor lighting, so it was always kind of dark out here. But that was okay with me since I parked near the building in one of the spaces designated for the customers.

As I approached my Honda I realized a man was standing near the front bumper. Great. Was I going to get a Holt's parking ticket now?

Then I saw that it was Ty Cameron. What was he doing here?

"Your car got hit," he said.

No, my car hadn't gotten hit. I had scraped the fender against the retaining wall when I'd run off the freeway the morning I'd left Pike Warner. But I certainly wasn't going to tell Ty that.

"It's nothing," I said.

He shook his head. "If it was hit here in the parking lot, you should file a police report."

Yeah, wouldn't that be great? Shuman and Madison could come out and God knows what they'd accuse me of.

"It's nothing," I said again. "Just a little mishap."

"You weren't hurt, were you?" he asked, looking concerned.

"No," I said. "No, I just ran—swerved off the road. To miss an animal. A dog. It was a puppy, really."

He ran his hand along the fender. "This looks pretty bad."

"I'm getting it fixed. I have an appointment. Tomorrow," I lied. "Tomorrow after work."

He frowned. "Tomorrow night? I've never known a body shop to be open at night. Which one is it?"

Didn't this guy have some place to go?

"It's a friend of the family. My uncle, actually. He's doing it as a favor," I told him.

"So you missed it, didn't you?"

"Missed what?"

"The puppy."

"Oh yeah," I said, forcing a reassuring smile.

"You didn't just leave it there, did you?"

"No. No, I . . . stopped and rescued it."

Ty frowned again. "You didn't take it to the shelter, did you?"

Jesus Christ, why wouldn't he just let it go? "No, I wouldn't do that. I kept it."

"What did you name it?" he asked.

"Pancake."

He looked at me for a long time, and I stared back for as long as I could stand it.

"Look," I said, moving toward the driver's-side door. "I've got to get going."

"You don't want to leave Pancake alone for too long," Ty said.

"Right. Well, good night," I called. I got into my car and backed out of the space.

A few employees were still leaving the store, so I had to stop while they crossed in front of me. Glenna Webb walked behind everybody else, and I was surprised to see a man with her. He wore jeans and a T-shirt, so I figured he wasn't an employee. Nobody at Holt's dressed that bad, even on casual day.

Then I realized it must be her husband. I sat in my Honda watching them walk past, wondering why he would be at the store. Was he worried for her safety because a murder had been committed in the stockroom? From the way they were walking—him out in front by two steps—I doubted it. Maybe, after seeing how distraught Glenna was, he suspected that she'd been having an affair with Richard. Maybe he'd figured it out, or someone had told him, and he'd decided to keep a closer eye on his wife.

They got to their car, an older model Buick, and as Glenna's husband turned to open the door, the security lighting caught him, and I realized I'd seen him before.

A few seconds passed before I placed him. Then I got a cold chill.

I'd seen him in the store. Near the lingerie department. The night Richard had been murdered.

CHAPTER 8

Not only were these few days off from Pike Warner a good opportunity to get my Christmas shopping done; it was also a great time to improve myself. I could stand to lose a pound or two—okay, maybe a few more than that—and it wouldn't hurt me to eat healthier. I mean, how often in life do you get this sort of chance? I couldn't see wasting it.

I sat at my kitchen table the next morning, drinking coffee and eating my second chocolate cupcake—better to be rid of them so I wouldn't be tempted—making a list of the things I needed to do.

First, set some goals. I decided to keep it simple, since I didn't want to overwhelm myself, especially at the beginning of my new lifestyle. I took another bite of cupcake, thought for a minute, then wrote down two goals.

One: to be the after-girl. You know, the one in those TV and magazine ads who looks great after finishing the diet and exercise program. And this tied in directly with my second goal: to be at my driver's-license weight.

Okay, simple enough. I jotted down a list of things I'd need to accomplish this, then put on jeans and a T-shirt, grabbed my orange Dior tote, and headed for the mall.

First, I hit the bookstore and picked up several eating-light cookbooks, along with every fitness magazine on the rack, all with an after-girl on the cover that I aspired to be. Great motivation. The sporting goods store was next on my list. I couldn't start a workout plan without workout clothes and shoes. I put together several really sharp outfits, picked up a couple of water bottles, then finished off each look with a coordinating duffel bag to carry it all in.

I hadn't made it to the health food store yet and my energy level was pretty low, so I went to Starbucks, just to get that one last mocha Frappuccino with whipped cream and extra chocolate syrup out of my system, and sat outside at an umbrella table to review my list.

I'd pretty much covered everything. Of course, it had cost me a couple hundred dollars, but hey, when it comes to changing your life you can't cheap it out and expect results.

I sat in the shade of the umbrella enjoying the sunny day and the light breeze, and looked across at the stores on the other side of the parking lot. Holt's popped into my mind and my mood soured a little. Then I picked up my cell phone I'd laid on the table and checked for messages. None. And that soured my mood a little more.

Why hadn't Kirk called me back? I'd phoned him yesterday and again this morning, and nothing. What was going on at Pike Warner with my investigation? How long was it going to take? I'm not really good at being patient.

Still, I needed some positive way to pass the time. I picked up my pen and started a new list, this one attacking the next big problem in my life: being a murder suspect. I flipped the page and made some notes.

First, the motives for murder. Why would a person kill another person? Ambition, greed, envy, love, money, revenge, of course, and I almost added "clearance sale on designer fashions" but decided that was more like assault, rather than murder.

Next I wrote down the names of the people whom I believed could have been involved in Richard's murder.

Sophia Garcia. Richard had threatened to fire her for abusing the employee discount. Would she have killed to keep her job? It was painful to think that someone would go to that extreme to keep a job at Holt's, of all places, but stranger things have happened. Besides, I don't think it was all about the job with Sophia. She didn't like Richard. Nobody did, but since she was a longtime employee, I couldn't help but think something else was going on there.

Then there was that bitch-hag Glenna Webb. Had Richard broken off their affair? Had she been so outraged she'd grabbed the rail off the U-boat and hit him in the head? Or maybe it had been the other way around. Maybe she'd broken it off, he'd become angry, and she'd hit him in self defense.

Now I could add Glenna's husband to my list. I'd seen him in the store that night. Why was he there? Had he come to the store to confront Richard after learning about the affair? I wondered if Craig Matthews had ID'd him on the stockroom surveillance videotape when he'd looked at it with the detectives and Ty. I have no way of knowing, of course, unless I saw the tape myself, and that didn't seem likely.

I took another sip of my mocha Frappuccino—the caffeine and chocolate had me buzzing pretty good now—and thought more about Richard's murder. Something had been bothering me about that night.

I'd gotten that one look at the employee work schedule by the time clock, before it disappeared, and it had been stuck in the back of my mind ever since. Now I realized why. Craig Matthews. He'd been in the store that night but I hadn't seen his name on the schedule. Why was that?

I sat there a while longer, thinking, then finished my drink and checked my watch. I had time to swing by the health food store, then head to the gym and get started on my new lifestyle before my shift started at Holt's. Plenty of time, actually. I could get some really healthy food, plus a really great workout.

But no need to rush it, I decided. I might manage the health food store better if I was fresh, and I hadn't worked out in a while and didn't want to risk pulling something. Maybe I'd check out those stores across the parking lot.

So here I was standing at the time clock again, more minutes of my life ticking away. Rita held the group captive, blabbing on about something; then everybody moved to the bulletin board that she pointed to and I meandered along with them.

A notice hung there advising all employees of a mandatory meeting in the training room. Several meetings were necessary, so that the sales floor could be covered. A schedule of who was to attend at what time was also posted.

Maybe I could stay for all the meetings? If I sat near the back, maybe no one would notice. Or, better still, I could hang out in the break room and claim I was at the meeting.

Life is full of so many great options, sometimes.

I was contemplating which way to go when Sandy came up beside me.

"I'm in the next meeting too," she said.

My fate was sealed, so I walked along with the crowd to the training room in the complex of offices in the back of the store.

"So, how was your date last night?" I asked. "Did he take you to Olive Garden?"

"No, he didn't have a coupon," she said. "He handed me a coupon book and said we could eat any place I wanted, as long as there was a coupon."

"Please tell me you dumped him on the spot."

"He invited me out again tonight."

"Please tell me you're not going."

Sandy shrugged. "I kinda like him."

The training room had rows of schoolroom desks, a chalkboard, flip chart, and projector, all the equipment necessary to lull the audience into a deep sleep. I got a seat behind this really big guy from Menswear so I could hide from the speaker when I dozed off.

Aside from peons like me, several of the area and department managers were there. Glenna Webb, of course, along with Craig Matthews. Didn't that guy have a home? I swear, regardless of what hours I worked, or which shift, he was here. Evelyn Croft was cowering in the corner.

Everyone came fully alert when Ty Cameron walked into the room. He looked good today, as usual, wearing a Gucci pin-striped suit. From the briefcase he carried, I figured he was running the meeting.

It surprised me a bit that he was still in the store. I figured, once the initial crisis of Richard's murder had passed, he would have gone back to doing whatever it was that chain store owners do all day.

There wasn't another man in the store as handsome as Ty, so I decided to enjoy the view while I could; most of the girls around me were doing the same.

Jeanette Avery, the store manager, came into the room wearing a hideous Play-Doh blue suit—ten of them were hanging on the clearance rack in the women's department at this very moment—and looking grim. Apparently she wasn't enjoying the sight of the store owner every day as much as the rest of us.

Ty had a way of captivating the audience—I'm certain it wasn't just me—as he walked about the room looking everyone in the eye and oozing sincerity as he spoke of the loss of Richard, the distress all the employees had experienced, and the need to heal. He told us how the Holt's "family" was committed to seeing each of us through this difficult time, then expressed concern for the employees who'd been so traumatized by events that they'd felt compelled to leave the company.

His speech rolled along pretty well until he got to the part where he apologized to us that we would have to take up the slack until replacements could be hired.

This had to be bad for us. Even with Christmas only about a month away and seasonal workers eager to make some extra cash for the holidays, I couldn't see a lot of people anxious to work at Holt's, where an employee had been murdered in the stockroom.

"The store values each of you," Ty said, "and we're committed to keeping you involved with what goes on here."

I doubted that, but didn't think it was a good time to interrupt.

"So we're asking for your suggestions," he continued, as he handed a stack of flyers to perfect, of-course-you-can-smile Julie to pass out. "We want you to give us your recommendations on what changes should be made here. For the benefit of employees and the customers."

Julie handed me the single-page flyer. I was definitely going to have to attach addendums.

"And we're going to hold more meetings to discuss your suggestions," Ty said.

I caught a glimpse of Jeanette. She didn't look happy.

The meeting broke up and I headed for the housewares department, my assigned corner of retail hell tonight. Shannon, the department lead, was waiting when I walked up. She, quite obviously, considered Rita a fashion icon because she dressed just like her, farm animal shirts, and all. But Shannon took it to the next level by wearing a fanny pack.

"I want you in the greeting cards," she told me.

Okay, this might be kind of fun. That area had stationery, gift wrap, those small, inspirational books with cloying verses and pictures of clouds, fields, and sleeping babies nestled inside giant fake flowers. I could pass a couple of hours reading.

"Some kid ripped open the confetti packages," Shannon said. She pointed to a huge mound of tiny pastel dots on the floor in front of the greeting card rack. "You'll have to vacuum them up."

I froze. Vacuum? She expected me to run the vacuum?

"I'm not the janitor," I told her.

"He quit. Too afraid to go into the stockroom, after you found Richard there," she said, and made it sound like it was my fault, somehow. "Just do it, will you, before some kid comes along and eats the stuff, or some old lady slips and falls in it?"

Shannon stomped away and I stood there stewing. Vacuum the floor? Me? What had my life become?

I could have ignored Shannon—which I was sorely tempted to do—but she'd probably write me up for insubordination, dereliction of duty, or disobeying a willful command, or something. I didn't know if Failure to Vacuum was grounds for termination here. They'd probably covered that in orientation.

I headed for the stockroom telling myself that this was actually doing a good deed. Someone might really slip and fall and, while the financial settlement from Holt's would surely be sizable, I didn't want anyone to get hurt.

The stockroom was silent as I wound through the tall shelves to the janitor's closet. I realized I hadn't been in here since the night I found Richard. It kind of creeped me out.

I stood at the bottom of the wide, concrete staircase, staring up at the second floor and visualizing the scene of

Richard's murder. The stockroom was so orderly, so clean it was hard to imagine something as awful as a murder could happen here. I tried to picture Sophia swinging that U-boat bar at Richard's head, or Glenna, or even her husband. Not a pretty image to have in my mind.

Then I wondered what else might have gone on back here. Richard and Glenna banging each other—on a Laura Ashley bed-in-a-bag set? Maybe the one *I'd* sat on? Ugh—gross.

I hurried to the janitor's closet, opened the big door, and found all sorts of commercial equipment and dozens of bottles and cans of cleaners inside. It didn't smell so great in here, so I grabbed the vacuum and wheeled it out—and ran smack into Craig Matthews.

I screamed. He yelped and jumped back.

"Jeez, you scared the crap out of me," I told him.

"I'm doing returns," he said, pointing across the room.

That area of the stockroom was where defective or unsaleable merchandise was packed in cardboard containers and wrapped in huge sheets of cellophane to await the arrival of what we called the "returns" truck. It came once a week, picked up the merchandise, and took it to the central warehouse. From there, it was either shipped back to the manufacturer for repair or credit, or sent to wherever unwanted merchandise went to die.

Craig sounded kind of defensive, and I knew I was on edge too. Guess neither one of us was too happy about being in the stockroom again.

"See you," I said, and pushed the vacuum out to the greeting card rack.

This thing was a beast. I hit the button and it roared to life, twice as loud as the one I had at home. Two customers looking at the stationery took off.

Wow, this is kind of cool. Maybe I should volunteer to vacuum the entire store every night. If I got skates, I could count this as my workout. I could wear my iPod and listen to music all night. And, best of all, no customer would come close.

I pushed the vacuum back and forth as I gazed around the store. Head up, eyes roaming, taking in everything—and not one worry that a customer would ask me to help with anything. Why, I could even—

Oh my God. Jack Bishop.

I dropped to my hands and knees and ducked my head.

Jack Bishop. That totally hot guy who works for one of the consultants on fourteen at Pike Warner. Here. In Holt's. Oh my God. Did he see me? *Vacuuming?*

He couldn't have. *Oh, please, God, don't let him have seen me—*

The vacuum suddenly died and I looked up to see Jack Bishop standing over me, his hand on the "off" switch.

I hate my life.

"Haley?" he asked, his head turned sideways as if he didn't believe this could possibly be me.

I couldn't quite believe it either. Jack was thirty-ish, tall, and rugged, with brown wavy hair and blue eyes that have, I was convinced, seen the dark underbelly of life. He made Eddie Bauer and J. Crew look awesome. And here I was, cowering on the floor in a pile of confetti, in *Holt's.*

"What are you doing here?" he asked, glancing around.

"Well, you know, just picking up some extra cash for Christmas," I said, as I got to my feet, trying to look casual and composed. "To donate, of course. To charity. I do it every year."

"Miss you around the office," Jack said.

"Yeah, I guess you know all about it," I said.

Jack worked for the private investigators employed by Pike Warner, so I was sure he knew all about my irregularities-investigation-pending situation, because he was involved with it.

"Know about what?" he asked.

Oh God. Did he not know?

"Something wrong, Haley?" he asked, because clearly he could see that there was.

Jack and I always hit it off at Pike Warner. We worked on the same floor, so we often ran into each other in the break room. We came together naturally, neither of us really fitting into the "corporate" atmosphere.

"I'm on administrative leave," I told him. "Mrs. Drexler said there was an audit and some irregularities were found with my work. Aren't you involved with the investigation?"

Jack shook his head. "That's not the kind of thing I do. Auditors and accountants would handle that."

"There's nothing to the charges, of course," I insisted. "Just some accounting code mix-up, or something. I didn't do anything fraudulent."

"Not your style," Jack agreed. "Let me know when you get back to work. We'll go out for a beer to celebrate."

"Sounds great," I called, as he walked away.

I stood there, watching him disappear down the aisle, wishing I could go with him, wanting my job back, desperate for that Louis Vuitton organizer and the—

"You're supposed to vacuum up the confetti," Shannon barked, suddenly appearing next to me. "Not play in it."

I looked down and saw dozens of little pastel dots stuck to my knees and my forearms. They clung to my shirt. Oh God, were they on my face too? While I was talking to Jack Bishop?

I hate this job. Hate it!

I hit the "on" switch. The vacuum roared to life and I aimed it straight for Shannon. She jumped out of the way and I pushed it toward her again. She yelled something, but I couldn't hear it over the noise; then she hurried away.

I hate this job. I hate my life. I want my old one back.

And I'm getting them, I swore as I banged the vacuum into the greeting card rack.

Tomorrow morning, I'm going to Pike Warner and I'm getting some answers.

CHAPTER 9

It was a Notorious day. Definitely.

I'd stood at my closet this morning studying my vast array of handbags, and decided that only my new, much-sought-after, everyone-will-be-jealous red leather Notorious bag would do for my trip to see Kirk Keegan. It teamed nicely with the Chanel suit my mom had bought for my first day of work at the firm. My hair in a little updo finished off my crisp, professional, conservative look. Very Pike Warner, I thought, as I took the elevator up to fifteen.

Last night I'd planned my arrival here very carefully. I knew Kirk had meetings most mornings, then worked through lunch—no one who expected to make partner at Pike Warner ever took lunch, unless it was with a client—so the best time to catch him was early afternoon. He didn't know I was coming. I'd tried to reach him again last night but hadn't heard anything, so I'd decided to just show up at his desk and find out what was going on with my job.

My knees shook a little as the elevator passed the four-teenth floor, where I—still, technically—worked in Accounts Payable. Then it stopped and the doors opened, revealing the dark, plush carpeting, the rich wood furnishings of fifteen. I moved out with the crowd and my heart nearly melted.

Prada. Gucci. Ferragamo. Designer fashions, everywhere I looked. This was my place. These were my people. I belonged here. I *had* to get my job back.

A large, curving receptionist desk sat in the center of the room; sumptuous chairs and a rain forest of green plants made up the waiting area. Along the back wall were large windows overlooking the city of Los Angeles. Secretaries sat at desks, ringing the reception area, standing guard over the lawyers' offices behind them.

I'd only been up to fifteen a couple of times, so I didn't know if anyone would recognize me. They'd probably know my name, though, thanks to the office-gossip super-highway. And if the receptionist or one of the secretaries recognized me, well, that would be embarrassing, but I was willing to risk it.

Wanda sat behind the large receptionist desk. She was in her fifties, with gray hair that she'd somehow managed to style so that she looked just like George Washington. Really. She wore a headset and operated a telephone control panel that could launch the space shuttle. She was always hitting buttons on the thing so you can never be sure whether she was talking to you, or the person on the phone.

"May I help you?" she asked.

I hoisted my Notorious purse higher so she couldn't help but see it. "Yes, I'm here to see—"

"Pike Warner." She hit a button on the console.

I waited; then she looked at me over the top of her glasses. "Who do you want to see?"

"Kirk—"

"Pike Warner."

I glanced around the reception area, hoping I might catch Kirk coming out of his office. I didn't.

"Miss?" Wanda asked, looking at me as if I'd somehow inconvenienced her. "You're here to see Mr. Keegan?"

"Yes, I'd like to—"

"Pike Warner."

I drew in a breath to calm myself and eyed Beth, Kirk's

secretary, seated at her desk. Maybe I should just go over and talk to her. She'd always seemed a little short with me when I called, but that was just the way lawyers' secretaries did their job.

"Name?" I heard Wanda say.

Was she talking to me, or the person on the phone?

"Miss?" she said, making the word sound a little like "stupid?"

"Haley Randolph," I said.

Wanda's hands froze over the telephone console. Slowly, her eyes came up and she looked at me as if she knew my innermost, shameful secrets.

Which, I guess, she did, thanks to the office gossip.

Okay, this is embarrassing.

"Do you have an appointment?" Wanda asked.

She could have checked the schedule on her computer, since she had my name, but I guess she just wanted to humiliate me further.

"No," I said, and felt my cheeks heat up.

"Have a seat," she said, as if I were being relegated to steerage.

I walked to the chairs in the reception area but didn't sit down. I kept an eye on Kirk's secretary, thinking I could just go over and speak with her, and saw her lift her phone. She made eye contact with Wanda. They were talking to each other. Beth froze for an instant, then sat up a little straighter in her chair, and her gaze swept to me. Wanda was looking at me now too. Both of them were staring. Then I heard the phone buzz on another secretary's desk. She picked up, listened, then stared at me too.

That awful Wanda was conferencing-in every secretary in the room. They were all staring, all talking about me and my irregularities-investigation-pending.

I clutched my handbag. It was a Notorious—in red leather, for God's sake. Only me and five of Drew Barrymore's closest friends had one. It *proved* I belong here.

Male voices came from the direction of Kirk's office and I turned quickly, praying that he was coming out of his office so I could rush inside. My hopes plummeted. It wasn't Kirk. It was another lawyer I didn't recognize, shaking hands with a client who was leaving—

Oh my God.

Ty Cameron.

I don't believe this. Ty Cameron? Here? At Pike Warner?

What if he sees me? What if he asks why I'm here? What if he learns about my irregularities-investigation-pending?

He'll fire me. I'll never get another decent job as long as I live. I'll have to spend the rest of my life saying, "You want fries with that?"

I whipped around and headed for the elevator.

"Haley?" Ty called.

I kept walking.

"Haley?"

I frantically punched the call button. Footsteps approached; then Ty was in front of me, smiling, looking outstanding in Versace, and waiting for me to say something.

"Oh, hi," I said, forcing a smile and pretending I just noticed him.

"What are you doing here?" he asked, looking genuinely perplexed.

Oh God. What was I going to tell him?

I waved my fingers indicating, hopefully, that it was nothing big, that being at the largest, most powerful law firm in the history of the world was just part of my normal routine.

"Taking care of some business," I said.

"Really? What sort?"

I punched the elevator call button six more times.

"My mom's latest venture," I said, remembering the

fund-raiser she'd roped me into helping with next week. "I handle the business end of things."

"No kidding?" Ty looked impressed. "What sort of venture is it?"

I've got no flippin' clue what she's up to now.

"We're expanding," I said, nodding and waving my hand as if I'd explained something rather than ignored his question. "I'm just here to look over the portfolio with Kirk. He's our attorney. One of them."

"My family has been with the firm for decades. Ted and Gerald," Ty said, as if I should know who these people were. "I saw Bob today."

"Bob's a good man," I said.

Behind Ty, I saw Wanda staring. I hit the elevator call button again.

"So, you're finished with your appointment?" Ty asked.

Wanda stood, then nodded to Kirk's secretary, Beth.

"Yes. For now. Sort of," I said.

Wanda unplugged from her console and came around her desk.

"Kirk's running behind so I had to—to reschedule. For later this afternoon," I said.

"Would you like to have lunch?" Ty asked.

Beth picked up her phone. Oh my God. Was she calling security?

"I've got to go," I told Ty.

"So that's a yes?" Ty asked.

"What?"

"To lunch," he said.

Had he just invited me to lunch? I couldn't go to lunch with Ty Cameron.

Wanda headed toward me. Beth spoke into her phone. The elevator dinged and the doors opened.

"Sure, lunch sounds great," I said and hurried into the elevator. Ty got in beside me, freezing Wanda in place.

"Messenger that package to me today, will you, Wanda?" I called, as the elevator doors closed.

I was so relieved to be off of fifteen that it took a few minutes to realize I was stuck in the elevator with Ty Cameron and I'd promised to have lunch with him. When we reached the ground floor, Ty said, "I know a little place near here. How does that sound?"

The guard at the security desk was on the phone. He turned and looked at us. Oh God, he was the one who had escorted me out of the building on Monday.

"Perfect," I told Ty. I hooked my hand through his arm and pulled him toward the door. "I'm starving. Let's go."

We walked in L.A.'s beautiful winter sunshine to an outdoor café furnished with wrought-iron tables and bright, blooming plants. Lots of well-dressed men and women were there. I spotted a Fendi tote, a Kate Spade satchel, and a—oh my God, a red leather Notorious, just like mine.

The maitre d' knew Ty by name and seated us right away at an umbrella table.

I was feeling a little jittery as I looked over the menu. I wasn't sure if that was because of my close call at Pike Warner, or the fact that Ty was seated across the table from me and the breeze had rumpled his hair so that he looked really sexy.

Ty ordered a steak sandwich and I asked for a salad. I didn't really want a salad, but women are expected to order one, and it did fit into my new, healthier lifestyle.

A couple of minutes passed in silence and I started to calm down. Then Ty smiled at me.

"How's Pancake?" he asked.

What the hell was he talking about?

"Pancake," he said again. "The puppy you rescued from the freeway."

Most men don't know the color of your eyes after six

dates and this guy remembers a story—a lie, really—that I told him about a dog?

"Fine," I said. "Cute as a button. Doing, you know, puppy things."

"Chewing up shoes and furniture cushions?" he asked and chuckled.

I don't know. My mom wouldn't let us have a dog.

"Right, right," I said. "Lost a great pair of Gucci sandals just last night."

"That's too bad. Listen, if little Pancake is too much trouble, how about if I find someone to adopt him?"

What?

"I couldn't have you go to any trouble," I told him.

"It's no trouble. In fact, I know someone who'd love to have a new puppy," Ty said.

"Really, that's not necessary."

"Why don't you bring him to the store?"

I shook my head frantically. "No, no—"

"I'll pick him up from you and take him to his new—"

"No!" People two tables away turned to stare. I forced a little smile. "I mean, I couldn't bear to part with little Flapjack."

"You mean Pancake?"

"Yes, of course I mean Pancake," I told him. Jeez, this guy gets me so rattled. I took a breath to calm myself. "We've bonded. I couldn't possibly part with him now."

"You're devoted to this little pup, aren't you?" Ty said, with a twinkle of admiration in his eye. "He must be very special."

"Oh, he is."

"I'd love to see him. Maybe I could swing by your place?"

What the hell is wrong with this man?

"Yeah, of course," I said. "Any time—oh, look, here's lunch."

I was never so glad to see a bowl of lettuce in my life.

We ate in silence for a few minutes; then Ty said, "I appreciate your hanging in there at the store, after Richard's murder. We've lost a dozen employees so far."

I wondered how many more would have quit if Richard hadn't been murdered and had continued to screw over all the employees. Probably more than a dozen.

"Have the detectives given you any new info?" I asked.

Ty shook his head. "They're not saying much. Something about Richard being involved with a neighbor's wife."

His neighbor's wife *and* Glenna Webb? How many women was that rat-bastard carrying on with?

"How are the other employees handling it?" Ty asked. "Have you heard anything?"

He seemed really concerned, as if the people who worked at the store mattered to him. I guessed he must be sincere, since he'd come to the store himself and had instituted programs to make some changes.

"To tell you the truth," I said, "nobody really liked Richard."

"They didn't?" he asked, looking surprised.

Why is it that people in management rarely know what's going on in their own companies?

"Why did you hire him?" I asked.

"My dad hired him, actually, a couple of years ago," Ty said. "The company was founded by my great-great-grandparents when they opened the first store in Los Angeles in the 1890s. It's been passed down, generation to generation."

"Five generations?" Wow, and I thought I had some family baggage to drag around.

"And you're running it now?" I asked.

"Yep," he said, with a tight smile. "Richard was good at his job. He worked in our Northridge store, helped make it the most profitable in the chain."

"What happened to the assistant manager who worked at our store before Richard?" I asked.

Ty didn't answer right away, and I got a little nervous.

"Don't tell me he was murdered too," I said.

"No, nothing like that. Transferred to another store, that's all." Ty finished his sandwich. "So, what do you think about working at Holt's?"

My throat went tight, but I managed to swallow. "Fine. It's fine," I said.

"Really?"

How could I sit here and criticize the store his great-great-grandparents had opened a hundred and some years ago? It was his legacy, his heritage, his future. Yet I'd just been dying for someone from management to ask me what I thought.

"Well," I said, "a few changes wouldn't hurt."

"Such as?"

I couldn't hold back.

"Throw everything out and start over," I said.

He winced. "That bad?"

I shrugged. "The housewares and domestics are okay, and I don't know much about the kids' clothing. But the women's fashions are just hideous, the shoes are awful, and the handbags—oh my God . . ."

Ty didn't say anything, just sat there. I don't think he was too happy about what I'd said.

"Write up your suggestions on the form I handed out," he said, as he frowned and looked at his wristwatch. "I'm afraid I've made you late for your appointment with Kirk."

Oh yeah, my nonexistent appointment.

"No big deal," I said. "I'll catch him later."

"You should call and reschedule," Ty suggested, looking slightly out of sorts and hurried.

I made a face. "You know, I don't have my cell with me," I said, even though I knew it was tucked inside my purse; I never went anywhere without it.

"Use mine."

"No. Really, that's not—"

He pulled his phone from the inside pocket of his jacket, punched in a number on speed dial, and passed it across the table to me.

Now what was I supposed to do?

I took the phone just as Wanda came on the line. Ty was watching me from across the table and Wanda was repeating, "Pike Warner, Pike Warner" over and over in my ear. I had no choice.

"Wanda, this is Miss Randolph," I said in my I'm-better-than-you voice. "Cancel me with Kirk for this afternoon. And did you messenger that package to me? Very good. All right. Thanks, dear."

I hung up.

Wanda had hung up right after she heard "Miss Randolph."

I smiled and passed Ty's phone back to him.

"Everything all right?" he asked.

"Perfect."

A couple moved past our table and I saw that it was the woman with the red leather Notorious handbag just like mine. Our eyes met.

"Will you be at Drew's this weekend?" she asked.

Oh God.

"Sure," I said. What else *could* I say?

"Great. See you then," she said and moved on.

Ty's brows pulled together. "Do you know Drew?"

I was *not* getting into this with him.

"I really need to go. Thanks for lunch," I said, as I got to my feet.

Ty rose beside me and reached for his wallet. "Could we do this again some—"

My cell phone rang.

Ty's brows drew together and he glanced down at my bag.

"Is that your phone ringing?" he asked.

"I don't hear anything."

"I'm sure—"

"It can't be my phone. I don't have mine with me," I insisted. "Thanks again for lunch. Good-bye."

I rushed out of the café and down the street.

Oh my God. How humiliating.

At the corner I dared to look back. Ty stood outside the café, watching me.

Chapter 10

"You. Come on."

Thinking it was a customer, I acted as if I hadn't heard anything and kept straightening the socks. I was working in ILA tonight, Craig's area, Intimates, Loungewear, and Accessories. Accessories covered socks, flip-flops, and purses, among other things. I was concentrating my effort—such as it was—on the sock displays, since I tended to lock up in the presence of nondesigner handbags.

"Haley, move it," the voice said again.

A customer who knew my name? More reason to keep looking down.

Then Rita stomped over—I knew it was her because I recognized her Pick'n Save footwear—and I was forced to look up.

"You're cashiering. Come on," she barked, and started walking toward the front of the store.

"Cashiering?" I exclaimed, as I hurried after her.

Oh my God, my second-worst nightmare—the first being working in the customer service booth.

"I've never cashiered before," I told her.

"You were trained on it in orientation," said.

I was?

"Yeah, but that was a long time ago, and—"

"Quit complaining," Rita snapped.

She was in high bitch mode tonight. Just my luck.

"Two more people quit today," she told me. "We're shorthanded. You're cashiering."

We turned the corner and I froze. Only three of the eight registers were open and the lines were incredible.

"Where did all of these people come from?" I blurted out, remembering how dead the store had been since Richard's murder.

"Our weekend sale started today. You're supposed to read the notices in the break room so you'll know these things," Rita said. "Take register three. It's already open. I'll be back to check on you later."

She stomped away. The customers turned to me, watching to see which register I'd go to so they could jump lines. And I was frozen in place.

Which register was number three?

Then I spotted a big gold 3 on the back of one of the registers and went to it. Customers rushed to follow. First in line was a tiny, gray-haired woman holding three blouses on hangers. Whew! Should be an easy first sale.

"Do you have layaway?" she asked.

Good question.

"No," I said, because it sounded as if it would cause more work for me.

"Is today seniors' discount day?" she wanted to know.

Holt's offered a seniors' discount day?

"No," I told her.

She sighed heavily. So far she hadn't put a single item on the counter. Six people were in line behind her and were staring—at me, for some reason.

Another minute passed.

"Well, okay," she finally said and laid one of the blouses down. "Ring this up, honey."

I glanced over at the three other cashiers. Their fingers

flew across the keypad, they swiped cards, made change, and bagged merchandise in one fluid movement. One of them was Colleen, who, from what little I knew of her, must have come to work here on a hire-a-nitwit program. If she could do it, so could I.

I read the screen on the register and saw that the instructions were all there. Cool. This wouldn't be so hard at all.

"You want to move your ass, honey?" the gray-haired woman said. "It's not like I've got a lot of time, you know."

I smiled—it in no way resembled an of-course-you-can smile—and scanned her blouse.

"Is that on sale?" she asked.

"No."

"It's supposed to be on sale. There was a sign," she told me. "Twenty percent off."

I was probably supposed to call someone from the misses department to verify that, but really, what difference did it make? Holt's was a big company; they could take a twenty-percent-off hit on a fifteen-dollar blouse. I gave her the discount.

I reached for the next blouse and she grabbed it away.

"What do you think of this?" she asked.

"It's ugly."

The woman held up the blouse and studied it. Now nine people were in my line.

"If it's ugly, I ought to get a discount for taking it off your hands," the woman told me.

"How does ten percent sound?" I asked.

"Make it fifteen and you've got yourself a deal."

"Done."

I scanned the last blouse and managed to wedge all three of them into a bag—she insisted on keeping the hangers— as I gave her the total.

"Is that with the discounts?" she asked.

"Yes."

"Is this seniors' discount day?"

"No."

"Seems to me if you people can give seniors a discount one day of the week, you could give it to them every day," she told me.

Now eleven people were in my line.

The woman grumbled under her breath, then opened her purse and pulled out a checkbook. A checkbook? I didn't think anybody used checks anymore.

"Well, I'll pay you for this stuff," the woman said, gesturing toward her bag, "but I don't think it's right."

By the time she filled out the check, three more people were in my line.

I was probably supposed to get an approval on the check, or something, but I had no idea how to do that. I dropped it in the cash drawer and she left.

Next was an old man with white, buzz-cut hair. He laid a pack of black socks on the counter.

"This is a damn long time to wait in line for a pack of socks," he complained. "Where are all the rest of the employees? Why would a big store like this have only four registers open? What the hell is going on here? Fine thing, come to a store and have to wait this long in line. I know what's going on here. Your store managers are saving on payroll to boost their own bonuses. What is this, some Communist country? I thought this was America."

He ranted while I scanned his socks and gave him the total.

"What about my senior discount?" he demanded.

Okay, so maybe today really was seniors' discount day.

I gave him a twenty percent discount, saving him a whopping sixty cents. But even that didn't suit him. He snatched the receipt out of my hand, grabbed up his socks, and stomped away.

Somebody should have gone the Old Yeller route on him ages ago.

The next customer rolled up with a cart and dumped a double armload of clothing on the counter. Four kids swarmed around her.

"Do you have layaway?" she asked.

"No."

Rita appeared beside me.

"Are you offering credit?" she demanded. "You're supposed to be offering credit."

I was?

"Of course I'm offering credit," I told her.

"What about the survey?" she asked.

There was a survey?

"Are you handing out the survey?" Rita wanted to know.

Jeez, credit, surveys. What did these people expect for seven bucks an hour?

"Look, Rita, you're holding up my line," I told her.

She glared at me for a few more seconds, then walked away.

"Do you take layaway?" the woman with the four kids and the double armload of clothes asked again.

"No."

"I haven't decided which of these I want," she said, "but go ahead and get started. I need you to tell me the regular price, the sale price, the percentage of the discount, how much that equals in real money, then give me a total of everything after each item. Then I'll tell you what I want. Okay?"

I looked at the mound of clothing and my line that now stretched down the aisle and out of sight.

Maybe going to prison wouldn't be so bad after all.

When the crowd died down, Rita released me from my cashiering bondage and sent me back to the accessories department. I went to the break room instead. We were still operating on the work schedule that Richard had set before he died and I wasn't supposed to have a break. But screw it. My feet hurt.

Sandy was there, munching on chips and flipping through a magazine. I headed for the vending machine. *Chocolate overdose—here I come.*

Then I saw that girl who'd lost twenty-five pounds eating what looked like a chuck of Styrofoam. Damn. My new lifestyle. Now I really hate her. I got a bag of trail mix from the vending machine, sat down with Sandy, and put my feet up.

"Have you heard what the Christmas merchandise will be this year?" she asked, nodding toward the wall.

I glanced over and saw a big calendar counting down the days until the surprise merchandise would be announced. Every year Holt's brought in a line of merchandise during the Christmas shopping season that they didn't usually carry, and offered it at a discount.

"Last year it was that new game system everybody wanted," Sandy said. "We sold tons of them. Craig carried them in ILA. He was pretty cool about it. He held some of them back and let some of us buy one. Store management got as many as they wanted, of course. Jeanette got three, I heard. I sold mine on eBay."

That reminded me of my last conversation with Marcie. She'd promised to think up a way for me to make extra money. Maybe she'd come up with something. I needed to give her a call.

"I hope it will be something cool this year," Sandy said, finishing her chips. "Can you find me another outfit tonight?"

"Oh yeah," I said, remembering her movie date with Coupon Boy last night. "How'd it go?"

"It was okay," she said, rising from her chair. "We saw that *Rocky* movie."

I frowned. "At the dollar theater? He couldn't spring for a first-run movie?"

"I paid," she said. "We got there and were in line and he said he didn't have any cash, so I gave him a twenty. Then he said he'd be embarrassed if I paid, so he bought the tickets."

"Let me guess. He kept the change."

"He bought me a popcorn," Sandy said.

"Dump his sorry ass," I told her.

She shrugged. "My old boyfriend called. He wants me to come over tonight."

"The tat guy?" I asked. "The one who said you had no soul?"

"He said what was really in his heart. Most people don't do that. Can you help me find an outfit for tonight?"

"Sure."

"I'm in Shoes," Sandy said, and left the break room.

I've got to get out of this place.

Kirk Keegan popped into my head. I got my phone from my locker to call him, and saw that I had a message. From Kirk.

Yes!

My heart raced as I punched in the code and waited. Kirk had called. My irregularities-investigation-pending nightmare was over. I could come back to work—tomorrow, probably.

Oh my God. What should I wear? Something fabulous. But not so fabulous that it distracted from my I'm-friends-with-Drew-and-you're-not Notorious bag. Something—

Kirk's voice came on the line. He sounded rushed, a little hard to hear with the traffic noise in the background.

"I told you not to come to the office. It makes you look desperate and guilty. Complicates things. I'm handling it. I'll call you."

He hung up.

I stood there for another minute with a death grip on my phone, then put it away and slumped into a chair again. Styrofoam girl was gone. I was alone.

Maybe Kirk was right. Going to the office made me look desperate—but not guilty. And what was I supposed to do, sit around and twiddle my thumbs, waiting?

I had to get my job back. Tomorrow was Friday. One whole week without my Pike Warner paycheck. I needed that job. For more reasons than one.

The money, sure. The Louis Vuitton organizer. My credit card balances and that overdraft the bank was making such a huge deal about.

But wouldn't returning to work prove to Detective Madison that, since I'd done nothing wrong, there was nothing to connect me to Richard's murder?

Although, maybe he'd already decided that. At lunch, Ty had said the detectives were looking at Richard's involvement with his neighbor's wife as a motive for his murder. Maybe they'd forgotten all about me.

I'd have to find out.

The break room door opened and Evelyn rushed in, looking wild-eyed.

"Oh, Haley, there you are." She plastered her hands against her chest. "I've been searching all over for you."

I just looked at her.

"You're supposed to be on the floor," she said. "Craig is having a fit."

I hate my life.

"Craig is very tense right now," Evelyn explained. "He's in charge of the special Christmas merchandise again this year and, well, he doesn't want . . . problems . . . again."

"There were problems?" I asked. Imagine that, the hottest game system in the world, and problems arose?

Evelyn twisted her fingers together. "Well, yes . . . yes,

there were problems. You see, some—several, really . . . well, quite a few, actually—of the game systems were shoplifted."

"How many is 'quite a few'?" I asked.

"Enough to make Craig very intense about this year's merchandise," Evelyn insisted.

"And me going out on the floor to straighten the socks is going to make everything better for Craig?" I asked.

"Yes, it will," Evelyn said, without seeming to realize how ridiculous it sounded.

"Whatever." I got up from the table and tossed my unopened bag of trail mix into the trash can.

"Things are very difficult for Craig," Evelyn went on. Okay, so maybe she did know how ridiculous she sounded and thought I needed more motivation to get out there and straighten the socks.

"His wife . . . well, his wife has cancer and the whole family has been struggling with it for a very long time now," Evelyn said, as she walked with me to the sock department. I guess she wanted to make sure I actually went there. "It's tragic, really. You can't help but feel sorry for them . . . no matter . . . what."

Evelyn looked as if she did, in fact, feel sorry for them, and I did too, of course. But it still didn't make straightening the socks the highlight of my life.

"The store owner asked about you," Evelyn said.

"Ty?" My heart did a little flip-flop. "What did he want to know?"

She smiled, as if this bit of news would somehow make up for her running me out of the break room.

"He asked if I knew anything about you . . . personally. If you had close friends here at the store, if you were dating anyone, who your family was. That sort of thing."

"What did you tell him?"

"The truth, of course," Evelyn said.

She hurried away and I dropped to my knees between the sock racks. Ty had asked about me? Why?

I guess he might be curious, after seeing me today. I mean, he must have assumed that when I said I was at Pike Warner regarding my mother's business I was telling the truth. After all, I had on a Chanel suit, so I looked as if I belonged there. He probably thought that I actually knew who Ted and Gerald were. You don't do business with Pike Warner in a Chanel suit if you don't have money.

Which would have led Ty to wonder why I was working at Holt's for seven bucks an hour.

Maybe that made him curious about me. Maybe he was enthralled with a person who wore Chanel by day, yet worked retail by night. To him, perhaps I was a woman of mystery, and he wanted to find out more, more, more.

Maybe he wanted to ask me out.

My stomach twisted into its something-thrilling-just-happened knot.

Oh my God. That would be great. No, it would be beyond great. Greater than great. Really, I'd had a little thing for Ty since the first time I saw him. So to date him would be just awesome.

I stared at the display of black socks, letting the scenario build in my mind.

Where would he ask me out? Here in the store? Probably. I mean, when else would he see me? Yes, he'd have to make his move here. Maybe I'd be working in Shoes, by those cool new boots we just got in. Or, better yet, in the lingerie section by the thongs and lacy high-cut bikinis. That would set a great mood. I'd accept his invitation, of course, but first I'd pause for a moment, so as not to look too anxious; then I'd say yes—no, first I'd toss my hair over my shoulder (I'd have to remember to wear it down from now on)—then I'd say yes. We'd have to keep our relationship quiet around the store, of course, so as not to cause a stir—oh my God, I can't wait until Rita finds out.

I love my life.

CHAPTER 11

For some unknown reason, Richard had not scheduled me to work tonight. I don't know how that happened, but since my week had been pretty crappy, with the exception of learning from Evelyn that Ty had asked about me, I decided not to question it, especially since it was Friday night and I wanted to go out.

Maybe that meant my fortunes were improving.

I was meeting Marcie in Old Pasadena, a section of the city filled with all the best shops, really cool restaurants and pubs, awesome apartment buildings, as well as art galleries and theaters for anyone who can stay awake in those places. The sidewalks were always jammed with pedestrians, making it a terrific place to see and be seen.

I was running a little late—one of the times I wish I had lesbian hair so I could just spike it and go—but I'd pulled together a really great outfit. Boots, gauchos, a crop jacket and bulky scarf, all in blacks and grays, then added a big splash of color with my purple, oversize Kate Spade tote.

I left my apartment and headed for the garage where my car was parked, feeling pretty good about things. Ty might ask me out. Kirk had called and, though his message was a little terse, he'd assured me everything was being handled at Pike Warner. Tonight I was hanging out with my best friend, in one of the most upscale areas of Los Angeles. And—best of all—I didn't have to work at Holt's.

Feeling optimistic, I decided to check my mailbox. I hadn't done that in a few days, but since I'd already gotten all my credit card statements this week, and the bank had sent its weekly overdraft notice—as if I could forget—I decided that nothing lurking in the box could upset me.

I pulled out the usual stuff, catalogs—ooh, Victoria's Secret—ads for dentists' offices, sheets of coupons for places I never heard of, and spotted an envelope from the Golden State Bank and Trust. Wow. The GSB&T. They'd been in business for a hundred years, or something, a very old, very prestigious banking firm. Why were they contacting me?

I stood next to the wall of mailboxes under the dim security lighting, debating whether to open it. Had my own bank alerted other banks to my overdraft? Had they all joined forces against me?

Since I'm not big on suspense, I opened the envelope and saw that—wow, this was cool—the Golden State Bank and Trust had reserved a credit card in my name. Preapproved. With a ten-thousand-dollar credit limit. Jeez, was this for real?

I checked the name and address on the envelope and saw that, yes, the offer was intended for me. I read the material once more, thinking it must be some kind of scam, but everything looked legit.

A firm like GSB&T didn't toss out credit cards, like some banks did. They had a reputation for carefully selecting their clientele, using exacting standards known only to them, and under which I was sure I didn't measure up to. So I figured it must have something to do with my mom. If anything were prestigious, my mom *had* to be a part of it, so she'd probably given them my info, thinking a GSB&T credit card would elevate my standing in life, somehow.

Then my heart started to beat a little faster. Ten grand? Preapproved? See, my luck had changed. And that made me think of—oh my God. What if I saw Ty in Pasadena? It was just the sort of place someone like him would hang out. What if he asked me out *tonight*? And what about Kirk? He'd hang out in Pasadena too.

I found a pen in my tote, signed the offer, shoved it into the self-addressed, postage-paid envelope, and pushed it through the outgoing mail slot.

Things were happening for me now. Any minute, my phone could ring and it could be Kirk telling me to report to work at Pike Warner on Monday morning—where Mrs. Drexler would apologize profusely and tell me she'd given me a raise—and that call would be followed by one from Detective Madison, who'd apologize just as profusely for wrongly suspecting me of Richard's murder, and tell me the case had been solved.

I let that little fantasy play out in my mind—along with the image of Rita being led away from Holt's in handcuffs—and felt my spirits lift. Yep, I was on a roll now. Everything was turning around. I'd get my old life back.

Perfect.

Marcie was inside the Gap on Old Pasadena's way-cool Colorado Boulevard, holding up two sweaters, when I walked in. We hugged and she asked me which I liked best.

"Get them both," I told her. "In fact, I'll get a couple too."

Marcie gave me that little frown of hers. "Did you get your old job back?"

"Not yet," I said, as I sorted through the sweaters on the display table. Why don't stores stack these things by size?

"I've been thinking about ways for you to make extra money," Marcie said. "The Internet's the way to go."

"I'm not doing porn."

"I meant selling things on eBay."

I paused with three sweaters draped over my arm. "You mean, like my clothes?"

"No, just stuff," she said. "You know, buy things cheap, then sell them. You can probably get lots of good deals on things at Holt's."

I jumped as if I'd been zapped with a cattle prod. "You want me to *buy* things, from *Holt's*, and bring them into my *home*? What sort of friend are you?"

"The sort that doesn't want you to go hungry," she said.

Okay, I couldn't argue with that. I could see that her heart was in the right place.

"Well, if I get desperate enough, I'll think about it," I told her. "But I don't think it will come to that. Kirk called. Everything's going to be fine."

"Is that what he said?" Marcie asked. "Exactly?"

"I know you don't like Kirk, but he's really sharp and he knows absolutely everything that goes on at Pike Warner," I said.

"I like Kirk just fine," Marcie said. "I don't trust him."

"I know," I told her. "But I've had a crappy week. I don't want to think about problems right now, okay?"

"Just promise me you'll be cautious of him," she said.

"Yeah, yeah, okay, whatever," I said

We paid for our sweaters and left the store. The night air was crisp, perfect for being outside. Lots of well-dressed people were there, store display windows were lit up, and delicious smells drifted from the restaurants. We decided to have dinner at the Cheesecake Factory. It was packed, as always, so we put our names on the list and went outside to wait, along with about a dozen other people.

"My mom and I stopped by Holt's the other night. She needs new pots for Thanksgiving next week," Marcie said. "I didn't see you."

Guess she didn't think to look for me hiding between the clothes racks somewhere.

"I saw that good-looking guy you mentioned," she said.

"Ty?" I asked, surprised. "How did you know who he was?"

"He was the only man in the store wearing a suit that looked like it came from Neiman Marcus," Marcie explained. "He's really good looking."

True. You could definitely leave the lights on with Ty.

"We had lunch together yesterday," I said.

"Oh my gosh," she exclaimed and her eyes got really big. "Are you two going out?"

"Not exactly," I said, then leaned in a little. "But he asked Evelyn at work if I was dating anyone."

Marcie's mouth flew open. "He's going to ask you out!"

"Maybe."

She squealed and latched on to my arm. "How cool!"

Then we launched into standard girlfriend mode: where would Ty and I go on our first date; what would I wear; what kind of car did he drive; what if we got serious; what if we got married; how would my first name sound with his last name; what if I hyphenated; how many kids would we have; what would their names be; would we hyphenate their names?

We covered all of that in about twenty seconds.

"Wow." Marcie sighed, then announced, "You and Ty would make the perfect couple."

"Do you think so?" I asked.

"Definitely," she declared.

We lapsed into a comfortable silence as the crowd milled around the entrance to the restaurant, and people walked past. Then Marcie turned to me and said, "There's this really cool guy at work that you just have to meet."

"What?"

Where had that come from, all of a sudden?

"He's so much fun," Marcie said. "He loves to ski and ride mountain bikes."

"What happened?" I demanded. "What did you see?"

And then I knew. I turned in the direction Marcie had been looking in, and there, across the street, stood Ty Cameron. With another woman.

My heart plummeted but I caught it before it hit bottom. Just because he was with a woman, it didn't mean she was his girlfriend. She could have been anybody—

She was gorgeous.

Mid-twenties, best I could tell from the distance. About the same age as me. Her blond hair was caught up in a casual knot. She wore black boots, a long leather trench coat, a bright red scarf, and carried a Marc Jacobs satchel.

The outfit screamed *sophisticated* and *successful*. Which meant she probably had a college degree and a good job somewhere. Which also probably meant she wasn't working at some crappy retail store for seven bucks an hour, wasn't being hounded by her bank for overdrawing her checking account. She probably wasn't considering selling stuff on eBay to pay her rent.

"She's not very tall," Marcie offered.

True. Her mother definitely wasn't a beauty queen.

"She doesn't have pageant legs," Marcie said. "You have pageant legs."

I do have great legs.

"Maybe they're just, you know, friends," she said. "They could be friends—oh."

Blondie walked to the display window at the next store and Ty obediently followed. Now my heart really plummeted and I couldn't catch it.

They were window-shopping.

I watched for another minute as she pointed at the dress in the window and he stood next to her, listening, looking at her, then at the dress, nodding, hanging on to her every word.

There are only two times in any relationship when couples window-shop. One is after they're married ten years and they've already talked about everything there is to talk about, and looking in shop windows helps pass the time. The other is in the first two months of dating when men will indulge their girlfriends' passion for clothes and shop with them because they're getting sex.

Oh God. Ty and Blondie were having sex.

I sighed and my shoulders slumped. I looked at Marcie.

"She's not his girlfriend," she declared. "Trust me, she is not his girlfriend."

Marcie is usually right about people, but still . . .

"And he did ask if you were dating anyone," Marcie reminded me. "Why would he do that if he didn't want to ask you out?"

"He probably just wanted to see if I was available to work more hours at Holt's," I said, feeling like a complete idiot because I let myself get so caught up in thoughts of Ty. Jeez, my life is so screwed up now.

"Does your mom know him?" Marcie asked.

"My mom?" I asked.

"The Cameron family has been in California for generations and so has your mom's family. Old money usually knows old money," Marcie explained.

"How do you know how long Ty's family has been here?" I asked.

"There's a plaque outside every Holt's store."

They probably covered that in orientation.

"You should ask your mom," Marcie advised.

No way in hell was I going to ask Mom about Ty's family. All I needed right now was for her to get a whiff of a possible boyfriend for me, and she'd be off and running, following the scent of a grand wedding.

I turned back to the restaurant. "I need cheesecake."

"What about your new, healthier lifestyle?"

"And a beer."

"But, Haley—"

I gave her my death stare and she backed off. That was the great thing about having a best friend. You could always count on her to be supportive, no matter how many slices of cheesecake you ordered.

My name was announced over the intercom, so we went inside to our table. Luckily it wasn't near the front window so I didn't have to look outside and see Ty and Blondie again.

Oh well, it didn't matter about Ty, I told myself. In a couple more days I'd have my job back at Pike Warner, and Ty, window-shopping Blondie, and Holt's would be but a bad memory.

"Want to go shopping tomorrow?" I asked Marcie.

"Aren't you helping your mom?"

Damn. I'd forgotten all about that, whatever it was. Some fund-raiser for sick people, she'd said.

"How about Sunday?" Marcie asked.

"Let me check my work schedule," I said.

"You're thinking about Ty," Marcie said.

How does she know these things?

"She's not his girlfriend," Marcie said. "I don't care what you say, he wouldn't have asked if you were dating anyone unless he wanted to date you himself. I mean, what other reason would he have?"

I thought about it for a moment but couldn't come up with any reasonable explanation. The whole thing didn't sit right with me, yet I couldn't say why.

Maybe something else was going on. Something I didn't know about.

CHAPTER 12

The Holt's chain had stores throughout California, as I recalled from orientation, before I drifted off, and right now I was headed toward the location in Northridge, a suburb of north Los Angeles. There was a great mall there where I shopped sometimes, but that's not why I was fighting the Saturday morning traffic out on the 118 freeway.

This was the store where Richard used to work.

At lunch the other day, Ty mentioned that Richard transferred from Northridge where, under his guidance as assistant store manager, the store had been a top profit maker for the chain. I couldn't help but wonder why, if Richard had been such an asset to the store, he'd transferred. So I decided to find out. Plus, it occupied my Saturday morning and kept me from wondering what my mom had in store for me this afternoon with her latest adventure in entrepreneurial la-la land.

I parked outside Holt's and went inside. The store was pretty crowded, which was a little surprising, since the biggest shopping day in the universe was this Friday, the day after Thanksgiving. Even more surprising was seeing that all eight of the registers were open—wow, what a concept—and manned with a cashier and a bagger. And absolutely every one of them wore an of-course-you-can smile. Real smiles. Not those fake ones at our store, where it looks like the Retail Outlet of the Living Dead.

I needed to talk to someone who'd worked here for a while and I knew just where to find her: the women's clothing department. That section, for some reason, is seldom busy on the weekends. I guess women who need bigger sizes prefer to shop during the week when it's less crowded. But there's always a salesclerk working back there and, sure enough, I found exactly who I was looking for.

Deb, according to her name badge, had a typical over-forty short haircut, and was decked out for the fall season in a denim vest with pumpkins on the pockets and a long-sleeve orange knit top. I flipped through a rack of skirts trying to decide how to start a conversation, when she threw me completely by coming over and asking if I needed any help. How weird is that?

"I need an outfit for my mom," I said, which was a total lie, of course, since my mom wouldn't even look at the sign if she drove past a Holt's, much less go inside.

"Christmas shopping early?" Deb asked with a smile. "Smart. Things will get crazy, starting on Friday."

I smiled back, which, oddly enough, was easy.

"I'm an after-Thanksgiving-sale virgin," I said. "I work in the Holt's store in Santa Clarita."

"No kidding," Deb declared, as if I'd just announced that I was her long-lost sister. Then she frowned. "Oh dear. I heard about what happened with . . . Richard."

"Yeah," I said and managed to look sad. "It was really bad."

Deb leaned closer. I knew what was coming.

"I heard that he was found in the stockroom wearing black fishnets and a garter belt," she whispered.

"Isn't it just awful?" I whispered back.

"I had no idea," Deb mused, then seemed to think she'd left something out. "Richard used to work here, you know."

"Really?" I asked and, wow, I sounded completely con-

vincing. "I'll bet everyone here was glad when he transferred out."

Deb pondered this for a moment, then said, "He wasn't
well liked, that's for sure."

I hate it when people make you drag things out of
them—especially when I'm trying to make it look like I'm
not doing just that.

"Oh?" I asked, raising my brows.

Again, Deb leaned closer, as if her info was hush-hush.

"Richard is—was—a bit of a troublemaker," she said,
as if she'd just told me how NASA had staged the moon
landing. "He came in here and cut back work schedules,
did away with employee incentive programs, cut expenses
to the bone. He fired people left and right. Why, we nearly
lost our store manager. Richard made him look like an incompetent old fool."

"Then they sent him to our store," I said, "and he did
the same thing all over again."

"Only I guess somebody in your store didn't like it very
much," Deb said.

Wow. I guess not.

At most every company or business there was some self-
appointed asshole who ratted people out, rolled over supervisors, and deliberately shook things up just so they would
look important. Did Richard consider himself the Holt's
hired gun? That would explain the screwed-up work schedules he came up with, and the lack of cashiers even during
busy times.

Maybe it explained something else. Like who killed
him.

"Oh, look at us and all this talk of murder," Deb said.
She waved her hands as if to erase our words from the air.
"You needed a skirt for your mom, right?"

"I'm going to look around a bit," I said, easing away.

"Let me know if you need any help," Deb said, with a
big of-course-you-can smile.

"Thanks," I said, and left the department.

I got in my car and glanced at my watch as I headed toward the freeway. Yikes. It was late. I'd taken longer talking to Deb than I'd meant to. I'd have to hurry to get to my mom's on time.

Jeanette Avery, the store manager, came to mind as I drove. She must have known what Richard was up to. She hadn't looked very happy and I'd figured it was because of Richard's murder, but now it seemed as if there could have been more to it than that.

Had Richard been spying on her, trying to come up with something that would show the corporate office that she was mismanaging the store? Richard was, after all, an assistant manager. He wanted to be manager. I wouldn't put it past him to try and get promoted by creating an opening himself.

Jeanette probably feared for her job. She was in her fifties, approaching retirement, and finding another high-paying, store-manager position somewhere else might be tough.

Was that reason enough to murder Richard?

I thought back to the night of the murder. Jeanette hadn't been in the store. I'd called her myself from the office while Evelyn was in the throes of a meltdown.

Or, at least, Jeanette wasn't in the store when I discovered Richard's body. I don't know how long he'd been dead before I found him. Hours, maybe? If so, Jeanette could have been in the store, killed Richard, then gone home.

And who was to say she was at home when I called? I couldn't remember what number I'd dialed, of course, so maybe it was a cell phone. For all I know she could have been outside in the parking lot, waiting for Richard's body to be discovered. Or, more likely, in the company of someone who could provide her with an alibi.

There was only one way to find out. I was going to have

to go through the records in the office and see what number I'd called that night.

I got to my mom's house just as two men I didn't know
were getting into a delivery van, and Mom was getting
into her Mercedes. She paused long enough to hand me a
folder, then pulled away, leaving me to follow in my own
car. As I drove behind the van, I tried to figure out what
sort of business she'd ventured into this time.

The first name on the sign was EDIBLE, which made everyone think of edible panties—or was that just me?—but Mom
had followed it up with ELEGANCE, so the whole thing was
sort of confusing. Luckily, there was a picture: slices of fruit
cut into the shape of flowers and arranged in pots.

I give it two months.

My spirits picked up when I followed the van through a
gated driveway in Brentwood, a fabulously rich neighborhood north of Sunset. Guess those sick people, whoever
they were, would feel better after today.

The house was a sleek contemporary, with carefully
manicured grounds. Really good looking guys in gold
valet vests waved cars toward the front of the house. I followed the catering van toward the rear where a security
guard checked IDs and consulted the list on his clipboard
before waving us through.

Jeez, whose event is this?

The event coordinator, Charla something-or-other (I
couldn't read Mom's handwriting), met the van and we
went through the usual first-meeting ritual of her telling
me how great my mom was, how wonderful her fruit bouquets were, and assuring me that she knew how proud I
was to have a mother like her.

Then we got down to business. I'd done this sort of
thing for Mom before, so I knew the drill. Charla counted
the fruit bouquets—some were dipped in chocolate and
really looked yummy—checked them over to make sure they

were up to the standards of whoever was throwing this fund-raiser, then directed the staff to take them into the house. We signed and exchanged forms. It was then that I saw Mom was donating the bouquets.

So much for turning a profit in the new business.

"You're coming in, aren't you?" Charla asked, as if she couldn't imagine why I wouldn't.

I'd dressed for the day in a black skirt and cowl neck sweater—I avoided fall colors so I wouldn't look like part of the decorations—and carried my Notorious bag, of course. Everyone in my mom's circle would expect a designer handbag and know about the Notorious.

"I'll stay for a while," I said, as if I had tons of other places in Brentwood to go today.

But, despite my arrival at the rear of the house with the other service personnel, I wasn't going to enter the house through the kitchen. I took the walkway around, past the gorgeous gardens to the front where a crowd of people, all women, gathered after valets whisked off with their Bentleys, Mercedeses, Beemers, and Porsches. I recognized quite a few of them as my mom's friends.

And I was relieved to see that I'd dressed appropriately. You never knew with these functions. The spring ones were the worst, where most of the women showed up in flowered dresses and big hats.

Most everyone was dressed conservatively—maybe the sick people would be here, after all—yet in expensive clothing. And everyone had a terrific handbag, mostly clutches from Ferragamo, Fendi, Prada, and—oh my gosh, there's a Notorious bag. In red leather. Just like mine.

Wow, I hadn't expected to see another Notorious here—oh, and look, there's another one. Two Notorious—three, counting mine—at the same fund raiser. Jeez, what were the chances?

Then I spotted yet another Notorious handbag, and this

one was on the arm of the woman I'd run into the day I'd had lunch with Ty. The woman who asked—

Oh my God. Am I at Drew Barrymore's house?

Wow, how cool! I'm at Drew's house with all her close friends, and I have a red leather Notorious bag just like they do.

The woman spotted me, smiled broadly, and waved. I waved back.

How great is this?

I pictured all of us inside, me with all of Drew's closest friends. I'd be drawn into the Notorious circle too, and we'd all compare our bags and say how marvelous they are, and then Drew would walk in and—

Oh, crap.

Drew would walk in, take one look at me, and ask, "Who are you?" Then everybody would turn and stare. They'd all back away a little, distancing themselves from me. Then someone else would call to my mom, and say, "Isn't that your daughter?" And then Mom would turn and look at me . . . like that.

Okay, I'm out of here.

I spun around and dashed—hopefully, I merely looked as if I were walking purposefully—toward the rear of the house. From the corner of my eye, I caught a glimpse of Charla waving at me, but thanks to my extensive customer service experience at Holt's, I ignored her with ease.

The rear parking area was congested. Vans were still pulling in, inching past vehicles that were trying to leave. My car was squeezed in between a florist van and some dumb-ass who'd parked crooked. All sorts of people milled around. Damn. This was the one time I wished I had one of those gas-guzzling SUVs. Even though you could only drive them from gas station to gas station, I could have used one of them right now to jump the curb and cut through the lawn and get out of here.

I dug in my bag for my keys as I walked, and when I glanced up I saw that a man was standing at the front of my car. He was—

Oh no. It can't be. It just can't—

"Hi, Haley," Ty called.

What the hell is he doing here?

"Are you following me?" I demanded.

"No," he said, looking a bit stunned and confused. He nodded toward the house. "I'm here for the fund-raiser."

Okay, that made me look stupid.

"Is that so?" I shot back, hoping if I sounded a little annoyed it might explain the embarrassing redness I felt on my cheeks. "You're the only man here."

"My mother hosts the event every year."

Good grief. I'm at Ty's mother's house.

"I'm running the auction," he said, and gave a rueful grin. "The day's big finale."

And his mom has him as part of the program, not schlepping food with the servants.

"I've got to go," I said, and started rooting in my bag for my keys again. Damn. This bag is a bottomless pit. Why can't they make a slot just for keys?

"You're here with your mom's new business?" he asked, and walked closer.

He looked relieved that what I'd told him that day at lunch was true, and that I wasn't some nutcase lunatic he'd had the misfortune of employing for seven bucks an hour.

I don't usually tell people who my mom is, especially if there's a chance they already know her and are aware that she's a former beauty queen. There's always the mental comparison. I can see it in their eyes. The shape of my face, then Mom's face. My hair, then Mom's hair. My nose, lips, chin, eyes, then Mom's. And, inevitably, they see that I don't quite measure up, that the goddess of stunning genes gave way at a crucial moment in my development so that I ended up merely pretty, and I get that look of disappointment and regret . . . just the way Mom looks at me.

"Yes," I said, finally—thank God—coming up with my keys. "But I'm only here to handle the business end of things. I have to go."

"You're not coming inside?" he asked, and sounded a little—something. Surprised, disappointed, I don't know what.

"No," I said, quickly.

"Why not?" he asked, and stepped in front of me.

Because it was his mom's house, way worse than its being Drew Barrymore's house. And I didn't want him to see my mom. And some of Mom's friends were here, so she was destined to mention my job at Pike Warner (after she'd worked her way through my brother and sister's update), and somebody would ask how I liked it there, and then what would I say? And how would I explain to Ty why I hadn't mentioned that I worked there—sort of—when I saw him that day at the office? Plus, for all I knew, everyone here actually knew Drew and would assume that I did too, and would ask how I enjoyed the Notorious bag she'd given me, and what would I say to that—with my mom listening?

There were a million reasons not to stay—and I couldn't give Ty a single one of them.

Yet there he stood, looking at me, waiting.

Well, I didn't have to give him a reason, I decided. It was none of his business, anyway.

"Long story," I said, and managed a you-know-how-it-is eyebrow bob.

I ducked around him and went to the driver's-side door. He got there first and opened it, but not wide enough that I could get inside, thanks to the florist's van parked next to me.

"I noticed you haven't gotten your fender fixed yet," Ty said.

Oh, Christ. That day I'd hit the retaining wall after I left Pike Warner, and the stupid story I'd made up about rescuing the dog.

"Wasn't your uncle going to fix it?" he asked.

Was every word I'd ever said to this man somehow emblazoned on his brain? Didn't he have something more important to remember?

"He was going to, but something came up," I told him. It was the quickest blow-off I could think of.

Ty frowned. "So important he couldn't fix his own niece's car?"

"It was an emergency," I said, edging closer to my car door. "He had to take his wife to the—the hospital."

"Nothing serious, I hope."

Christ.

"She . . . she went into labor."

Ty smiled. "Boy or girl?"

"Girl," I said, nodding so that I looked confident. "It was a girl."

"Please don't tell me they named her Pancake."

"Of course they didn't name her Pancake!"

I batted his hands away from my door, squeezed inside, and whipped out of the spot, nearly clipping a delivery van. I caught a glimpse of Ty as I sped away. Was he grinning?

Bastard.

I hit the freeway headed toward—I don't know where I was headed but I kept driving. A million thoughts were jumbled in my head, but the one I kept coming back to was Ty.

Why did I keep seeing him everywhere I went? What kind of crazy coincidence was that?

Well, I guess it wasn't a coincidence that I saw him at Pike Warner, since his family had done business there for generations. If I'd gone to fifteen more often, I'd probably have seen him there before. And lots of people go to Old

Pasadena on Friday night. The thing just now at his mom's fund-raiser, okay, that was just sort of weird, but not completely off the scale, considering that my mom's old-money family routinely gets involved with other old-money families. But, still, something bothered me about all of it.

Then it hit me: what if Ty were keeping tabs on me—for the police?

Ty seemed like an easygoing guy, but let's face it, he was the fifth generation in charge of a huge retail chain. Money—big money—was at stake, not to mention reputations, jobs, future income, and future generations. An employee had been murdered in one of his stores, at the one time of the year when retail outlets made the profits that would carry them through the lean times of the year.

I'd wondered before if Ty thought it odd that I wore Chanel and conducted business at Pike Warner, yet worked at Holt's, and I'd sort of mentally blown right past it. Now the thought gave me a sick feeling in my stomach.

Maybe Ty thought I had another reason for working there. An agenda. Revenge, maybe. A personal vendetta.

Against Richard.

Was that why Ty had asked Evelyn questions about me? Was that why I "ran into him" so often, why he took me to lunch that day?

Maybe he thought I was involved with Richard's murder.

And maybe he was working with Detective Madison to prove it.

CHAPTER 13

Thanksgiving was just a few days away but you wouldn't know it by the gorgeous afternoon sunshine at the Grove, one of L.A.'s ultrahip shopping destinations. The outdoor plaza featured kiosks, benches, flowers, and restaurants, surrounded by some of the priciest stores in the city. A trolley looped the plaza, taking shoppers to the adjoining farmers' market with its kitschy shops, souvenirs stands, and food stalls. The diversity of the place brought in all sorts of people.

Including me.

And Detective Shuman, I realized, as I saw him enter the Macy's store.

At first, it irked me that I'd seen him. I'd come here to spend a few hours Christmas shopping before I had to report for work at Holt's tonight. Seeing Shuman reminded me of everything I'd been trying to forget these past few days, since the fiasco at that stupid fund-raiser last Saturday.

But maybe this was a sign, I thought. After all, what were the chances I'd run into Shuman? Especially here. It probably wasn't the sort of place a homicide detective could routinely afford to shop. Plus, it was a weekday, so he was working, and he must have ducked in here to get something special.

It was destiny, I decided.

I hurried inside to catch up with him.

I doubted he was headed for the men's clothing department, so I checked out the perfume counter and found him gazing at the display cases, looking uncomfortable.

"Girlfriend's birthday," I said, coming up beside him.

Shuman turned, surprised to see me. But he recognized me immediately. I'm not sure having a homicide detective know you on sight is such a good thing, but that was what my life had turned into.

"How'd you know?" he asked.

"Elementary, my dear Shuman," I told him. "You're not married—no wedding ring, plus a wife would never let you out of the house wearing that tie—therefore you're not here for an anniversary present. You wouldn't buy your mom or sister expensive perfume, so it must be a girlfriend. The next gift-giving occasion is Christmas, and there isn't a man on the planet who shops any sooner than the week of Christmas Eve, so it has to be a birthday."

Shuman seemed impressed. He gestured at the display. "She mentioned something and I wrote it down, but I left it at home. Now I'm not sure which one to buy her. I thought if I came here and looked at the bottles, I'd remember."

Shuman looked kind of handsome today. He had on a tweed jacket that complemented his trousers and shirt. And I liked it that he'd written down his girlfriend's favorite perfume.

"We'll figure it out," I said. "Tell me about her."

"She's awesome." He got a dreamy look in his eye. "Smart, funny, pretty. She just went to work in the district attorney's office. She'll be a judge someday."

She was probably only a few years older than me, and already she'd finished law school. Wow.

"How long have you two been dating?" I asked.

"Two months, three weeks, two days."

I could see Shuman was taken with her, something beyond just a woman he was dating, and that required a special gift.

"Forget the perfume. Come with me," I said. We left the store.

"The three-month gift is crucial," I explained as we walked. "Too soon for lingerie, a little too late for perfume. You want to give her something special, memorable, and I know just the thing."

I took him to the Burberry store. He hesitated in the doorway.

"I can't afford something from here," he said.

I figured he couldn't spend five hundred bucks on a purse—though it is a very worthwhile purchase—so I took him to the counter and asked the clerk to show him a Burberry scarf.

"Cashmere," I said and held it out.

He looked at the tag. "It's over two hundred dollars."

"It fits her conservative, attorney image. It makes a statement. She'll love it."

"I don't know," he said, shaking his head. "I'm sure she'd like the perfume."

"The gift isn't about her, Shuman, it's about you," I said. "Think about it. What's going to happen when she gets to work with it? All her friends will notice, they'll crowd around, they'll be jealous, they'll ask who gave it to her. And she's going to stand there with a proud smile on her face and tell them her boyfriend gave it to her. Everyone will be impressed, not only with the scarf, but with the man she's chosen to date. See? It's really a reflection on you."

Shuman hesitated. He looked at the scarf, at me, then at the scarf again. I could see him thinking, processing what I'd said. I guess you didn't get to be a homicide detective by believing everything everybody told you.

"I'll take it," he finally said.

The clerk wrapped the scarf in their gorgeous beige gift box with BURBERRY embossed in gold letters and tied it with their luxurious ribbon, then slipped it into their impressive shopping bag.

We left the store and Shuman stopped. I thought he was having second thoughts about the scarf, but I was wrong.

"I can't talk to you about the investigation," he told me.

"I didn't help you with the scarf to get information," I said, which I sincerely meant. Yet I saw no reason to waste this opportunity, since he'd brought up the subject. "And I didn't kill Richard."

"Yeah, I know," he said, sounding weary. "But Madison . . . he's old school. He's retiring at the first of the year and—"

"And he wants to solve this case before he goes?" I asked, stunned. Great. Just what I needed. Some old guy wanting to leave a clean desk behind when he walks off the job.

"Other people had a strong motive for wanting Richard dead," I said.

He looked concerned now. "Stay out of it. You'll wind up in more trouble."

"I'm a murder suspect," I said. "I don't know how it can get much worse than that."

Shuman shrugged. "We're looking at the neighbor. They were having an affair."

I already knew that, but at least now he was talking about the case. And I realized what had been bothering me all along about the neighbor's supposed involvement.

"Richard's neighbors were in Holt's stockroom?" I asked.

Shuman didn't say anything so I figured I was on to something. I waited, hoping I could outlast him. I did.

"There was a truck unloading around the time of Richard's murder," Shuman said. "Anybody could have come and gone through the loading dock doors. The camera back there is limited. Big blind spots. So the stockroom surveillance video is—"

"Worthless," I said.

Shuman nodded reluctantly. "Of some value, but not conclusive."

So maybe it was a Holt's employee who murdered Richard, and maybe it wasn't. I didn't feel any better knowing that.

"How long was Richard dead before I found him?" I asked.

"About an hour," Shuman said.

"Prints on the murder weapon?"

"Dozens."

I should have known that, given how many people in the store use those U-boats for moving merchandise.

"Look, I've got to get back to work," Shuman said.

I could tell I'd pushed him too far, but so what? I need information and he had it.

"Just one more thing," I said. "Please tell me you and Madison are still looking for suspects."

"We're working the case," Shuman said. His eyes narrowed. "Is there something you want to tell me?"

I wasn't sure what leads he had or which suspects he knew about, and I wasn't sure if he'd listen to my list of names. Since I was a suspect myself, wouldn't my info be, well, suspect?

Besides, I didn't like the idea of naming names, possibly getting an innocent person into trouble. I was in the glare of the detectives' spotlight myself; I wouldn't wish that off on anybody—anybody who wasn't guilty, that is. And how many times could I "cry wolf" to Shuman and expect him to follow up? I decided to keep my ideas to myself until I had something to back them up with.

"Yeah," I said and pointed to the Burberry shopping

bag. "Start saving now. You can get her a matching wallet for Christmas."

He grinned, raised the bag in a little salute, then left.

"Let me know how she likes it," I called.

I stood there for a moment looking at him, then at the store.

"What the hell . . ." I muttered.

I went inside and bought myself a scarf—with a matching wallet.

"You want to go to a hair show?" Bella asked me.

"A what?"

"A hair show."

We were standing in line at the time clock, waiting for our shift to start. Bella had outdone herself with her do today. It looked sort of like a tsunami wave crashing up the back of her head.

"You know, a show where they preview the latest hairdos and all the new beauty products," Bella said. She pulled her cell phone from her pocket and flipped it open. "Give me your number. I'll call you."

"Sure," I said, and rattled off my number as she punched it into her phone. The line moved toward the time clock. "When is it?"

"No cell phones on the sales floor." Rita's voice blared from across the break room.

"She's so good at riding asses, she ought to get a job at the rodeo," Bella muttered.

"She's already got clown clothes," I added, and we both laughed.

We punched our time cards and went out onto the sales floor.

"Where are you going?" Bella asked.

"I'm in Housewares tonight."

"No, you're in the meeting," Bella told me. "Didn't you read the notice by the time clock?"

There was a notice by the time clock?

"I'll call you about the show," Bella said, and headed toward the front of the store.

Apparently, a lot of us were scheduled for the meeting so I followed the crowd to the training room. Sandy fell into step beside me.

"So, how's it going with Mr. Sensitive, the tattoo artist?" I asked.

Sandy looked a little miffed. "Do you know what I found out? I found out he has a profile on match-dot-com, and it's been there ever since we started dating."

"He didn't take it down while you two were going out? What a jerk," I said. "So you're dumping him, right?"

"I read his profile. He's really an interesting guy," Sandy said. "I'm kind of lucky to have him for a boyfriend."

Okay, the closest thing I have to a psych degree is the two-day *Oprah* marathon on Lifetime I'd watched last spring when I called in sick for cramps, but, jeez, this wasn't right.

"Sandy," I said and tried to look wise. "You can do better."

"You just don't understand what it's like to be an artist," Sandy said, sounding even wiser.

That's for damn sure.

Inside the training room I looked for that big guy from men's clothing, hoping I could get the seat behind him and hide, but he wasn't there. But I snagged a spot on the back row between Colleen, the sort-of retarded girl, and Grace, the poor sap who was permanently assigned to the customer service booth.

The woman in front of me turned around and I saw that it was Shannon, the lead in the greeting cards section, the one I'd tried to run down with the vacuum cleaner.

She narrowed her eyes at me.

"Thanks a lot, Haley." She sneered.

What grade are we in?

"On account of you, we're all stuck in these meetings," Shannon said.

Just because you're in a meeting doesn't mean you have to pay attention. Was I the only one who understood that?

"And we're working longer shifts because nobody wants seasonal jobs here," Shannon added. "You shouldn't have made such a big deal out of finding Richard dead. You should have kept it quiet."

Shannon gave me one last scathing look, put her nose in the air, and whipped around.

"You found Richard?" Colleen asked. She gazed at me as if I were a front-page tabloid celebrity. "Did he really have on spandex leggings?"

Rita pushed her way into the aisle and stood over me.

"You're training in the customer service booth tonight," she told me.

"What?" I bolted upright in my chair.

"It's your new assignment."

"I don't want to work in customer service."

"Well, you're going to." Rita sneered and walked away.

God, I hate that bitch.

And I hated the customer service booth. It was the worst place in the entire store. I couldn't work there. There was absolutely no way to hide from customers and you had to actually wait on them.

Rita knew I didn't like it there. She'd managed to put me there, somehow, and she'd done it to make my life miserable.

As if it could get any more miserable.

I realized that Colleen was still staring at me, still looking awestruck, still waiting for an answer to her question.

"No. Richard wasn't wearing spandex leggings," I told her. "It was a teddy and the name 'Rita' was embroidered across the butt."

The room quieted as Jeanette Avery came in. I don't know how anybody expected me to pay attention in a meeting now, after just hearing devastating news.

The customer service booth? It was the crappiest job on the planet. I had to get out of it, somehow.

Jeanette started rambling on about how great we all were as employees, and what fine jobs we were doing under difficult circumstances, and how much she appreciated us all working together, blah, blah, blah. I was deep into my how-can-I-get-out-of-this thoughts when Ty walked into the room.

He looked a bit breathless and rushed, as if he were running late. But other than that, he looked impeccable, as always. And handsome. I hadn't seen him since the fiasco in his mother's driveway on Saturday. That day I'd wondered if Ty suspected me of Richard's murder, if he was working with the police to prove it. I hadn't learned anything to change my opinion.

Ty stood off to the side while Jeanette talked; then something caught his eye, so he walked to the door. A woman waited there. Blond, really nice looking, dressed in a suit that fit her perfectly, carrying a folder.

My heart jumped. It was the woman I'd seen him window-shopping with in Pasadena that night I'd gone out with Marcie. What was she doing here?

Jeanette kept talking but I watched the two of them. They spoke quietly for a few seconds, and then Blondie pulled a document from the folder. She flipped a page, pointed to something, and Ty studied it.

Oh my God. She works for Holt's. For him. His secretary.

Marcie had said Blondie wasn't Ty's girlfriend—when will I learn to listen to her opinion?—and she was right. But instead of feeling better, I felt worse.

The two of them stood side by side, looking over the document. Not touching, but connected. Both understanding it, working together to solve a problem or handle some situation.

And suddenly, I wanted to be the one working on a problem, solving something, handling a situation. I didn't want to be sitting here in this stupid meeting, watching Blondie in her great outfit, conferring quietly with Ty.

He nodded, finally, and glanced at her. She nodded too, then walked away.

"Sarah?" he called softly, and took a step toward her.

She stopped and turned back. I couldn't see Ty's face, but whatever he said made her smile.

I hate my life.

Sarah left, Jeanette finished her spiel, and Ty took over the meeting. He thanked her and echoed her words about what great employees we all were, before he finally got down to business.

"As you all know, this Friday is the biggest shopping day of the year," he said. "And, due to tragic circumstances, we find ourselves short on personnel. Our annual surprise merchandise campaign kicks off and we have to be ready when we open the doors at five a.m. on Friday."

A groan rumbled through the room.

Ty smiled, then said, "But in order to be ready, that means some of us will have to work on Thursday. Thanksgiving Day."

An even bigger groan erupted. Employees rolled their eyes and shook their heads, and complained to everybody seated around them. Shannon turned and glared at me again.

"And to compensate for time away from your families on this very special day," Ty said, "everyone who works will receive four times their usual hourly wage."

The room got quiet.

Mom had been planning Thanksgiving for a couple of weeks now, and from what I'd overheard, our usual family holiday gathering was expected. Juanita and her daughters would spend two days preparing the feast; then some of my parents' friends would come to eat, along with a few aunts and uncles, and my sister, of course, on break from UCLA.

This year Mom was serving Russian cuisine—who knew?—and while several cases of vodka would surely get everyone through the day much easier, blinis, smoked fish, and beef Stroganoff didn't seem all that festive to me, no matter how fresh the noodles.

My sister would tell everyone about her classes—Mom would mention her 4.0 GPA—and then she'd talk about her last modeling assignment, then her next modeling assignment, and before the day was over we'd all end up in the den watching the webcast from my brother in the Middle East, looking very handsome in his flight suit and surrounded by all his friends, and Mom would ask questions; then Dad would remind her that everything my brother did over there was top secret. Then we'd all have dessert, which could have been the saving grace of the occasion, and while I don't know what Russians have for dessert, I'm pretty sure it's not pumpkin pie.

I raised my hand. "I'll work."

CHAPTER 14

"Things are absolutely frantic here today," Mom declared as she let me in the front door of her house. She had a glass of white wine in her hand and wore a YSL blouse and pencil skirt.

I followed her through the silent house to the kitchen. Juanita and her two grown daughters were chopping, grating and mixing, and chatting quietly in Spanish. Pots were boiling on the stove. Something smelled funny.

Mom dropped into the chair at the little table across the room and gestured with her wineglass.

"Guests will arrive tomorrow at noon, and I have many, many things to handle before then," Mom said. "It's frantic here. Just frantic."

In front of her on the table were three lists she was making. One list was for the gardener. The second was a list of things for Juanita to do, and the last was a list of things Juanita had to tell the staff to do. Beside these lay a copy of *Vogue* magazine Mom was flipping through.

My mom's idea of frantic.

I hadn't told her I wouldn't be here for Thanksgiving dinner, even though I'd known for a few days now. I decided it was better to tell her in person.

"About tomorrow," I said, and sat down across from her.

She tapped a photo in the magazine. "Have you seen what Michael Kors is doing this season?"

"I know it's Thanksgiving, a family occasion," I said. "But I won't be here."

Mom paused, a well-manicured fingernail pressed against the glossy page. "Do you realize what this means?"

Okay, at this point a number of things might come to mind: it's a family holiday and my brother is in the Middle East; two of her children will be absent; relatives and family friends will miss seeing me; it just won't be the same without me there.

But my mom said, "This will completely throw off my dinner table seating."

She launched into crisis-management mode. I waited while she added more items to all three of her lists—even the gardener's, for some reason—and had Juanita refill her wineglass.

"So, why won't you be here?" Mom asked, finally.

"I'm feeding the homeless."

She wrinkled her nose. "Where?"

"Bel Air," I said.

She thought about it for a moment, and I knew she was imagining how this story would play tomorrow when her guests arrived and asked where I was.

"Oh. Well, all right." She turned back to her magazine. "That reminds me. Do you know Ty Cameron?"

I jumped, but Mom was looking at an Oscar de la Renta evening wear photo spread and didn't notice. I'd never gotten around to telling Mom that I'd taken a part-time job at Holt's, so I didn't know how she'd linked us.

"Maxine Davis was at the fund-raiser on Saturday," Mom said.

None of this connected but I knew to wait. It would come.

"Honestly, you wouldn't believe what that woman had on," Mom said, flipping the page.

Patience . . . patience . . . patience. . . .

"She pointed him out to me—good gracious, he's a handsome thing—and mentioned that she saw him talking with you." Mom looked up at me. "Do you know him?"

Lying to someone straight to their face, especially someone you care about, isn't easy. Luckily, I've had years of practice. Not to be mean. It's more instinct. Self-preservation.

Mom had asked the question easily enough, but I knew her too well to fall for her casual, innocent tone. She sensed a possible relationship on the horizon.

I frowned, as if I were thinking hard, then shook my head. "No, the name isn't familiar."

"Maxine is positive she saw you talking to him," Mom insisted. Now I could see that her thoughts had raced on. She was mentally picturing our engagement party.

I deepened my frown, as if I were thinking really hard this time, then said, "Oh, I know. It was probably that guy I talked to out back."

"Oh, so you *did* meet him." Mom's exquisitely arched brows drew upward and I knew she was picking my wedding colors.

"Doesn't he already have a girlfriend?" I asked, thinking of Sarah, the blonde I'd seen him window-shopping with that night in Pasadena, then again at the store. I was pretty sure of my instincts when I'd seen them discussing business—and, of course, Marcie is always right about these things—but I figured it wouldn't hurt to get a confirmation.

"Not according to Maxine," Mom said with the conviction that only comes from talking smack with the biggest gossip in your social group. "So, what were you two chatting about?"

She tried to sound casual, but behind those innocent eyes of hers, I could tell she was deciding on my veil and headpiece.

"He'd noticed your fruit bouquets. Said they were fabulous," I told her.

"Really?"

I saw my imaginary walk down the aisle vanish from my mom's mind.

"He thought they were the hit of the day," I added.

"Well, how nice." Mom smiled and went back to flipping pages again.

"Okay, so I've got to go," I said, getting up.

"Did you bring the paperwork for the fruit bouquets at the fund-raiser?" Mom asked. "The accountant, what's-his-name, is having a hissy fit for all sorts of records."

I had it in my car but I wasn't going to risk coming into the house for a second time today.

"I'll bring it over next time," I promised.

Mom didn't seem to hear me. She was studying a Lord & Taylor ad.

"Maybe I'll ask around," she said.

I knew what she meant but I didn't want to give her any encouragement.

"Maxine might not be completely up to date," Mom mused. She gazed off across the kitchen, but I'm sure she wasn't noticing how hard Juanita and her daughters were working. She was thinking about Ty and any possible girlfriend he might have.

"I'll let you know," Mom promised, turning back to her magazine.

I wanted to wave her off, tell her not to, but decided it was better to let it go.

"Okay, Mom, bye."

She flipped to the next page, and I left.

When I got to my apartment I turned the TV to the Food Network. It had become my porn channel, thanks to my new healthier lifestyle. I salivated through a half hour of Italian cooking, then actually started to drool when that woman who starts every recipe with a stick of butter came on.

That's when it hit me: I needed to modify my new lifestyle.

No sense in knocking myself out with an improved diet and increased exercise, I decided. I could cut back—just a little—and still achieve outstanding results. Tackling both was too big a first step. I should pick just one.

Exercise, of course. It made perfect sense. I walked all the time at Holt's, which increased my heart rate and boosted my metabolism, so if I added a couple of days at the gym, that should be more than enough. And I could incorporate better eating later.

Relieved, I scrounged in the back of my cupboard for my emergency bag of Oreos, and sat down on the couch.

My list of murder suspects still lay on the coffee table where I'd left it several days ago. I picked it up.

The only two names on the list were Sophia Garcia, whom Richard had threatened to fire for supposedly abusing the company discount—which I still found incomprehensible—and Glenna Webb, Richard's lover—which I still found repulsive. I had no new info on either of these suspects, but I had more names to add to the list.

First, the neighbor whom Richard was having yet another fling with. I hadn't pictured Richard as such a stud that women would be clamoring for bedroom time with him, but I hadn't imagined you could die of being an asshole either; Richard had proved me wrong on both counts.

Also, the neighbor's husband. Both of them had motive for revenge, even if I didn't know the specifics. I could assume that Detective Shuman and his soon-to-be-retired partner Detective Madison had come up with something substantial, since they considered one of this husband and wife team a suspect. Yet those same detectives had put me on their suspect list, so did their suspicions about these two have any merit?

I looked at the list of suspects and, with some reluctance, added Jeanette Avery's name. She had reason to want Richard out of her store. Jeanette was privy to store gossip and surely knew what sort of employee Richard was, that he'd nearly succeeded in getting the manager of the Northridge store fired. She probably figured he'd transferred to her store, gunning for her position.

Shuman had told me that Richard had been dead for about an hour before I found the body. I had to find out where I'd reached Jeanette when I'd phoned her that night, before I'd know if she was a viable suspect.

Then I got a little chill. That night, Detective Madison had asked if I'd seen or heard anyone in the stockroom. I'd blown off his question, but now that I thought about it a little more, it wasn't so unreasonable. The stockroom was huge, two stories, with gigantic shelving units that reached the ceiling, a janitor's closet, a forest of mannequins, plus that huge machine near the loading dock that wrapped merchandise awaiting the returns truck.

Maybe the murderer had actually been in the stockroom, hiding. Maybe I'd seen him—or her—come or go through the entrance by the intimates department.

Oh my God. Had Richard's killer been right in front of me—and I hadn't seen him?

Grace deserved a medal. An award, a plaque, a historical marker, a new car. Something. Not only did she know and understand each of the zillion tasks required of a customer service booth employee; she also had to train *me*.

The girl who usually worked here *supposedly* had food poisoning, but I thought she was off shopping, or something. I hoped she got back here soon so I could go back to the sales floor; straightening socks didn't seem so bad right now.

I'd been at this for a few days now and I was still as overwhelmed as when I started. And no matter how many times I screwed up, Grace never got upset or short with me, just explained things one more time, and told me to try again.

I was never going to get out of this place.

The customer service booth was at the back of the store near the public restrooms, the customer convenience phones, the bridal registry, the offices and training room, and the employee break room. The counters were high, the ceiling was low, and we were locked in here behind a door with a keypad. Grace said it was to discourage would-be robbers from jumping the counter to get to the cash office and safe, located behind a partition at the rear of the booth, but I was convinced it was to keep us employees from escaping.

"Can I help you?" I asked, facing the woman at the head of the long line awaiting service.

It was Wednesday night. Tomorrow was Thanksgiving. Why weren't these people at home cooking?

"Do you have layaway?" the woman asked, dumping an armload of men's briefs on the counter.

"No."

"Why not?" she demanded. "You should have layaway. Customers need layaway."

People think that because you work in the customer service booth, you know everything and are responsible for everything.

"That's our policy, ma'am," I said, and made "ma'am" sound like "bitch" with almost no effort at all. I'd been practicing.

"I want to speak to your supervisor," the woman announced.

"Sure. Grace?"

She was working at the computer at the back of the booth, looking up stock numbers, something I was destined to spend hours on. She walked over.

Grace was barely five feet tall—I towered over her—

petite, with short blond hair she could roll out of bed with, not touch, and still everyone would think a stylist on Rodeo Drive had spent hours on it.

"This woman thinks we should have layaway," I told her.

The woman made some sort of noise.

"You know, we get requests for that all the time," Grace said, with the most charming of-course-you-can smile I'd seen in the entire store. She pulled a customer comment card from under the counter. "Would you fill this out?"

"Darn right I will." The woman snapped it out of Grace's hand, gave me a withering look, and moved down the counter to write, taking her briefs with her.

"Can I help you?" I asked the next person in line.

"I'd like to return this," the woman said, handing me a blouse.

"Do you have a receipt?" I'd said that about a million times, today alone.

"No. Sorry. I lost it," she said, with an apologetic smile. "But I paid twenty-five dollars for it."

"I'll have to look it up," I said.

This part of the job wasn't so bad. Grace had trained me on the inventory computer and it was kind of cool to scroll through the thousands of items and see everything Holt's stocked. I spent a lot of hours looking up merchandise returned with no tag or receipt, searching for the description and the manufacturer, then seeing the original price and the clearance price, how many were in stock here and in other Holt's locations, and how many had been returned to the manufacturer as defective or unsaleable. It was a quick way to get an overview of what customers bought. I wondered if anybody ever brought the corporate buyers into the store, showed them the god-awful clothes on the clearance racks, and asked what the hell they'd been thinking.

I found the info on the customer's blouse. She wasn't going to like it.

"It's been marked down for clearance," I told her. "The price now is six dollars."

"Six dollars?" she exclaimed. "I just bought that blouse."

"In June," I told her, and nodded toward the inventory computer. "We stocked these in June and clearanced them in August. It's November."

"But I paid twenty-five dollars for it," she said.

"Without a receipt, all I can give you is six dollars."

"But—"

"That's our policy, ma'am," I said.

She drew in a big breath, stewed for a minute, then said, "Fine."

I entered the transaction on the register, gave her six bucks, and she left. The next customer in line came forward.

"Do you have layaway?" she asked.

"I need a break," I told Grace.

Our line had disappeared and the store was quiet, since it was almost closing time. I was nearly cross-eyed from looking up stock numbers on the inventory computer, and decided my evening needed a boost.

"Sure," Grace said. "But before you go, do you want to handle these customer comment cards?"

I looked at the half dozen forms that had been filled out by disgruntled customers during our shift, lying in a basket on the back counter.

"Just file them." Grace grinned and nodded. "Over there."

I grinned too because I realized what she meant. The trash can.

"Standard procedure," Grace said.

I dropped them into the trash.

Okay, I'm kind of liking this job now.

Since I'd modified my new lifestyle to concentrate on exercise, I decided to take a walk through the store, and for that I needed some energy food. A Snickers bar from the vending machine in the break room sounded like just the thing.

I went inside and there sat that girl who'd lost twenty-five pounds. She was always in here—eating. How could anybody lose that much weight, constantly eating? Okay, so it wasn't exactly a Snickers bar she was munching on—more like a piece of shoe leather—but still, it wasn't fair. No wonder I hated her. I was surprised she had any friends at all.

But I couldn't bring myself to get a Snickers bar in front of her, so I left the break room and headed for the front of the store. A few days ago Bella had asked if I wanted to go to a hair show with her, and I hadn't heard anything else about it. I'd seen her name on the work schedule—there was a copy in the customer service booth in case employees needed to call in and be reminded of when they worked—so I figured she was on a register tonight; she split her time between there and the housewares department.

Bella had outdone herself with her do tonight. It looked like the Great Pyramid atop the Giza Plateau. She was busy with a customer so I kept walking, circled through the men's department, picked up my pace past the luggage and shoes, then slowed at the accessories section.

Merchandise had been removed, the shelves had been repositioned, and four workmen were busy installing glass display cases. I figured this was for the surprise Christmas merchandise that would be unveiled on Friday. Craig was there—didn't that guy ever go home?—looking over some paperwork.

I guess I had to admire him, in a way. After the problems last year when those game systems had been shoplifted, he was apparently working hard to keep a better eye on things this year. But I suppose it wasn't just commitment to Holt's he was thinking of. He probably didn't want to lose his job. Especially since his wife had cancer. He needed his pay-check and his medical benefits.

I looked around to see if the Christmas merchandise was there, ready to be stocked—it would be really cool to be the first to know what it was—but I didn't see anything. I'd checked the inventory computer earlier, but Grace had told me the info wouldn't be downloaded from corporate until the wee hours of Friday morning.

"Hey, Craig," I said. "What's up with the surprise stuff?"

He frowned at me. "It will be here when we open on Friday morning. Aren't you supposed to be working in Customer Service?"

"On break," I told him, then walked away. Jeez, what a crank-ass. I guess it takes somebody like Evelyn to be able to work for him. She actually seemed to have some com-passion for the guy.

As I walked through the intimates department, I glanced at the entrance to the stockroom and got a little chill, re-membering the night Richard was murdered. I'd gone over that whole thing in my mind again and again, and hadn't come up with anything new, anything more than what I'd remembered when I'd spoken to the detectives that night. But the truth was, I really might have seen the murderer and not known it.

The thing is, employees roamed the store all the time. Unless you were tied to a register or held hostage in the customer service booth, you pretty much had the run of the place, as soon as your supervisor's back was turned, anyway, or if you were on your break or lunch. The work schedule meant nothing, really. The store manager, the as-sistant manager, the area and department managers came in for their designated shift, but they could be here at any time of the day or evening to handle paperwork or prob-lems. Hourly wage employees swapped shifts with other workers, or came in to shop on their time off. So there was no way to know exactly who was—or wasn't—in the store that night.

Yet someone had removed the work schedule for the night Richard was murdered from the clipboard beside the time clock and from the customer service booth. Somebody was trying to hide something.

But who? And what?

I didn't know the answer to those questions, but there was another one I could answer tonight.

Jeanette's phone number.

I got a little tingle in my belly. I headed for the offices in the back of the store, but made a detour to the toy section next to the kids' clothing. I walked down two aisles before I spotted the Lil Campers set. I glanced around, saw no one, then ripped open the package and popped out the kid-size flashlight. I flipped it on. The light was feeble, but it would do.

Grace was busy with a customer when I walked past the customer service booth, so she didn't notice when I headed down the hallway toward the offices. All the doors were closed. It was silent back here. I looked up and down the hall, saw no one, opened the door, and slipped into the office used by the department managers. I closed the door quietly and turned on the flashlight. The beam looked brighter here in the total darkness.

Jeez, I can't believe I'm really doing this. My palms started to sweat and my insides jiggled.

Okay, I have to focus. And I have to hurry. If somebody found me in here, I don't know how I'd explain it.

I whipped the light around the room. The place looked the same as when I'd been in here twice before with Evelyn. I went to the desk, trying to remember which drawer she'd found the phone numbers in. I hadn't been watching her all that closely.

I pulled open the top drawer. It was a mess. Papers,

pens, pencils scrambled together. I opened another drawer. File folders. Yeah, okay, this might be something. I flipped through them and found a corporate directory, a softcover pamphlet slightly bigger than a paperback book.

I yanked it out and fanned the pages. This had to be the book Evelyn had used the night of the murder. The corporate structure, flowcharts, a store directory, names, titles, contact numbers—

Footsteps in the hallway.

I dropped to my knees behind the desk and switched off the flashlight.

Oh my God. What if someone comes in here? What if it's Craig? Or Rita? Or Jeanette—

The footsteps got louder. I crouched lower and held my breath.

I'll get fired. They'll call the police. Shuman and Madison will show up and this will convince them that I'm involved in Richard's murder.

Don't come in here. Please, don't come in here.

The footsteps faded. Thank God. . . .

I waited, listened hard. Nothing.

The office was totally black. I couldn't see my hand in front of my face. I waited, counted to one hundred, then counted again. Nothing. Slowly I got to my feet—I don't think I have the knees for too much of this covert activity—and crept to the door. I listened while I shoved the corporate directory into the back waistband of my pants and pulled my shirt over it. I heard nothing, so I opened the door just a crack.

Nobody in sight. I eased out and pulled the door closed. I'd made it.

Wow, this was actually very cool. Sneaking around undercover—

The door to Jeanette's office flew open. I jumped. Craig appeared in the doorway. He jumped. Damn, we were always meeting up like this.

I heaved a big sigh. "You scared the life out of me."

"What are you doing back here?" he asked.

Good question.

"Looking for you," I said, and it came out sounding really reasonable. "A customer had a question about some luggage."

Craig's eyes narrowed. "So?"

"So," I said, hoping I didn't sound as if I were stalling for time. "Luggage is your department so I wanted to ask you about it."

His eyes narrowed farther. "Okay, ask me."

Jeez, now what was I going to do?

"Well, okay, the customer wanted to know if they could get replacement parts," I said, totally winging it. "One of the wheels came off."

"You should know this by now. How long have you been working in the customer service booth?" he grumbled and walked past me. "Ask Grace. She knows."

Craig disappeared, leaving me standing alone in the hallway with the store directory shoved into the back of my pants.

Something about Craig always hit me funny. I guess he was just really stressed, with his wife's medical problems and everything. Anyway, I was glad he'd believed my feeble question about the luggage.

But that left me with another question: why had Craig been in Jeanette's office?

Chapter 15

Thanksgiving is a time for family. Warm houses filled with the aroma of roasting turkey, sweet potatoes, and apple pie. Pumpkins, cornstalks, and gourds decorating the hearth. Family and friends gathered.

But that's what other people were doing today. Not me. I was at Holt's. Working.

Lots of people have to work on Thanksgiving. Police, firemen, medical people, the military, all giving up their family time for a good cause.

My good cause today? Me. And the thirty bucks an hour I was making.

They'd told us to come today prepared to work hard and get dirty. I dressed in a pair of jeans with a red paint stain down the leg (my brief flirtation with furniture refinishing), a faded 'N Sync T-shirt (I'm still in love with Justin), and a ratty old pair of Skechers I'd dug out of the back of my closet.

"We'll be lucky to get this stuff stocked by New Year's," Bella muttered.

She was working in Housewares, unpacking and setting up displays of Christmas dinnerware. I was an aisle over in Domestics, putting out holiday table linens. Between us, we had five U-boats of merchandise to stock.

Other employees were spread out through the store,

doing the same. The merchandise display people were finishing dressing the mannequins in holiday clothing and hanging the store decorations. Though the whole operation had been carefully planned, we still expected to put in a lot of hours.

Ty was here. I'd seen him earlier in jeans and a T-shirt, loading boxes onto U-boats in the stockroom. He looked great. Too bad I couldn't work next to him. He was probably all sweaty by now.

In the stockroom on the loading dock was a mountain of boxes that had been delivered yesterday, all the holiday-themed items, plus the special after-Thanksgiving merchandise that would be featured in the sale ad. Every box came with a store map and department diagram designed by somebody in the corporate office, so minimum-wage peons like me would know exactly where to stock it.

"I'm supposed to be home right now eating turkey," Bella said, and held out her hands. "And here I am wrecking my nails instead. What kind of Thanksgiving is this?"

"Your hair's great," I offered. In keeping with the tradition of the holiday, she'd fashioned her hair in the shape of a cornucopia tipping forward on her head. No fruit, though.

Bella patted the back of her hair. "This is nothing. When I enroll in beauty school, you're gonna see some dos. Stylist to the stars. That's what I'll be. Just wait. You'll see my creations on the red carpet. All them hot stars, prancing around like show ponies, wearing my hair designs."

"So, when's the hair show?" I asked, as I pulled the plastic off another four-pack of Santa place mats.

"Didn't I call you? I thought I called you. It's next week. Three days, but I'm only going on Thursday. That's the day they show the new dos," Bella said. She hoisted another box of Snowmen plates off the U-boat.

"Did you ask for Thursday off?" I asked.

"You bet I did. Two weeks ago."

I wasn't scheduled to work on day shift during the week, because of my job at Pike Warner, and since I figured I'd be back in the accounts payable unit any time now, I hadn't changed my availability here at Holt's. The weekly work schedule wasn't announced until Sunday, but I had no reason to believe my hours would be any different.

"I'll have to be back here for my shift Thursday night," I said, as I pulled red-and-white-striped napkins out of a box.

"No problem," she said. "Hey, that reminds me. When we're out on Thursday, can you take me to get one of those knockoff purses like you carry?"

I froze, a dozen red and white napkin rings in my hand. My mind locked up. Knockoff purses? As in fake, counterfeit, rip-off? Bella thought my handbags—my genuine, authentic, extremely expensive, gorgeous designer bags—weren't the real thing?

"I saw them on the Internet, but you just don't know about some of those Web sites," Bella said, arranging Snowmen plates on the display table. "They might be selling second-rate fakes, you know? I tried to find them on eBay, but they're just a bunch of uppity assholes. They don't allow knockoffs. Just the real ones. I can't afford those real ones. So, believe me, I got no qualms about sporting around town with a fake on my arm, as long as it's a good-quality fake."

I didn't want to tell her that I bought the real thing. She'd want to know how I afforded them on my Holt's salary, and I didn't want to get into the whole Pike Warner irregularities-investigation-pending thing.

But Bella didn't have time to notice that I hadn't answered her question. Rita suddenly appeared in the aisle.

She, like Craig, seemed to always be in the store. Like they were afraid something would happen and they wouldn't be there to see it.

"Schedule's changed for tomorrow," Rita announced, jabbing a clipboard in my direction. "You're in Customer Service."

"I'm restocking tomorrow," I told her, glad that, for once, I'd looked at the work schedule.

"You're in Customer Service," Rita barked. "Permanently."

"Permanently? No way!" I exclaimed. "What about what's-her-name? With the food poisoning? She's supposed to be back—"

"She's not coming back. You're in Customer Service."

"But—"

"Get over yourself, princess," Rita said, then walked away.

Customer service? Permanently? As in, forever?

No. No, it couldn't be true. What had I done to be thrust into the bowels of retail hell?

Whatever it was, I wasn't going to take it.

I started down the aisle after Rita, ready to rip that schedule out of her hand and change it myself—in *her* blood, if necessary—but Bella touched my arm.

"She's not worth it," she said. "She's a bitch, but she's not worth it."

I hate it when other people are right.

"I detest working in Customer Service," I all but screamed.

"It's a shit hole, all right," Bella agreed. A moment passed; then she nodded toward the U-boat. "Let's get this stuff stocked so we can get out of here. Get home in time for pumpkin pie, or something."

I guess that thought would have lifted another person's mood, but not mine. It was nearly noon now, and by the time we got all this stuff unpacked and displayed, Mom's guests would be eating Thanksgiving dinner.

No way was I walking into the middle of that. It would throw off Mom's seating arrangement, for one thing. And she'd want me to talk about feeding the homeless today, and though Mom hadn't noticed (she won a beauty contest, not an I'm-planning-the-Mars-mission contest, luckily), one of the guests would question the plausibility of a homeless shelter in Bel Air, and then what would I say?

I got another box of place mats from the U-boat, ripped off the plastic, put them on the shelves like a robot. It was mindless work, leaving my brain available for more pleasant thoughts.

My gorgeous red leather Notorious handbag popped into my mind. It would look great at Christmas. I mentally flipped through the clothing hanging in my closet at home and selected a perfect outfit to wear with it. Then Detective Shuman's girlfriend appeared in my thoughts, and I wondered how she liked the Burberry scarf I'd helped him pick out, and whether he'd buy her the matching wallet. Before long my mind was filled with handbags, racing along at top speed, hopping from Dooney & Bourke to Coach to Kenneth Cole, until it reached the Holy Grail of my desire: that Louis Vuitton organizer.

I must have moaned aloud because Bella looked at me funny.

"You okay?" she asked.

"Yeah. Great," I said.

"I'm great too," Bella said, "because I'm done."

I realized she'd finished. I only had another couple of boxes to go, so I ignored corporate's merchandise display diagram, crammed everything onto the closest shelf, and followed Bella to the stockroom, towing two U-boats.

When I got there, the towers of merchandise had disappeared, but there was still a lot of commotion. The big doors on the loading dock were open and people in white coats were streaming inside carrying folding tables, chairs, and chafing dishes. An older woman stood by the doors, watching over everything, giving quiet instructions to the workers as they filed past. I walked over and saw a furniture rental truck and a catering van parked outside.

"Happy Thanksgiving," the woman said, smiling pleasantly at me. She had gray hair and wore a very nice grandma-style suit in fall colors.

"What's up?" I asked, nodding outside. It was a really great Southern California day, sunny, clear, warm.

"Thanksgiving dinner," she said, still smiling. "Courtesy of Holt's."

I turned, looking for Ty in the crowd, and spotted him talking with two employees I didn't know. He'd done this? Arranged Thanksgiving dinner for us?

"Wow . . ." I said, and I know it came out in a breathy little sigh because I was very impressed.

"It's the least that could be done," the woman said, "since all of you gave up your holiday with your family."

With some effort, I pulled my gaze from Ty and turned it to the woman again. Her smile was warm and hinted at some pride at her involvement, so I figured she was the caterer.

"I'm sure your family misses you today," she said.

Actually, I hadn't heard from my family, but managed to say, "They understand."

"I'm Ada," she said, and held out her hand.

I wonder why my mom hasn't called me today.

"Haley Randolph," I said, a little surprised she wanted to shake hands knowing how grimy I was from handling the boxes.

Ada studied me for a minute. "You look familiar."

I'd never seen her before, but since she was a caterer, she might have seen me at some event my mom had attended or hosted.

And my dad. Why hasn't he called? I've had my cell phone on me all day.

"Oh yes, of course," Ada said. "The fund-raiser last Saturday. Edible Elegance."

I figured she must have catered that event too. But, as usual, I wasn't going to get into my family history.

"I help out with the business end of things," I said.

"And you work here too?" She nodded her approval, then paused and smiled, as if she'd just uncovered a secret. "Your name was on Saturday's guest list. Now I understand why Ty was suddenly so anxious to help out with the fund-raiser."

I didn't really think my sister would call, but jeez, it would have been nice. I mean, I wouldn't get to see any of them tomorrow either. Since I knew Pike Warner would be closed on the Friday-after, I'd scheduled myself to work at Holt's 5:00 a.m. opening.

Oh God. Now I'd have to work in the customer service booth.

How much more crappy can my life get?

"Everything going smoothly?" I heard someone ask.

I turned to see a young woman bound up the stairs onto the loading dock. Oh my God, it was Blondie, Ty's secretary. Sarah, or something. What's she doing here?

"Fine, fine," Ada said to her. "Have you met Haley Randolph?"

She turned to me, a practiced smile in place. She didn't offer to shake, but I saw her glance at my hand. No way was she touching me.

Bitch.

"It's good of you to give up your holiday for us," Blondie said.

"This is Sarah Covington," Ada said. "She's vice president of marketing for Holt's."

Vice president? Of marketing? Oh my God, she's hardly any older than me. And she's got a really great job. She's probably never worked in the customer service booth, and she doesn't have to have an of-course-you-can smile. And she's wearing a fabulous sweater. And she's clean. And she's—

Oh my God. She's—she's carrying a—a Louis Vuitton organizer. *My* Louis Vuitton organizer. The one I'm dying to have. The one I can't afford. The one I'm probably going to have to actually kill someone to get.

This is awful. Just awful.

I'm crushed. I don't think I can stand up. My breathing is all ragged and I could faint any second now.

Sarah gives me a pitying stare—I haven't said a word and I know she's slotted me in the minimum-wage-half-wit category of her mind—then smiles at Ada and walks away. Straight to Ty. She leans in and says something. Then he looks up—at me.

I launch into panic mode. I have to leave. I have to get out of here. I know my cheeks are red and I'm standing here like a complete idiot, unable to say a single word.

But, God, he looks handsome. The jeans fit great and the T-shirt is snug—I didn't know he had such a good chest. His bangs are loose and hanging over his forehead, and he's all rugged and masculine, and I want to throw myself on him and—

Oh no. He's walking over. He's looking me straight in the eye and I'm caught like a deer blinded by headlights. I can't move.

He leans down and kisses Ada on the cheek. "Hi, Grandma."

Grandma? *Grandma?*

She pats him on the arm and smiles up with pride. "Everything's moving along nicely, dear. The caterer will be set up in a few minutes."

She's his grandmother. One of the five generations of the Holt's Department Store family. And I thought she was the *caterer.*

Oh, crap. This is so embarrassing. She probably thinks I'm an idiot. And Sarah—Blondie—is probably watching too, and making notes in the Louis Vuitton organizer I can't afford. And my whole family must be sitting around the dinner table laughing because somebody told Mom there's no homeless shelter in Bel Air and they think I'm driving around in circles looking for it. And I have to be here at 5:00 a.m. to work in the customer service booth from hell.

"Have you two been introduced?" Ty asked and grinned. "Grandma, this is Haley Randolph. She's our quality assurance specialist in charge of the Laura Ashley bed-in-a-bag sets."

The breath went out of me.

He knows. He's always known. He watched the stockroom surveillance tape and saw me sitting on the Laura Ashley bed-in-a-bag set when I was supposed to be working. He goaded me into that ridiculous story about rescuing a puppy on the freeway, and my uncle taking his pregnant wife to the hospital instead of fixing my fender. He's known the truth all along.

And all along, he's been laughing at me.

Suddenly, I wasn't mindless anymore. I wasn't paralyzed with embarrassment. Sarah wasn't better than me. Ty wasn't handsome anymore. I was calm and collected, and I knew exactly what I needed to say and do.

I looked up at Ty. "Screw you."

Then I realized that I'd said it in front of his grandmother, so I said, "Sorry" to her, then walked out through the loading dock doors to my car parked in the front of the store.

I yanked the keys from my pocket and punched the "unlock" button. I was angry, furious, and about ready to cry when I heard my name. I turned and saw Ty jogging toward me.

I should have gotten into the car and driven away—or circled back and run over him—but I didn't. I stood there. I couldn't believe he had the gall to come after me.

"Shut up!" I yelled, even though he hadn't said anything.

He froze in place in front of me.

"You think you're hot shit, don't you?" I screamed. "You and your Holt's Department Store! Well, you know what? Holt's is the crappiest store on the planet! The clothes are horrendous! They're embarrassing! If my family owned this shit hole of a store and they gave it to me to run, I'd blow it up, and then I'd set what was left on fire, and then I'd plow it all into a big hole! *Then* I'd leave town and change my name!"

Now Ty has that deer-in-the-headlights look.

"You think you're all cute and funny and clever, but you're not!" I shouted.

I'm not really sure he knows what I'm talking about.

"So go ahead and bang your blondie girlfriend until you get skid marks on your knees—see if I care!"

Now he definitely has no idea what I'm talking about.

I stomped over to my car. "I quit! I'm done here. I'm leaving and I'm never coming back!"

I yanked open my car door and yelled, "And I'm getting that Louis Vuitton organizer if it's the last thing I do on this earth!"

I got in and whipped out of the parking space.

Don't look in the rearview mirror . . . don't look in the rearview mirror. . . .

Damn. I looked.

And there was Ty, still standing in the same spot, watching me.

CHAPTER 16

Okay, so now I didn't have a job. Any job. Not even a thankless job at a crappy store.

I stretched out on my sofa in my apartment, Oreos on my right, Snickers on my left, watching the Food Network. After blasting Ty in the Holt's parking lot earlier today, I'd driven around for a while to tap off some energy, then come home. Now I was exhausted.

Here was where my new lifestyle might do me some good. Exercise was exactly what I needed right now. It releases endorphins in the brain, which improves your mood. I could use an improved mood, but I wasn't so anxious for it that I could pry myself up off the sofa and hit the gym.

I popped another Oreo into my mouth.

Maybe I'd just lie here and eat. Like those morbidly obese people the Discovery Channel shows sometimes. All they do is eat and lie in bed. They lose the remote but don't understand why the channel changes every time they sneeze, then find it when the crane finally comes in to move them.

I couldn't really see me doing that, but I was going to have to think of a different lifestyle change. This whole exercise and improved diet just wasn't working for me.

I'll start on that tomorrow.

Today, I had other things to decide and the sugar rush was giving me a good buzz. I needed it, because I had to figure out how I was going to live until Pike Warner called me back to work.

I had no income now. My rent and utilities were due on the first, and without my paycheck from Pike Warner . . .

I shoved two Oreos into my mouth.

I hadn't heard from Kirk about the investigation. It had been nearly two weeks. I thought everything would be cleared up by now. Maybe things were slow there, since it was Thanksgiving week. Yeah, maybe that was it.

Then it hit me. What about that Golden State Bank and Trust credit card I was approved for? Oh my God. Perfect.

I sat up on the sofa and unwrapped a Snickers bar.

As soon as that credit card arrived, my troubles would be over. I could pay my rent, my car payment, utilities, everything. And I could finish my Christmas shopping. Wow, what a relief.

I bit off a big chunk of the Snickers bar and decided to make a list. There's nothing like having a list to make you feel organized.

I'd dropped my purse on the coffee table when I came in, so I dug through it and found an old envelope and a pen. This was why I desperately need that Louis Vuitton organizer. It would make my life flow so much more smoothly.

Then why not make it my first purchase with my new GSB&T credit card?

The idea hit me like seeing a "sale" sign in Macy's shoe department.

I couldn't think of a better way to break in new plastic, so I made it the first item on my list. Next: pay back my checking overdraft.

I sprang to my feet, envisioning myself strolling into my bank, which, apparently, will go under if they don't receive my eight hundred dollars along with their astronomical fees (which I'm not sure are even legal and maybe I should sue them when I get my job back at Pike Warner), presenting my prestigious GSB&T credit card, and signing away my overdraft with a casual signature and a shrug. That will show them.

I was pacing now, writing furiously.

My rent. I could get a cash advance and pay my rent—maybe I'd even pay it for January too. I'd send away my utility bills without a thought. Wow, that would be great.

And I could take my mom out to lunch. To that tearoom she loves that's so freakin' boring you want to slit your wrists just looking at the menu. Yeah, she'd be really impressed when I take her there.

I started a second list. This one was for things I wanted to follow up on. First: call GSB&T and find out when I'd get the credit card. I put a star by that one. Second: call Kirk Keegan. Third: if no definite response from Kirk, call Mrs. Drexler.

Wow, I was feeling pretty good now. Organized. Focused. A little light-headed from all the sugar, but that was okay.

I paused and read over my two lists. Everything looked good. But maybe there was something else? I'd filled the back and front of the envelope, so I went to my purse for something else to write on. I dug down and came up with the Holt's store directory.

When I'd gotten away from Craig in the hallway that night, I'd slipped into the break room and put it inside my purse in my locker. I'd forgotten all about it.

Now it occurred to me that, hey, I had time on my hands. I might as well solve Richard's murder. It would be good to get that cleared up.

I flipped through the pages to the personnel directory. No addresses were listed, just phone numbers. I found Jeanette Avery's name and looked at her contact info. Only one number was listed—other than the store's main number, of course—and, I swear, I couldn't remember if it was the one I had punched into the phone the night of Richard's murder.

But I supposed it didn't matter. This was the only number available, so it had to be the one I called. It looked like a landline number and that brought into question my suspicion that, if I'd reached her on a cell phone, it could put her close to the store within the right time frame to murder Richard. Yet I wouldn't know for sure, couldn't mark her off my suspect list, until I knew where she lived. It was possible her house was only a few minutes' drive from the store.

I went to my laptop on the kitchen table and logged on to the Internet. I knew there were sites where you could find addresses that matched phone numbers, and after a few minutes, I found a couple, but nothing corresponded to Jeanette's number.

Huh. Now what?

I turned a few pages in the store directory and my gaze homed in on Ty's name. My stomach got that gooey feeling and my heart ached a little. I'd told him off pretty good in the parking lot today—and he totally deserved it—but now I wasn't feeling so great about it.

Maybe I was just coming down from my sugar high.

Because I couldn't quit torturing myself at the moment, I flipped to the page to where Sarah Covington's name was listed along with her title. Vice President, Marketing. I felt a little envious. But I still hated her, of course.

I closed the book and forced myself to concentrate. Just because I'd left Holt's, that didn't mean Holt's had left me, regarding Richard's murder, anyway. In fact, I now got a weird feeling, wondering if my sudden departure might play into Detective Madison's hands, that he might twist this around, somehow, and make it look like further proof that I'd murdered Richard.

I hunted up my list of suspects. Nothing new to add. Nobody I could remove. I needed more information.

I found my cell phone and scrolled through the directory until I found Jack Bishop's number. He was the only person I knew who could help me, presuming he was willing. When I'd seen him in Holt's that night when I'd been vacuuming—which is still humiliating to think about—he'd said to let him know how things were going. I wasn't sure this was what he had in mind.

It was Thanksgiving Day, late, and I doubted he'd even answer his phone—although it was hard to imagine, he probably had a family somewhere—so I was surprised when he picked up.

"Haley, how's it going?" He sounded friendly enough. Sexy too.

"Great," I told him.

"Liar."

Jack doesn't waste time.

"How'd you know?" I asked.

"Because you're not back at work yet," he said. "Missed you at the Thanksgiving feed. Smuggled in a six-pack of Corona, just to share with you."

"Wish I'd been there," I said, and never meant anything more in my life.

"What's up with the investigation?"

"It's coming along," I said, then changed the subject. "Listen, Jack, I was wondering if you could help me out with something. I can pay you, of course."

"It's not your money I'm interested in, Haley."

He said it in that deep, Barry White voice men use sometimes. It sent a warm shiver up my spine, and down to some other places.

"So what do you need?" he asked.

My thoughts had raced ahead to something that had nothing to do with Jeanette Avery's phone number. It took a minute to reel myself back in. "Addresses."

"You stalking somebody?"

"Trying to."

Jack chuckled. "What have you got?"

I gave him Jeanette's phone number, and then, on impulse (not really, I'd planned it all along) I read off Ty's and Sarah's numbers.

"I'll get back to you." Jack hung up.

Since it was Thanksgiving and most everything except stores and restaurants would be closed tomorrow and the weekend, I figured it would be late Monday before I heard back from Jack. That left me with a lot of days to find something to do.

A number of things came to mind, but I didn't really want to do any of them, so I grabbed another handful of Oreos and started flipping channels. An hour later, my doorbell rang.

Could that be Ty?

The fantasy sprang into my head that he'd ransacked every office at Holt's looking for my home address so he could rush over and apologize, beg for forgiveness, tell me how great I was and how he'd lusted after me since the first moment he'd laid eyes on me, and how, if only I could find it in my heart to give him another chance, he would move heaven and earth, and try to live up—

My doorbell rang again.

I really need to ease up on the sugar.

My heart rate amped up considerably when I looked through the peephole. Jack Bishop.

What was he doing here? How did he know where I lived? Jeez, did I have time to run to the bathroom and brush my teeth? Maybe put on some makeup?

I had to settle for flicking the cookie crumbs off of my shirt, as I opened the door.

God, he looked gorgeous. Black pants, black sweater, deep blue eyes. I stepped back and he came inside.

He took in my apartment with a sweep of his gaze, then turned to me.

"Eating chocolate alone?" Jack shook his head. "Worse than drinking alone."

"My life has gotten complicated."

"Because you're a murder suspect?"

How did he know?

Jack seemed to read my thoughts, and said, "I've got friends in low places."

"I'll get you a beer."

When I came back from the kitchen with two Coronas, Jack was sitting on the end of my sofa. I took the other end. I didn't ask him why he wasn't with his family on Thanksgiving, and he didn't ask me that either. I guess we both already knew the answer.

I didn't ask how he knew where I lived either. If he could find Jeanette's, Ty's and Sarah's addresses, I guess he could find mine.

Suddenly, I got a sick feeling that Ty and Sarah's addresses might be the same.

"So, how did your friends in low places get involved with the murder at Holt's?" I asked, just to get the ball rolling—and to keep me from looking too deeply into his warm blue eyes, and to quit thinking about Ty.

Jack was a licensed private investigator working as a consultant for Pike Warner on discreet matters, which really meant that he dug up dirt on anyone or anything that served Pike Warner or its clients. He was bound by moral obligation—and the ironclad contract he'd been forced to sign—to keep things to himself. But Jack played by his own rules.

"The Holt's head honcho was worried about their exposure. Lawsuits from the widow of the deceased, employees, employees' spouses. All sorts of rodents crawl out of the bushes when there are deep pockets to gnaw on. I checked it out with the cops and who did I find?" Jack saluted me with his beer bottle. "You."

A knot of dread tightened in my belly. My future flashed

in front of me—which was really an empty black hole, because now I had no future. Pike Warner would never let me work for them again—even after my irregularities-investigation-pending problem was cleared up—if they knew I was the prime suspect in a murder investigation. Especially an investigation that involved one of their longtime, wealthy clients. Pike Warner was huge on reputation. They'd tolerate nothing that tarnished their carefully perfected image.

"I had nothing to do with Richard's murder. All I did was find him dead in the stockroom," I told Jack. "Damn. Next time I find a dead body somewhere, I'm just walking away. Let somebody else find it."

Okay, that made no sense but, hopefully, it was just the Oreos, Snickers, and beer, and I hadn't burned out some important brain cells with chocolate overload.

"That dumb-ass old fart of a detective is trying to railroad me just so he can retire with a clean desk," I said. Then, because my suspense factor is really low, I asked, "Did you mention my name in your report to Pike Warner?"

Jack gave me a little grin. "Discretion works one way—mine."

Wow. That was a relief.

"I'm keeping you out of it," Jack said. "For now."

"For now" had to last as long as it took for me to find Richard's murderer, if I ever hoped to have my old life back. And I was getting that life back.

"I guess it has something to do with this?" Jack asked as he pulled a slip of paper from his shirt pocket.

The addresses I'd asked for. Jeanette's home. Its location could prove—or disprove—my suspicion that she murdered Richard.

Of course, Ty's address would be written on there too. And Sarah's. I wasn't sure I wanted to see that.

But I took the paper anyway and unfolded it. Only Jeanette's info was listed. I figured that was because, as the store manager, she had to be on call twenty-four/seven for any problems that arose. Ty and Sarah, further up the corporate food chain, didn't. Plus, they wouldn't want anyone with access to the store directory to have their info and just drop by their place.

"The other numbers were for the corporate offices?" I asked Jack, just to be sure.

He nodded. "Should have their personal info first thing Monday."

So I'd have to wait the whole weekend to find out if Ty and Sarah were living together. Great.

I looked at Jeanette's address and my belly did a little flip. Stevenson Ranch. It was an upscale community just west of Valencia, close to the Holt's store. But "close" in California doesn't mean much. Here, distance is measured in time. Traffic flow—actually, the lack of it—determines drive-time.

"Want to check it out?" Jack asked, gesturing to the paper with his beer bottle.

Why not? It beat the heck out of me sitting here alone. And I could do without the last dozen or so Oreos and Snickers bars left in the bags.

I changed into jeans and a dark sweater—which was kind of weird, with Jack waiting in the other room—and debated on which handbag would be appropriate for a covert op. I finally decided on a black Marc Jacobs satchel. If it worked well for me tonight, maybe I'd write them a letter, let them know. Maybe they could use it in their advertising.

See? I have a sense of marketing, just like Sarah Covington. And I'm doing it without a Louis Vuitton organizer.

"I'll get the direction off MapQuest," I said to Jack when I came back into the living room.

"Got it covered," he told me.

We finished our beers and I dropped the bottles in the kitchen trash. Jack waited at the front door.

"Listen, Jack, I don't expect you to do it for free," I said, though I'd have to wait for my GSB&T credit card to arrive before I could pay him.

Jack eased a little closer. "Who said I was doing it free?"

The Barry White voice again. I got that warm shiver once more that, somehow, froze me in place.

"I'll tell you what sort of payment I want." He angled his body closer. "And when I want it."

Oh my God. . . .

CHAPTER 17

Jack and I just stood there for a few seconds, him looking sexy and hot, and me looking, I feared, like a dork. Was he going to kiss me? Take me in his arms? Head back to my bedroom?

Every time I'd seen Jack in the office building at Pike Warner, even when he'd caught me vacuuming the floor at Holt's, I'd sensed this heat between us. But now that the moment was here, I wasn't so sure.

He must have sensed it—or maybe my radar was way off—because he walked out the door ahead of me. I fumbled with locking the door, and followed.

His Range Rover—I guess private investigation paid pretty well—waited in the parking lot outside my building. It was dark now, the security lights were on, and they reflected nicely off the gleaming black paint job.

We got in and I saw that he had a navigation system. Jack punched in Jeanette's address and we took off. He was in private investigator mode now. Maybe it was for the best.

"What's the connection with this Avery woman?" he asked.

I gave him a rundown of my suspicion about Jeanette's involvement with Richard's murder. He listened, but when I was finished, he didn't say anything. I'd hoped he'd give me some feedback—that I was either nuts or on to something—but he didn't. I'd like to have some of the info he'd garnered from his friends-in-low-places who'd divulged the official police insider stuff on the murder investigation, but he didn't offer that either. I guess Jack didn't trust me yet with everything he knew.

The route plotted out by the Range Rover's navigation system took us past the Holt's store in Santa Clarita, through the city itself, across the 5 freeway overpass, and into Stevenson Ranch, a master-planned community covering thousands of acres. We wound through the foothills, through tracts of homes, to Jeanette Avery's house.

Jack slowed, but didn't stop.

Hers was one of the smaller models, but still expensive, appropriate for a store manager who easily pulled down a hundred and fifty thousand annually, not including bonuses, benefits and other perks. All the motive Jeanette needed, I figured, to kill Richard, if he was after her job.

"Thirty minutes from the store to here," Jack said, as he circled the block. "It fits."

Plenty of time for Jeanette to kill Richard, then get back home in time to receive my call, giving her the bad news.

My belly ached a little. I thought this would make me happy, but it didn't.

Jack made another circuit around the block and I looked at Jeanette's house again. Several cars were parked at the curb. Lights were on downstairs. I wondered if her kids and grandkids were there for Thanksgiving dinner. I wondered what they'd do next year, if Jeanette was in prison.

"Motive, means, and opportunity," Jack said, driving out of the subdivision.

"But no evidence," I said.

The police could find the evidence. I could call Detective Shuman, tell him what I'd learned and let him take it from there. But without something concrete, something more than suspicion, I was no better than Detective Madison when he'd decided I was a suspect. I couldn't do that to Jeanette. I couldn't do that to anybody—well, okay, maybe Rita—until I had something more.

But how would I get it?

"Think she could have done it?" Jack asked. "Physically, I mean."

I thought about it for a minute. Jeanette was in her fifties, shaped like a cylinder, and probably not very strong. But it wouldn't take much strength to swing one of those U-boat bars.

"Yeah, I think she could," I said.

"What about—"

Jack fished his vibrating cell phone from his pocket and flipped it open. He listened for a while, then closed it and glanced at me.

"I've got some business to take care of," he said.

Jack's eyes burned with a new kind of passion. Intense. Like something was going down.

"Cool," I said. "What's up? A case you're on?"

Jack flipped a U and headed back toward the 5 freeway. "Grab that briefcase out of the back, will you?"

I pulled it onto my lap and snapped it open. The smell of rich leather floated up. Inside was—wow, cool!—a handgun, a camera, and some file folders.

"Hasselhoff," he said.

"David Hasselhoff? The actor?" Hey, this was getting cooler by the minute.

Jack shook his head. "Aaron Hasselhoff. Claims to be the actor's brother. Uses the name to work his way into the lives of lonely, rich women. Then takes them for what he can, and moves on."

"What a dick," I said.

"Most of the women are too embarrassed to come forward, but he ran into some rich old broad in Laguna

Beach who wouldn't play his game. Now he's claiming he fell at her house. Ruined his back. Can't work anymore. Suing her for millions."

"And Pike Warner is handling her case?"

Jack hesitated a minute. "I do a little freelance work, on the side. Court date's Monday."

I figured Jack had just been handed this case and was expected to pull off a miracle, or he'd worked it for a while with no results. Either way, time was critical and his reputation—along with that rich old woman's millions— were on the line.

"So, what's the deal?" I asked, pulling the Hasselhoff folder out of the briefcase.

"Just got a call from a contact that he's at a bar down on Sunset."

Jack's got *contacts*. Wow, this is so cool.

"The address is in the folder," he said. "Find it for me, will you?"

"You're trying to get a picture of him dancing on a table, or something that proves he's not injured?" I asked.

This is way better than Thanksgiving dinner at Mom's.

"The guy's a pro. Figures somebody is after him. He's careful. I haven't been able to find where he lives, or who he's shacking up with. Nothing."

We were on the 5 now, going south toward L.A. Not a lot of cars were on the freeway tonight; most people were still at home, I figured, too stuffed with turkey to go anywhere.

I opened the Hasselhoff folder. There was a typed report, then handwritten notes that Jack, I suppose, had made. I found the address of the bar on Sunset and read it off.

Then I checked out the guy's photo. It looked like a posed shot of friends gathered, only everyone else had been cropped out. Hasselhoff was smiling at the camera in full color. Late thirties, I figured, with brown hair and a cheesy mustache. He looked like an '80s porn star.

Except—

"Stop. Turn around," I said. "You're wasting your time."

Jack cut his gaze to me.

"I know this guy."

My cell phone rang, waking me from a deep sleep. I opened one eye. Still dark. Jeez, what time was it?

I squinted at the phone. Four thirty-two. In the morning? Who the hell was calling me at this hour?

The phone kept ringing.

I pushed my hair back over my shoulder and flipped open the phone. I meant to say "hello" but nothing came out.

Not that it mattered.

"Haley! Where are you, girlfriend!"

I winced and eased the phone away from my ear a bit. "Bella?"

"Get your skinny white ass down here! Now!"

Okay, obviously I'd missed something.

"What—what's going on?" I managed to ask.

"You're supposed to be at work!" Bella shouted.

Then everything came rushing back. It was the Friday after Thanksgiving. The biggest shopping day of the year. Holt's would open in twenty-five minutes and I was supposed to already be there.

Except that I quit. Yesterday. I'd tendered my resignation, so to speak, by screaming at Ty Cameron in the parking lot. I guess word hadn't gotten around the store yet.

I hoped Rita didn't hurt anyone when she got the news and did cartwheels through the aisles.

"You got to get down here, girl!" Bella yelled. "Now!"

"Look, Bella," I said. "Something happened. I'm not—"

"I don't care who you're in bed with, girl!"

I looked around at my empty bed. Just me. No Jack. He'd walked me to my door last night, then gone on his way.

"It's not that," I said. I liked Bella, and I wished I didn't have to tell her like this. "It's just that—"

"Listen up," Bella told me. "I got four words for you: Lou Eee Va Ton. It's here! In Holt's!"

Lou Eee Va Ton? What was she talking about? What was Lou—

I bolted straight up in the bed.

"Louis Vuitton?" I asked, my heart suddenly racing. *"Louis Vuitton? At Holt's?"*

"Right here in the store. It's the surprise Christmas merchandise. Every kind of fancy handbag you can think of."

"Are they—" I couldn't say the words. I was so afraid the answer would be "no" that I could barely bring myself to speak.

I forced myself. "And they're *real?*"

"Hell yeah, they're real. None of that fake shit. This is the good stuff," Bella told me. "You've got to get down here! Craig is handing them out to the employees like candy—at cost!"

"Cost?"

I sprang out of bed, caught my ankle in the covers, and hopped on one foot to the closet, dragging the quilt with me.

"Hurry!" Bella told me. "Management is getting as many as they want, but us peons can only get two. You'd better get down here before they're all gone!"

"I'll be right there!" I shouted into the phone, then tossed it over my shoulder.

Oh my God. Designer handbags? And Craig was letting employees buy them at cost?

That Craig, he's a great guy. I always liked him.

I pulled khaki pants off the hanger. I had to get there.

I glanced at my clock. Twenty-five minutes until the store opens. Twenty-five minutes until those hordes of crazed, after-Thanksgiving shoppers descend on the accessories department, and the designer bags disappear like a grain field beneath a swarm of locusts.

I yanked a black T-shirt out of the closet.

This is too good to be true. Too good!

But I don't have a second to spare. Forget taking a shower—I'll double up on the cologne. I can dress in four minutes (my personal best is two minutes, but that was back in high school when Bobby Holland's mom came home early). Twist my hair into a bun on the way to the car. Put on makeup as I back out of my garage. Drive to the store in seven minutes, six if I run the light at the corner.

Plenty of time.

I'll get to the store ahead of the shoppers and before the other employees—

Wait. I'm not an employee.

Oh my God. I'm not an employee. I quit. *Yesterday.*

I slapped my hand against my forehead. *"Noooo!"*

Shoppers were three and four deep in a line that stretched the width of the store, then disappeared around the corner. The parking lot was jammed. It was still dark. Security lights were on. I whipped into a spot and sprinted to the front door.

The crowd undulated as everyone turned to look at me. They checked their watches. Only a few minutes until the store opened. Some of them glared at me thinking, I'm sure, that I intended to cut in front of the line.

I waved my lanyard with my Holt's name badge—thank God I hadn't thrown it in Ty's face yesterday—and rushed to the door.

Rita stood inside, holding the key. She crossed her arms and looked at me, then pointedly gazed at her wristwatch.

I hate that bitch.

Taking her sweet time, and just before I was ready to rip

the door off the hinges, she turned the key and opened the door. I dashed inside.

"You're late."

"No, I think everybody else was early," I shot back.

"You didn't punch out yesterday," Rita told me. "You can't punch in this morning until you get your time card cleared from yesterday. That means you have to—"

"I know what it means," I snapped and took off.

Okay, I didn't really know what it meant. Something about having a supervisor sign off on the time card. But I didn't care about that.

I jogged past the checkout registers. They were fully manned, cashiers at the ready. Bella hooted as I ran past.

I skidded to a stop at the accessories department, frozen in humble reverence in front of the newly installed display cases, stuffed to the hilt with gorgeous, designer handbags.

Coach. Dior. Chanel. Ferragamo. Betsey Johnson. Marc Jacobs, and more. And there, in their own private case, were the Louis Vuitton bags.

I walked forward slowly and laid my palms on the glass.

I thought I would cry.

"Aren't you supposed to be in Customer Service?" Craig barked.

I turned and saw him watching me. For a moment, I was too overcome to speak.

"Bags," I finally managed to whisper. "Can I have the bags?"

Craig looked annoyed. "How many do you want?"

"All of them."

"Employees get two." He huffed and glanced at his wristwatch. "We're opening in three minutes. Come back on your break."

"No!" If he'd been closer, I might have grabbed for his throat. I calmed myself. "I mean, no, I'm afraid they'll all be taken by then."

He waved me away like an annoying fly. "Stockroom's full of them. Come back later."

Craig walked away.

The stockroom? Of course. I could spend hours selecting bags at my leisure in the stockroom. No need to rush now.

Since I had tons of time, I headed for the back of the store. Grace was in the customer service booth.

"I'm so glad you're here," she said, and sounded as if she really meant it.

"Sorry I'm late," I told her, though I didn't really mean it.

"Don't worry about it. We don't do sales so we won't get busy for a couple of hours," Grace said.

Perfect. I could slip away and into the stockroom.

No one seemed to know that I'd quit yesterday. Lucky break for me. Not that I really wanted to work here. But, I figured, if I could stay here long enough to get the handbags I wanted, then it would be worth it. And I wasn't worried about Craig's decree of two purses only for employees. No way would Bella, Sandy, Colleen, or most of my other friends buy more than one bag. I'd simply give them cash and ask them to buy one for me. Dozens—for me!

My stomach fluttered a little as I realized I could buy *everyone* I knew a gorgeous designer bag for Christmas. Wouldn't that be great?

Of course, I didn't really have the money for that right now. And, while I've made a few bad moves financially, I'm not crazy enough to spend the last of my savings—my rent money—on handbags.

But my new Golden State Bank and Trust credit card should arrive any day now. I could hold out here at Holt's until then.

I put my purse in my locker and grabbed my time card

from the slot beside the time clock so I could get it cleared from yesterday and punch in this morning.

Might as well get paid during my stockroom shopping extravaganza.

I stopped at the customer service booth and Grace told me to have my time card initialed by a supervisor, so I headed down the hallway toward the offices. Just then, all hell broke loose behind me, as waves of customers surged through the aisles.

Yikes!

The door to Jeanette's office was partially open, so I knocked quickly and stuck my head inside. She sat behind her desk wearing a suit the color of eggplant (which, with her shape, made her look sort of like an actual eggplant), shuffling papers. She looked up as I walked in.

"Would you initial my time card so I can punch in?" I asked, holding it out.

"What for?"

Ty's voice came from the corner of the room. And it wasn't his Barry White voice. More like Darth Vader.

He scowled at me and said, "You don't work here anymore."

Chapter 18

No. No, this could not be happening. Not now. Not when something good had finally happened in my crappy life.

I was not leaving Holt's. I was keeping this job—and my employee discount.

So what could I do but turn to Ty quite calmly and say, "What are you talking about?"

He raised an eyebrow. "Yesterday. You resigned your position here."

I managed to look mildly puzzled. "You must have me mixed up with someone else."

Ty took a step closer, his gaze boring into me. "I remember distinctly—very distinctly. You quit."

I know he was remembering what happened in the parking lot. I could see a weird kind of fire in his eyes. I was remembering it too, and for some reason, it sort of fired me up too.

But I couldn't afford to lash out now. I shook my head and offered a tiny apologetic smile.

"No, that wasn't me," I said.

From the corner of my eye I saw Jeanette, still seated at her desk, bouncing her gaze between the two of us.

"It was you," Ty said, more forcefully now, as he came even closer.

I couldn't tell if he was mad, or upset, or hurt, or what. He probably deserved to be all of those things, after the way I'd screamed at him in the parking lot.

But that was his problem. I had my own to deal with.

I held my time card out to Jeanette. "Would you sign this so I can get to work?"

Jeanette stole a quick glance at Ty, uncertain of what to do. She was the store manager, but he was the owner. Finally, she reached for my time card, but Ty plucked it out of the air between us with such a look of smug satisfaction that I wanted to slug him. Or kiss him. Maybe both.

We were locked in some sort of primal stare-down. Two warriors battling for dominance. Ty's chest had puffed out and his shoulders were squared, his jaw had gone rigid.

God, that's such a hot look on men.

Ty held on to my time card—the path to the one good thing that had happened to me lately. But if he thought I was going to beg for it, he was sadly mistaken. There's only so far I'll go, even for designer handbags at cost.

Still, I'd said awful things to him yesterday in the parking lot. Some of them, he actually deserved. Most, he didn't.

"Oh, now I remember. I did leave a little early yesterday," I said, as if the recollection had just come to me. I looked at Jeanette. "I left to celebrate my promotion. I'm head of QA now, specializing in Laura Ashley bed-in-a-bag sets."

Jeanette's eyes widened. She knew, of course, that no such position existed at Holt's, but she didn't dare say anything.

"If you'll excuse me." Jeanette popped out of her chair and scuttled out the door.

I turned to Ty. His gaze still pierced mine but his lips were pressed together, and I could see he was trying hard not to smile.

I'm cute that way.

"So you do want to keep working here?" he asked.

I suppose I could have lied, plastered on a big of-course-you-can smile, and gone on and on about how much I wanted to be part of the Holt's "family," but I couldn't do it. And, after the things I'd said in the parking lot yesterday, Ty wouldn't have believed me anyway.

"Look," I said, "my life is kind of complicated right now. Believe it or not, this job is the best thing I've got going, which is really sad, but there it is."

He just stared at me for another few seconds, then pulled an ink pen from the inside pocket of his jacket. He didn't take his eyes off me as he clicked it, and held up my time card, poised to scrawl his initials in the margin.

Maybe he was expecting me to say something else. I didn't know. But I was done.

I guess he saw that in my face because he initialed my time card and handed it back to me. I took it, but he didn't let go. We held it between us for a few seconds, connected in a weird way, and the heat seemed to leave the room. I headed for the door.

"My grandmother liked you," Ty said.

I looked back. Something entirely different was in his expression now. I wasn't sure what it was. I'd like to think he'd said it just to keep me from leaving, but that didn't seem realistic.

Still, if he could attempt to be civil, I could too. Really, how could I walk away without a word after he'd mentioned his grandmother?

"Sorry about what I said in front of her," I said. I'd apologized to Ada yesterday, but figured Ty deserved the same.

"She said you had spirit."

"Even after I said 'screw you'?"

Ty grinned. "That's what she liked best about you."

Okay, well, at least I hadn't insulted her.

Ty shifted, as if he were about to say something important, but the door flew open and Rita planted herself in the doorway, hands on her hips.

"What are you doing back here?" she demanded. "You're supposed to be in the customer service booth. Grace is by herself. You need to get over there."

"Get out of the way and I'll go," I told her.

Rita glared at me, then stepped back. I left the office.

From a hot, private moment with the store owner, to being reprimanded by the biggest bitch in the place.

My life sucks.

Just as Rita claimed when she'd rousted me out of Jeanette's office, Grace was by herself in the customer service booth. But what Rita didn't mention was that there were no customers there either.

"We'll be busy in a few hours," Grace said, as she straightened the counter. "Customers will think they got the wrong price, or didn't get their discount, or something, and they'll come here for us to do price adjustments."

We could see the line of customers now. It snaked from the registers up front, down the aisle, and halfway across the back of the store. Mostly women shoppers, only a few men. I spotted some mother-daughter teams, struggling to hold all their purchases, inching ahead slowly in the line, smiling and laughing, making plans for where they'd shop next, where they'd go for lunch. It seemed like fun.

"You want to look up those stock numbers?" Grace asked, nodding toward the mound of merchandise on the back counter.

I didn't see any reason to knock myself out working. All the action was on the sales floor and at the registers. Nobody was paying attention to us.

Then Grace bobbed her brows upward to the security cameras overhead, hidden behind smoky panels in the ceiling. The customer service booth had several, one for each of the three cash drawers we had, plus others that covered the entrance to the cash office. The store hadn't hired a new loss prevention team yet, that I knew of, so management was taking turns in the security room monitoring everything.

I forgot, sometimes, that the cameras were all over the store, recording everything that went on, and since I didn't want any trouble from store supervisors—at least, not until I got my purses at cost—I figured I'd better stay busy.

I grabbed a blouse from the top of the clothes heap, but before I looked up its stock number I decided to check out the info on the handbags that had been downloaded overnight.

Wow. My heart fluttered slightly as I scrolled through dozens of handbags, all the latest styles from the most desirable designers. I couldn't wait to get into the stockroom and see them all in person. Touch them. Run my fingers over the leather. Feel the fabric. I could try them on, one at a time, or a dozen at once. Maybe I would put them all in a big pile and lie in them—

No, wait. That's how I'd gotten into trouble with the Laura Ashley bed-in-a-bag sets.

"I need you up front," Rita announced, her voice blaring in my ear.

I froze. No. I couldn't cashier. Not today. Not with this frantic crowd of holiday shoppers. Besides, if I was working at a register, how was I going to slip away into the stockroom to look at the purses?

"I'm really busy here," I told her. "Swamped."

"Move it," Rita said, then walked away, expecting me to follow.

I hesitated, but since I didn't want to get fired at this very moment, I went with her.

The front of the store was controlled chaos. Instead of a line for each register, one lane had been roped off, and Evelyn stood at the head of it directing customers to the next available cashier. Things were moving pretty smoothly, considering.

"Take over for Evelyn," Rita told me.

Okay, this might be kind of cool.

"Do I get a whistle?" I asked Rita.

"No."

"A bullhorn?"

She rolled her eyes. "Just get to work."

Evelyn, in a dither, twisted her fingers together and bobbed up and down on her toes, trying to see which cashier was ready for another customer. She seemed relieved to see me.

"You have to keep the line moving," Evelyn said in a low voice.

"Got it."

She passed me her clipboard. "And see if they'll complete one of these surveys."

I had no intention of doing that.

"No problem," I said.

"Be sure to ask everyone if they'd like to open a charge account," Evelyn said.

No way in hell was I doing that either.

"I'll handle everything," I told her, and she left.

I felt like a traffic cop, or something, motioning customers forward, putting up my hand to stop them, directing them to an available register. I had to hand it to the cashiers, they were hustling pretty good. Baggers would have helped, of course. More carts would have been nice too. Some people were having a hard time holding on to everything they'd selected.

From what I saw, customers were buying just about everything in the store. Clothes, shoes, toys, housewares. Lots of people had selected the red and white holiday table linens I'd stocked yesterday. It was kind of cool, seeing them go through the line.

Then it occurred to me that the one thing I wasn't seeing

much of was the designer handbags. What was wrong with these people? True, they couldn't get them at cost like employees could, but Holt's was offering them at a great discount. I'd seen a copy of the sale ad earlier in the customer service booth, and the bags were featured on the front page. Why weren't they selling?

Then it came to me. I should work in handbags. Oh my God, what a fabulous idea. I was perfect for that position. I had to find Craig.

When Rita finally walked by a few minutes later, I flagged her down.

"I need a break," I told her.

"It's not time for your break."

"It's an emergency," I insisted, which was ridiculous since I was an adult and shouldn't have to beg for a bathroom break.

She huffed. "Oh, all right. But hurry."

Yeah, I'll do that.

I headed for the back of the store, then cut across to the accessories department. Three customers were there. Evelyn was behind the counter, showing a Chanel tote. No sign of Craig.

The biggest shopping day of the year, a department full of hot, expensive purses, and Craig wasn't there? Jeez, what was up with that?

I hurried to the offices in the back of the store, but didn't find him there. That left the stockroom. The entire store was stocked to the brim, so I couldn't imagine he'd have a reason to be there, but I spotted him moving the luggage around.

"Hey, Craig," I called.

He jumped and whipped around. I'd startled him, or maybe he was still sort of punchy about being in the stockroom.

"What are you doing back here?" he demanded.

"Looking for you," I said.

Okay, we'd gotten off to a bad start, but I was pumped, ready to impress him with my almost infinite knowledge of designer handbags.

Now he looked suspicious, or maybe worried. "What's wrong?"

"Nothing," I said quickly. "Listen, Craig, I want to work in Accessories selling the new line of purses. I know absolutely everything there is to know about those handbags."

He frowned. "Yeah?"

"First of all, Louis Vuitton. Oh my God, they're the best," I said. "The company started out in the nineteenth century making traveling trunks. So did Prada and Gucci. Fendi sold leather goods and furs. Then gradually, over the decades, lots of handbags came along. Chanel is fantastic. Dior, Ferragamo, Hermes. Judith Leiber makes the glitziest evening bags on the planet. And—"

"Hold on," Craig said, waving his arms for me to slow down. "How do you know about these purses?"

"I own dozens," I declared. "They're my passion. My life's blood. The very fiber of my being."

Okay, I knew I was laying it on really thick, but I wanted to work in his department.

He studied me for a minute, then asked, "You own real ones? Not fakes or counterfeits? Not knockoffs?"

"No, of course not," I told him. I waved my hand around the stockroom. "Bring out a handbag. Any handbag. Just hold it up and I can tell you who made it, the style, the color of the lining, how many interior pockets and zippers. Believe me, Craig, you won't find anybody in this store— or most anywhere else—who knows designer handbags the way I do."

Craig didn't say anything, just stood there beside the luggage staring at me as if he couldn't believe what he just heard. I guess I impressed him pretty good.

"I'll take a look at the schedule," he said.

Yes!

"Thanks, Craig," I said, and headed out of the stock-room.

"Haley?" he called. "Go ahead and pick out all the handbags you want. I'll give them all to you at cost. But get them today, before they get picked over."

I guess Craig hadn't noticed that the handbags weren't exactly jumping off the shelves, but that was okay. All the best purses would be available for me.

"Cool," I said.

"But keep this between you and me," he said. "I don't want to have to do this for everybody."

"Thanks."

I left the stockroom.

That Craig. What a great guy.

Under normal circumstances, getting off work at 1:00 p.m. would seem early. But not if you've been on the job since 5:00 a.m.

The Holt's parking lot was full as I left the store. It was still packed inside too. The crowds hadn't let up since we'd opened. The only difference was that now most everyone was tired and cranky.

But not me. I was happy, thrilled beyond belief as I was struggling toward my car with three huge shopping bags, full of purses. Designer purses. Gorgeous, designer purses. Purchased at cost—cost!

Yeah, yeah, I know I said I'd wait until I got that Golden State Bank and Trust credit card, but I couldn't hold out. Not after Craig had made me that great offer. All the purses I wanted—only management got that opportunity. I couldn't let it slip past. What if somebody found out he'd offered me that deal and put a stop to it? What if he changed his mind?

I couldn't chance it. So I'd done what any crazed, obsessive, handbag whore would have done: whipped out my debit card and spent my rent money.

"Hey, trouble," a man said.

Jack Bishop walked toward me. Oh my God, he looked awesome. Jeans, a snug crew-neck sweater, and a sport coat. Great shades of blue and gray.

And I looked like crap. I suddenly remembered that I'd left home in a hurry this morning. No shower. Little makeup. Yikes.

Jack took the bags from my hands and walked along with me to my car. I popped the trunk and he put them inside.

Then he turned to me, a dark—smoldering?—look in his eyes.

"You owe me," he said. "Last night. Remember?"

Of course I remembered. The contact info he'd gotten for me for Jeanette Avery, Ty, and Sarah Covington. Jack had said he'd tell me what sort of payment he wanted. And when.

"I'm ready to collect," Jack said. "Now."

CHAPTER 19

I haven't done this in a long time—a really long time. And it shows. I'm out of breath. My heart is racing. My thighs are killing me.

I stole a peek at Jack—he'd told me not to look at him—and he's reared back enjoying himself. And why shouldn't he? I'm the one doing all the work.

Sweat runs into my eyes. I swipe it away. I want to quit, but I can't. Not yet. Not at this crucial moment. With a quick burst of energy, I give it all I've got, then—whew!—we're done.

With a round of polite applause from the sideline, I jogged over to the net and extended my hand. The dirtbag, known here at the Foothills Tennis Club as Aaron Carson and elsewhere as Aaron Hasselhoff, shook and threw me a smug smile.

"Good game," he said. "Just work on that backhand."

"Yeah, I will," I said, panting like a dog. "Thanks . . . for the . . . last-minute lesson."

"No problem." Aaron gave me a quick once-over. "Any time."

I wished I could come up with a witty slam, but I was partially brain-dead from lack of oxygen. The bastard deserved it. Pretending to be David Hasselhoff's brother.

Cheating lonely old women out of their money. Faking a fall, then suing.

Aaron gave me a salute with his racket and jogged off the court. I dragged myself to the umbrella tables nearby and opened my bag, struggling not to look at Jack, cool and relaxed, sitting at the next table with a frosty mug of beer in front of him.

"Nice form," he said, gazing in the other direction.

"I've played for . . . years," I said, forcing myself not to knead the stitch in my side. "Get what . . . you needed?"

"Perfect." Jack opened his palm and I saw the tiny camera. "Picture perfect."

When Jack and I were out scouting Jeanette Avery's house and I'd seen the photo of the con man Aaron Hasselhoff, I'd recognized him at once. He'd changed his appearance after disappearing from the scene in the San Diego area. Mustache shaved, hair shorter and dyed blond. New name too. He must have felt pretty secure working as the tennis pro here at the club. It was very old—my mom's family helped found it—and very exclusive—I was only a member because I was born into the family.

That night, Jack and I had come up with this plan, but I hadn't expected him to show up at Holt's this afternoon. I'd signed Jack in as my guest, scheduled a tennis lesson, and run my ass off while he snapped all the pics he needed for his client's lawsuit.

I pulled a towel from my bag and wiped my brow.

"So," I said, "I've paid my debt to you. Now you owe me."

Jack sipped his beer, then turned to me. His gaze felt like a laser blast going through me.

"Are you ready to collect?" he asked, his voice as rich as the belt of whiskey I could have used at the moment.

I started to heat up all over again, but managed a casual shrug.

"I'll tell you what I want," I said. "And when I want it."

Jack nodded slowly, then finished his beer and rose from the chair. He stopped in front of me and slipped a folded piece of paper into my tennis shirt between my breasts.

"You owe me," he said, and walked away.

Oh my God, he's so hot.

My knees gave out and I collapsed into a chair as Jack disappeared around the corner. With what little strength I had, I pulled the paper out of my top.

Phone numbers and addresses. What the . . . ?

Then my heart jumped. Ty's address. And Sarah's. Jack had gotten them for me.

Now my brain blasted into fast-forward. For a few seconds I wasn't sure I wanted to look at them. What if Ty's and Sarah's address were the same?

Since my suspense factor was really low, I unfolded the paper.

Sarah Covington, vice president of marketing for Holt's Department Store, resided in Glendale. I didn't recognize the name of her street. Ty lived in Pasadena, in an apartment on Colorado Boulevard. I knew the place. I remember when the building opened. It was a really cool complex where a two-bedroom unit ran about four grand per month.

Wow, what a relief. Sarah lived in Glendale, and Ty in Pasadena. I was almost giddy.

My mind raced on. That's why I'd seen them in Pasadena the night Marcie and I were shopping and having dinner at the Cheesecake Factory. Ty lived there. He and Sarah weren't on a date, weren't boyfriend/girlfriend, they weren't window-shopping, or having sex. They were simply—

What?

Well, I didn't know exactly what it meant, except that they weren't seriously involved enough to live together.

It was too much to think about in my weakened condition. I grabbed my bag and went home.

*   *   *

My cell phone rang as I pulled out of my apartment complex. It was nearly 10:00 a.m. and already the street was crowded with cars headed toward the shopping areas near my home. Saturday. It would be like this right up until Christmas Eve. And I'd be in the thick of it, as long as I worked at Holt's anyway.

I dug around in my purse for my phone as I raced through a yellow light, and finally came up with it. For an instant I thought it was my mom's number on the caller ID, but realized it was just my guilty conscience at work. I still had to bring her the Edible Elegance paperwork from the fund-raiser, but I'd been putting it off.

I answered the phone. It was Marcie.

"Your problem is solved," she announced, as I cut in front of an SUV. I almost asked her "which problem," since they seemed to have piled up on me lately, but I didn't. If any one of them were solved, it would be great.

"We're having a purse party," Marcie said. "You and me. At my office building. I'll reserve the big conference room, send out e-mail invitations, and post a flyer in every break room. It'll be great."

A million questions zinged through my mind, but Marcie didn't give me a chance to ask them.

"I don't know why I didn't think of this sooner," she said. "We can get purses for pennies on the dollar, sell them for half their retail value, and make a fortune."

"You mean fake bags?" I asked, panic jolting me. "Counterfeits?"

"Replica bags," Marcie corrected.

"Isn't that illegal?"

"Not if we're up front about saying they're knockoffs. All we have to do is explain that a purse is, for example, made in the same style as a Dior clutch, or whatever. That's all," Marcie said.

I flashed on beating Richard's murder rap, only to be imprisoned for dealing in counterfeit merchandise.

"You're sure?" I asked.

"Well, yeah. Pretty sure," Marcie said. "Don't worry. People do it all the time. I know where we can buy the purses. Zillions of them. In stores, shops, out on the street. It's no big deal. We don't need a wholesale license, or anything. Just cash. What do you think?"

I thought it seemed too good to be true.

"And you think the women at your office building will buy fake bags?" I asked. The concept went against my grain, big time.

"Are you kidding?" Marcie said. "I just mentioned a purse party in the break room yesterday, and a dozen women nearly stampeded over me wanting first chance at the bags. I'm telling you, Haley, this will work."

Most things that sound too good to be true usually are. But Marcie sure sounded as if she knew what she was talking about.

"All we have to do is buy the purses," Marcie said. "We'll go fifty-fifty on everything. What do you say?"

I didn't know the first thing about hosting a purse party, where to buy them, how much they'd cost, how much profit could be made, or whether I could get arrested for being involved. I would be totally in the dark with this.

"Sounds great," I said, as I whipped into the Holt's parking lot.

"I figure we'll need about four hundred dollars each," Marcie said. "We'll triple—maybe even quadruple—our investment. You'll see."

We agreed on a day for the purse shopping trip, and hung up. I put my phone away and sat in my car for a minute, looking up at the blue Holt's sign.

Four hundred dollars? Wow. Where was I going to get that kind of money? I'd spent my savings—my rent money—

on the gorgeous handbags I'd bought yesterday—courtesy of my good friend Craig—so things were a little tight. More than a little tight, really. But not so bad that I wouldn't take a chance on quadrupling my money selling knockoff handbags.

I heaved a heavy sigh, still looking at the Holt's sign. Besides, I had my job here, plus my GSB&T credit card that would arrive any day, and I'd be called back to work at Pike Warner at any minute now.

My spirits lifted. I felt sort of like an entrepreneur, wheeling and dealing in a high-stakes business venture. Yeah, this was great, I decided as I got out of my car. I'd score a ton of cash in this purse deal. And who's to say that one party would be all we'd have? Marcie and I could have these parties everywhere. We'd be rich.

I got to the break room just as the early-morning shift was clocking out. The store was opening at 6:00 a.m. this weekend, way too early for me. I punched in and headed for the customer service booth, but Jeanette stopped me before I went inside.

"Could I see you for a moment?" she asked quietly.

"Sure," I said, glad to avoid the long line awaiting me, and followed her down the hall. Inside her office, Jeanette closed the door and took a seat behind her desk.

"Please, sit down," she said, gesturing.

This all seemed eerily familiar. Unpleasantly familiar. Jeanette, in her fuchsia and gold plaid suit, somehow morphed into Mrs. Drexler. Oh my God, was I going to get fired?

No, no, I realized, as I sat down. This had to be something good. And I knew just what it was. I'd talked to Craig about working in the accessories department selling the designer handbags. Obviously, he'd been so impressed with my extensive knowledge he'd gone to Jeanette right away, told her what a rare find I was and how I would be an immense asset to his department, and asked—no, begged, probably—that I be reassigned.

And I was getting a raise.

My heart thumped a few quick times.

Yes, I was getting a raise. That had to be it. With my new, more important position in the accessories department, I deserved a substantial raise. Maybe I'd ask for a promotion too. And a percentage of the department's profits. Wow, that would be so cool. If I got that, I'd sell the hell out of those bags. Maybe I'd even perfect my of-course-you-can smile. I'd earn so much money I could—

"Haley," Jeanette said. "Something's come up."

"Yes?" I said, trying to hold in my smile so as not to spoil her surprise.

"There have been some complaints," she said. "About you."

The smile froze on my face. I stopped breathing.

Jeanette didn't seem to notice.

"A number of complaints, actually. From customers. And from members of our management team."

This could not be happening.

Jeanette reached into her desk drawer and pulled out a personnel file. *My* personnel file.

No. Not again. Not here at *Holt's.*

She opened my file. "I've written up an employee action form that I'll go over with you. Then you'll sign it, acknowledging that—"

"I'm not acknowledging a goddamn thing!" I sprang to my feet.

Jeanette rocked back in her chair.

"Who complained about me?" I demanded.

"Haley, let's try to remain calm—"

"Who was it!" I screamed.

"Craig," Jeanette blurted out. Her face went white. "He—he said he'd seen you roaming the store, and—and he said that a number of customers had come to him, complaining that you weren't assisting them."

"Yeah, he saw me in the store, but I was on my break and he knew that," I shouted. "And these *supposed* complaints from customers? Why the hell would a customer go to Craig about me? Did any of them come to you? Or any other store manager?"

"Well . . ."

"Did they?" I shouted.

"No," Jeanette said quickly.

"Then it's all crap!" I told her. "You know what, Jeanette? You're just lucky I still work here. I found a dead body in your stockroom, for God's sake. I worked on Thanksgiving Day. I've covered nearly every department in this store, I've cashiered, I'm in customer service booth hell—and I even ran the vacuum cleaner one night! So don't come to me with some half-ass complaints about my work!"

I stormed out of the office and slammed the door behind me.

My heart pounded so hard I heard it in my ears. My hands shook. I couldn't believe I'd gone off like that to Jeanette.

Why hadn't I done that to Mrs. Drexler? Maybe I'd still have my job there.

But I'd really laid in to Jeanette—and she was the store manager.

I froze. Oh my God, I just told off the store manager. What the hell was I thinking?

I felt dizzy. I braced my arm against the wall to steady myself.

She was going to write me up—the prelude to firing me—for real this time. Firing me!

Then I had a terrifying thought. What if she knew I suspected her of Richard's murder? Had she somehow learned that I'd been in the Northridge store asking questions? Did she know I'd stolen the store directory, gotten her home address, gone to her house?

How could she have known that?

She couldn't have, I decided. No, it was impossible. Oh God, I hoped it was.

So did that mean that Craig had actually complained about me? Why would he do that? I'd gone out of my way to offer to work for him, help him sell those purses. I thought he liked me. He'd let me have as many of the handbags as I wanted.

This made no sense. Any of it. The only reliable fact in this mess was that I was about to get fired from Holt's. Sure, I'd blown right by Jeanette just now, but that didn't mean this was the end of it. She'd just document more derogatory info about me, pile on the complaints until the evidence was so compelling I couldn't fight it off.

I couldn't lose this job. It was my only income. I just spent my rent money, and I was on the hook with Marcie for four hundred bucks worth of fake purses. How was I going to live?

Wait.

I dashed down the hallway. At the customer service booth, Grace tried to wave me down.

"Somebody is looking for you," she called.

"In a minute," I said, and dashed into the break room. That girl who had lost so much weight was at the table eating fruit. *Fruit!* Somebody told me she'd lost another five pounds. God, I hate her!

I grabbed my purse from my locker, dug out my phone, called directory assistance for the number of the Golden State Bank and Trust, and tried to calm down. I couldn't talk to them if I was all hyped up like this. It's simply not the way things are done at GSB&T.

I took several deep breaths while my life flashed in front of my eyes and I wove my way through the telephone maze to the customer service department. I got a human on the line right away. Good sign. Especially on a Saturday.

"This is Haley Randolph calling," I said, using my I'm-better-than-you voice. "I'd like to find out when I can expect to receive my credit card."

"Certainly, Miss Randolph. One moment, please."

Some dreadful classical music played while I waited. My palm was so sweaty I thought I might drop the phone. I *had* to get that credit card soon. If it was ready, I'd tell them I would come down and pick it up. I *needed* that credit card. If I didn't get it immediately, I was sunk.

Oh God, why had I spent my rent money on those handbags?

"Miss Randolph?" This was someone different. An older man. He sounded like a supervisor.

Oh, crap. Did this mean they decided not to give me the credit card? No, no, it couldn't be!

"I'm Mr. Olsen, vice president," he said.

Why was I talking to a vice president? This couldn't be good.

"I have your file right here," he went on. "Thank you for so graciously accepting our credit card offer. We're so pleased to have someone of your caliber banking here with us."

What the hell is this old guy talking about?

"Yeah, sure. You're welcome," I said. "I just need to find out if I can expect the card by Monday. I'm—I'm leaving town—the country, really."

"Permanently?" Mr. Olsen asked, sounding a little concerned.

Oh no. Now he thinks I'm going to take his credit card and skip the country.

"No, no," I said, trying to sound light and airy. "Just . . . just going abroad . . . for the holidays. Same as last year."

Mr. Olsen chuckled. "Of course. Well, let me look at your paperwork. Yes, I see it right here. Everything is in order, and I'm pleased to say you can expect to receive our credit card by the second week of January."

January? *January?*

"But I need—that is, I was hoping to get it sooner," I said, trying not to sound desperate.

Mr. Olsen chuckled again, a don't-you-know-anything-about-business chuckle. "That's the best we can do."

"But your offer indicated I'd receive priority processing," I told him.

"This *is* our priority processing."

Oh God.

I hung up the phone.

This can't be happening. It can't. If I don't get—

The break room door opened and I braced myself to see Rita glaring at me, but it was Grace.

"This really hot-looking guy is looking for you," she said. "Says he's a friend of yours."

It wasn't like I had so many hot-looking guy friends that I didn't know who this might be. I followed Grace out of the break room and there stood Jack Bishop.

I smiled. I actually smiled. I was so glad to see a friendly face.

Only Jack didn't smile. He walked over and leaned in.

"Is there some place we can go to talk privately?" he asked.

Now what?

We stepped into the break room. That girl who'd lost all the weight was still there, still eating fruit, so we went to the back corner by the lockers.

"I got some information about the investigation at Pike Warner," Jack said.

"About my job?" I asked.

He nodded and my hopes soared. Oh my God, this is great. I'm getting my job back. And not a minute too soon. This is perfect. Absolutely perfect.

Except that Jack looked grim.

"What is it?" I asked, barely able to get the words out.

"There is no investigation."

I just looked at him.

"Pike Warner laid you off with no intentions of investigating anything," Jack said. "They figured you wouldn't cause a problem. You'd just go away quietly."

"But . . . ?"

I couldn't process what he was saying. It wouldn't penetrate my brain. "But Mrs. Drexler told me—"

"You're not getting your job back at Pike Warner, Haley." Jack shook his head. "You're done."

"I—I don't understand."

"I'm still checking. I'll have more info for you soon," Jack promised. He looked at me harder. "You okay?"

I was not going to fall apart in front of Jack Bishop.

"Oh yeah, sure," I said, and even managed to smile. "Just . . . just let me know what you find."

"Sure," he said, and left.

I stood there for a minute, all alone beside the lockers. Then one single tear seeped into my eye. Another followed.

I hurried out of the break room, down the hall, and into the stockroom. Thank God, no one was there. I went to the domestics section, pulled out a king-size Laura Ashley bed-in-a-bag set, and plopped down. I pressed my lips together to hold in my feelings, but it didn't work. I burst out crying.

Then the stockroom door opened and there stood Ty.

CHAPTER 20

I tried to gulp back my tears as I looked up at Ty. I was hiding in the stockroom, sitting on a king-size Laura Ashley bed-in-a-bag set when I was supposed to be working.

Oh my God, he was going to finish off what Jeanette had started. He was going to fire me.

Instead, Ty pulled another bed-in-a-bag set off the shelf, dropped it onto the floor, and sat down beside me.

I burst out crying again. I sobbed and wailed. Ty put his arm around me and pulled me against his shoulder. I cried harder.

When I finally wound down, Ty asked, "Bad day?"

And there I went again crying, only this time I tried to talk at the same time. All that came out was blub, blub, blah, waah, blub, blah. He couldn't possibly understand what I was saying. *I* couldn't understand what I was saying.

When I stopped crying for the second time, Ty didn't ask me anything, which was for the best. Instead, he pulled a handkerchief out of his pocket and gave it to me. I dabbed my eyes and my mascara came off. Jeez, I probably looked like crap. I'm not a pretty crier.

Another minute or so passed while I sniffed and tried to

wipe off my makeup, and we were quiet. Finally, Ty said, "Want to tell me to get screwed again?"

Horrified, I looked up at him—smeared mascara and all. "What?"

"It seemed to make you feel better the other day," he pointed out, with the tiniest hint of a grin.

I burst out laughing. I couldn't help myself. He chuckled too, a silly, high-pitched laugh you wouldn't expect from a guy his size, and that made me laugh harder.

His arm was still around me, which was okay with me, and he didn't seem to be in a hurry to move it. It was kind of nice, sitting there together like that. I'm pretty sure it's the only time Ty ever sat on a Laura Ashley bed-in-a-bag set inside the stockroom of one of his stores.

"Sarah's not my girlfriend," he said.

His comment came out of nowhere, and it rattled me a bit.

"That's who you meant, wasn't it?" he asked. "In the parking lot the other day?"

"I know she's not your girlfriend," I said.

He frowned a little. "How did you find out?"

Oh, crap. I shouldn't have said that. What was I supposed to say now? That I'd broken into Richard's office, stolen the store directory, and had a private investigator run their phone numbers?

That might spoil the mood.

"I figured it out. She's very professional. It's obvious from the Louis Vuitton organizer she carries," I told him. "Besides, it's none of my business anyway."

"Just so you know," Ty said. "Sarah and I aren't personally involved."

So why were they window-shopping in Pasadena? What was going on with them? I wanted to ask but didn't want him to get the idea that I was spying on him, which, of course, I was, but still.

"I'd better get back to work," I said.

We'd been cuddled together in the stockroom for a while now and lucky no one had walked in and found us, which would have been way cool, if it had been Rita. But, really, I didn't want to be at the center of store gossip.

We got to our feet and everything suddenly seemed sort of awkward.

"Did you mean what you said in the parking lot?" Ty asked. "About the Holt's stores being so bad?"

I'd thought we'd just had a personal moment, but now it seemed he wanted to use me as a focus group.

I was emotionally drained, too exhausted to lie or sugar-coat the truth.

"Yeah," I said. "I meant it."

Ty nodded and I could see that his mind had wandered off. I left.

I went to the restroom and washed my face. Jeez, I looked a wreck. My makeup was in my purse inside my locker, but I didn't have the strength to get it, or apply it. I'd just spend the rest of my shift in the customer service booth looking like hell; I doubted anyone would notice.

I needed to think about the news Jack had given me earlier about my job—or lack of a job—at Pike Warner, and figure out my next step. But it was just too much. I couldn't get my brain around it right now.

As I was drying my hands, Evelyn rushed in, wild-eyed and frantic.

"There you are," she declared, planting her palms against my chest.

Couldn't I get a minute's peace in this store? I wasn't even assigned to Evelyn's department and she was coming after me.

"Haley, are you all right?" she asked.

"Fine," I said, though I wasn't, of course.

She caught my arm and urged me into the corner beside the baby changing station. Customers came in and out. Toilets flushed. The water ran.

Evelyn glanced around and leaned closer. "You have to stay away from Craig."

Okay, so that was it. She'd heard that Craig had ratted me out to Jeanette. Guess I should be glad she'd tried to warn me, even if it was too late. Wish I'd had this kind of friend at Pike Warner.

"Don't worry about it," I told her. "I already—"

"No. Listen to me." Evelyn shook my arm. "Stay away from Craig. Don't talk to him. Don't go near him, or his department. Please, Haley, you have to stay away from Craig."

Now she had me concerned. Something else was going on here, something beyond her apparently learning that Craig had complained to Jeanette about me.

"You know something," I said. "What is it?"

"Nothing," she said quickly, and dropped my arm.

"Yes, you do," I said. "Tell me what's going on."

"It's—it's nothing, really," Evelyn said, twisting her fingers together. "I—I just wanted you to—to remember that Craig is under a lot of stress right now. His wife, she's not well, you know. Cancer. And it's the holiday season, our busiest time. Craig isn't in . . . well, he isn't in the best of moods right now."

"Because he's worried about the designer bags? Afraid they'll get shoplifted like the game systems last year?"

Evelyn winced and looked away. She would have made a horrible poker player.

"You know something, Evelyn," I said. "I can see it in your face. You have to tell me what it is."

More finger twisting. She pressed her lips together, stared at the ceiling, drew two big breaths, and just when I thought I might actually shake her, she looked me straight in the eye.

"The night of Richard's murder," she said softly.

Suddenly, she stopped, looked around, then leaned closer.

"That night, I heard Richard in his office arguing with someone," she whispered.

I gasped. "Who was it?"

She shook her head frantically. "I don't know. I was in the hallway. I only heard their voices."

"Was it a man, or a woman?"

"A man."

"And you didn't recognize the voice?"

Evelyn pressed her lips together, then gave a weak head shake. "I couldn't say for sure."

I wasn't sure she was telling the truth about knowing who Richard's argument had been with, but this information had obviously weighed heavily on her for a while now.

"Did you tell the detectives?" I asked.

"There was nothing to tell," she insisted. "I heard a voice. It sounded like an argument, but I don't know for sure. It could have been anyone, talking about anything. It probably had nothing at all to do with Richard's death."

Sounded to me as if Evelyn had spent a lot of time rationalizing her decision not to share this info with the homicide detectives. I wondered why.

She touched my arm again. "Just promise me you'll stay away from Craig. You don't want to upset him."

I didn't give a rat's ass if I upset Craig, especially after what he'd pulled with Jeanette. But it seemed the only way I could calm Evelyn.

"I'll keep my distance," I told her.

She looked relieved, then hurried out of the bathroom.

By noon each Sunday, the week's work schedule came out. A copy was posted in the break room beside the time clock and another was snapped into the binder at the customer service booth. I knew this because it was noon on Sunday and I'd talked to more employees about their work schedule than I had customers.

"This is bull," Sophia Garcia declared.

She stood outside the booth looking at the work schedule. Grace had a customer and I was sorting merchandise to return to the sales floor. Sophia wasn't happy.

"Bull," she said again. "Complete bull. Working me thirty-nine hours this week."

After learning that Richard had written Sophia up for abusing her employee discount and threatened to fire her, I'd put her on my list of murder suspects. She sure seemed mad enough to kill, at the moment.

"Thirty-nine hours," Sophia said, slapping her palm against the schedule. "Thirty-nine hours, not forty. They expect me to work that many hours, but won't make me full-time so I get benefits."

"That's bull, all right," I said.

"Damn right it is," she said. "I thought things would get better with Richard gone. But they're not. Same old bull."

Sophia stomped away.

Maybe I should ask Detective Shuman to check Sophia's alibi.

A few minutes later, Sandy came by to look at the schedule. I hadn't seen her in a while.

"How's it going with your tat guy?" I asked.

"Great," she said, copying her work schedule onto the back of a customer comment card. "Taking a sabbatical to San Francisco for a week."

"Cool," I said. "Want me to help you pick out some clothes to take?"

"Oh, I'm not going," she said. "It's an artist thing."

Far be it from me to knock art, but come on, the guy did tattoos.

"Yeah," I said. "But couldn't you go anyway?"

"I'm keeping his dog," Sandy said.

"Stand back!" Bella declared, barreling up to the counter beside Sandy. Today, she'd done her hair in a long braid and coiled it on top of her head. It looked like Half Dome.

"Give me that work schedule. My future awaits. I've got my hair show to go to on Thursday and I'm—what the hell?"

Bella's eyes were wide and her mouth hung open as she stared down at the binder. This wasn't good.

"Don't tell me . . ." I muttered, as I looked down. Sure enough, she was on the schedule for Thursday.

"What the hell? What the *hell*?" Bella jabbed her index finger into the schedule. "I'm supposed to have Thursday off. I asked two weeks ago—two weeks ago! I got it cleared, just like I was supposed to do. I'm supposed to be off on Thursday!"

"Everybody's got tons of hours," Grace said, joining us now that her customer was gone.

"I'm supposed to have Thursday off!"

"You should talk to Jeanette," Sandy said.

"It won't do any good," Grace said.

I knew she was right. Already this morning, most everyone had complained about their schedule. I'd had the misfortune of answering the phone when employees called in and I'd gotten an earful every time.

"I'm supposed to have Thursday off!"

"Maybe somebody can take your shift," Sandy suggested. She put up both hands. "But not me. I'm maxed out on hours this week."

"Me too," Grace said. "Everybody's working nearly forty hours this week, since we're short-staffed."

We couldn't work forty or more hours in any week because of some state law, or so Holt's claimed. I think they just didn't want to pay us overtime.

"I'm supposed to have Thursday off!"

"I'll work for you," I said.

Everybody looked at me. I still hadn't notified store management of the change in my availability. I was still working evenings and weekends. There didn't seem any reason to change it now since Jeanette probably planned to fire me; I figured she'd bring backup next time.

And I sure as hell wouldn't be called back to work at Pike Warner on Thursday.

My stomach twisted into a gooey knot at the thought, sort of like the kind you get when you're a day late. I'd lain awake last night, staring at the ceiling, trying to understand what was going on at Pike Warner, why I'd been treated this way. I'd gone over everything I'd done there—until around 3:00 a.m.—and still didn't have a clue why they'd let me go with that trumped-up story about irregularities with my work and an investigation, when they had no intentions of following up on anything. I'd called Kirk twice, but hadn't heard back. Maybe Jack would have some info for me soon.

"Really. I'll do it," I said to Bella. "I'll cover your shift on Thursday."

I didn't mind. Seeing the hair show would mean the world to Bella. She was the kind of friend who'd have done the same for me.

"You're supposed to come with me," Bella said.

"Yeah, but this way, at least you can go."

She stewed for a minute. "You sure?"

"Positive," I said.

"Cool," Bella declared. She pointed her finger at me. "When I graduate from beauty school, I'm going to do your hair for free."

She headed out to the sales floor again.

I sure hoped Jeanette didn't get around to firing me until after Thursday. For everyone's sake.

I went back to sorting merchandise, looking up stock numbers on the inventory computer, and answering the phone while Grace handled the customers at the counter. We took turns, swapping duties.

The phone rang. I answered it.

"Holt's customer service," I said. I was supposed to say this with an of-course-you-can smile. Yeah, right.

"It's Rita," she barked into the phone. "Check the schedule. Tell me what time I'm supposed to be there tomorrow."

I pulled the binder closer and flipped the page. Rita was scheduled to come in at two o'clock tomorrow afternoon.

"Six in the morning," I told her, and hung up.

I love working the customer service booth.

CHAPTER 21

"Look for Maple Street," Marcie said. "That's where we'll park."

We were on Olympic Boulevard in downtown L.A. heading toward the Fashion District. Marcie had called in sick and borrowed her mom's Honda Pilot so we could load up on knockoff handbags for the purse party we were hosting at her job later this week. Midmorning on a Monday and the traffic was light, considering.

Downtown had begun to revitalize in the past few years into an entertainment and cultural hot spot. New developments were going in. Historic buildings were being converted to high-rise housing units. As usual, Los Angeles's past struggled for a place amid its flashy present, and apartments for ten grand a month made for an uncertain future.

"There," Marcie said, pointing. "That's where we're going."

A big yellow and black banner announced Santee Alley. I caught a glimpse as we drove past the narrow passage between tall buildings, crowded with shoppers.

I'd never been here before but Marcie had, luckily. She turned onto Maple Street, then drove up a narrow ramp to a rooftop parking lot. Around us, the buildings told the history of downtown. Ornate ones from a time when craftsmanship mattered, some with broken windows, crumbling facades, others faring marginally better. Traffic noise rose from the street.

"Here's the plan," Marcie said as she gave the keys to the parking attendant and we headed for the stairs. "We'll get the best bags at the best prices. The vendors will cut their prices, sometimes, if we buy in quantity."

We took the stairs and emerged near the entrance of a men's clothing store in Santee Alley. This place was *the* spot to shop for bargain hunters, according to Marcie. It was only four blocks—tiny compared to the ninety or so blocks of the Fashion District—but the deals didn't get hotter anywhere than in the Alley.

Two- and three-story buildings backed up to Santee Alley, their rear doors open, inviting shoppers in. Booths, stalls, racks, makeshift tables spilled out into the Alley, crowded together, loaded with formal wear, sport clothes, Italian menswear, lingerie. Sunglasses, toys, portable stereos, pirated DVDs and CDs.

We made our way through the crowd past displays of shoes, iPod and cell phone cases, cigarette lighters. Spanish music blared from somewhere. The rich aroma of food wafted past.

"Okay, this is it," Marcie announced with a grand gesture.

My heart jumped.

Oh my God. Purses. Everywhere. Hanging on hooks, displayed on tables, piled up in boxes, dangling over doorways. Walls of purses. Kate Spade, Gucci, Prada, Burberry, Ferragamo, Louis Vuitton, Chanel. Coach—I loved their line last spring. I spotted a half dozen Marc Jacobs. And— oh my God—the latest Kenneth Cole. A huge display of Chloe and Mulberry. Satchels, clutches, hobos, buckets— every style imaginable. Great fabrics, leathers, colors.

"These are all knockoffs?" I asked Marcie, hoping

against all hope that she'd tell me they were the real things.

"Faux," Marcie corrected. She studied me for a moment. "Are you okay with this?"

Marcie knows my aversion to nondesigner handbags, but she didn't know how desperate I was for the money our purse party would generate. There are some things you can't tell even your best friend.

I'd gone by the bank this morning and taken a cash advance on my last credit card—running it to within thirty dollars of the limit—to buy the bags today. This was my chance to make some serious cash. I wasn't turning back now, even if I had an all-out allergic reaction to the fauxs, and broke out in hives.

"Let's hit it," I said.

I can be really strong when I need to.

We went from vendor to vendor, checking the quality of the bags. Some weren't so good. Crooked stitching, loose clasps and handles. No way were we buying those. I mean, we had a reputation to uphold with our purse parties.

A few of the merchants had second-rate knockoffs, though you might not think that was possible. Marcie had a good eye. She showed me what to look for—Louis Vuitton bags without the "LV," Dooney & Bourke bags printed with the initials "DP"—and, thanks to the many years I'd dedicated to serious shopping, I caught on right away. We spotted the less-desirable bags and moved on.

We stopped at a display of Gucci, Prada, and Ferragamo bags.

"How much?" I asked the woman standing beside a table of terrariums filled with live baby turtles. She was young, Hispanic, dressed in jeans and a T-shirt, and spoke with the customers in both Spanish and English.

"Twelve dollar," she said. "Ten for wallets."

My eyes widened. Twelve bucks? For a Gucci purse? I

couldn't believe these prices. The genuine bags go for three hundred, four hundred—some for over a thousand.

"How much for ten?" Marcie asked. Wow, she was a real pro at this.

The woman didn't hesitate. "Ten dollar. Eight for wallets."

Perfect. Just the sort of deal we needed.

We dug in. Marcie picked out purses while I found matching wallets. The Hispanic woman saw we were into volume buying so she went to a stockroom somewhere and brought out a few bags that weren't on display. They looked great. We bought them all. We paid in cash, received no receipt, and moved on.

I was into it now. Ready to wheel and deal.

We bought Burberry bags and cosmetic cases and I talked the guy down on those. Then we found a Kate Spade vendor and got a half dozen bags. Same with Prada and Chanel, and just about every other designer I could think of. The Louis Vuitton handbags were pricey, up to about seventy-five dollars each, but we got several. I mean, come on, they were Louis Vuitton. How could we possibly have a purse party without Louis Vuitton bags?

For a crazy second I looked for that organizer I was dying to have. But I couldn't do it. I just couldn't buy a faux for myself, no matter how much I wanted it.

Guess I'm really a designer handbag snob.

Near the end of the Alley a guy stood on the crate calling, "Five dollars, five dollars. Everything five dollars. Good price," in English and in Spanish. We checked it out. No designer bags but some really hip styles. We bought five, just to see how they sold at the purse party.

Two hours later we were exhausted, broke, and struggling to carry huge bags of purses back to Marcie's Pilot. Luckily, some of the vendors had stuck self-adhesive handles onto the black plastic bags, making them easier to manage.

On the drive home we decided on pricing and calculated the profit we'd make from the party. A nice chunk of change, if they all sold.

For a minute I thought about selling my own, genuine purses, the ones Craig had given me for cost. The horror of parting with them gave me brain-freeze for a few seconds. Then I realized that, even at cost, those bags would still be too expensive for the average person. Only someone devoted to designer purses would part with that kind of money. A store might buy them from me, though, but they would be interested in quantity, not the few I'd bought from Holt's. And besides, I'd need a connection to a store buyer, which I didn't have.

"If this purse party goes well, we can have them all the time. Our own business," Marcie said. "Do you think you'll want to do this after you go back to work at Pike Warner?"

I hadn't told her about my job. I hadn't told anybody, but I couldn't keep the truth from Marcie, my best friend, so I told her what Jack had learned. Marcie was livid, as a best friend should be.

"I called Kirk but I haven't heard from him yet," I said. I'd tried him on his cell phone; I couldn't bring myself to call him at the office. Not after what had happened with his secretary when I was there the other day.

"Forget Kirk," Marcie told me. She can be really forceful sometimes. "You need to go to the top on this. Start with Mrs. Drexler."

"I don't want to go in blind," I said. "I need more info. Jack's still checking into things."

Marcie didn't disagree so I guess she was satisfied with my plan.

She dropped me off at my apartment, and I had just enough time to change and get to Holt's for my shift. But as I dodged customers coming out of the store, and saw who waited there, I knew I was going to be late.

Detective Shuman.

For a second, I considered running back to my car, hauling ass out of the parking lot, making a run for—somewhere. But then I figured that if Detective Madison wasn't with him, I probably wasn't about to be arrested. Madison wouldn't want to miss that.

"My girlfriend loved the scarf," Shuman said.

He had a big, goofy grin on his face so I figured my birthday gift recommendation must have led to a night of wild sex. I didn't think Shuman had it in him.

It's always the quiet ones, you know.

"Do you think I should get her the matching wallet for Christmas?" Shuman asked. He frowned. "I don't want to look too anxious."

"Timing's perfect."

He thought over my advice, then nodded. "Okay. I'll do it."

We stood there for another minute just looking at each other. Cars crowded the parking lot, racing from aisle to aisle, trying to get a good space near the doors. Customers hurried into the store, then out again, struggling to carry big bags of merchandise.

I thought about Grace inside at the customer service booth, facing a long line, expecting me to show up and help. I didn't like leaving her hanging, but I couldn't go in. Not yet.

I didn't know if Shuman had come all the way to the store just to ask me what to get his girlfriend for Christmas, or if he had something else on his mind. Something unofficial.

"So," I said, trying to sound cheery. "Solved any good homicides lately?"

Shuman grinned. He had a great grin.

"No, but I'm making progress," he said. "Ruled out a few suspects."

"Anyone I know?" I asked, as if we were discussing the weather.

"Neighbors," he said. "Both have alibis."

Damn. Richard's neighbors weren't suspects anymore. They'd both been cleared. So who was left?

Me.

I felt a little queasy, realizing that this was why Detective Shuman had come here tonight. To warn me. He'd have known I'd ask about the investigation. This way he could give me a heads-up, off the record.

I glanced at my car in the parking lot. Maybe making a break for it wasn't such a bad idea.

It might be kind of cool. Me, loose on the open road, taking in the sights, shopping my way from state to state. Of course, I'd need money for that. Money I didn't have.

So much for that little fantasy.

I'd have to stay. But that didn't mean I intended to go down for Richard's murder.

"You know, he was involved with someone here in the store," I said, trying not to sound desperate.

"Glenna Webb," Shuman said, and I was surprised he already knew about her. I wondered who in the store had told him. "Air-tight alibi."

"What about her husband?" Okay, now I was sounding desperate. "He was at the store that night. I saw him."

Shuman frowned. "You're sure?"

"Positive. And Richard threatened to fire one of the employees the night he was murdered."

I'm sounding really desperate now.

"Sophia Garcia," Shuman said, then shook his head. "The surveillance tapes show her in the shoe department at the time of the murder."

Damn. Those surveillance cameras and tapes. I kept forgetting about those things.

"What about Jeanette Avery?" I asked.

Shuman looked interested now. "What about her?"

Jeez, what was I going to say? I didn't have any evidence, just suspicion and theory. But now that I'd mentioned Jeanette, I couldn't back away.

"I think Richard was after her job," I said. "He'd done that before, in the Northridge store. She's kind of old and probably can't get another manager's job very easily."

Now that I'd said it out loud, it sounded really lame. But Shuman had the good grace not to laugh in my face.

"I guess that sounds crazy," I admitted.

He shrugged. "Not as crazy as some of the tips we get. Somebody phoned in an anonymous tip that Richard was a cross-dresser working in a transvestite club in Hollywood."

"How do these rumors get started?" I mused.

"Any more suspects?" he asked, nodding toward the store.

I supposed he was just being nice so I wouldn't feel like such an idiot, and I liked that about him.

"No, that's it," I said.

"Sure?" Shuman tilted his head. "Nobody else?"

If I'd suspected anyone else, I'd have told him. But I didn't, so I just shook my head.

"I'll check out the store manager," Shuman promised.

I wish I could put him to work investigating my job at Pike Warner, but I didn't want him to know about it. He'd be obligated to share the news with Detective Madison and I didn't want to give that old bastard any more ammunition he might twist to use against me.

I wished too that Shuman could take me to the police station so I could get a look at those stockroom surveillance tapes. While I didn't really want to see myself lounging on the king-size Laura Ashley bed-in-a-bag sets when I was supposed to be working, I knew—just knew—that, if I looked at those tapes, I'd see something that the lazy-ass, soon-to-retire Detective Madison had missed.

But I didn't waste my breath asking. No way would Shuman agree to that, no matter how wild a night of sex he'd had with his girlfriend, thanks to my Burberry scarf birthday gift idea.

"If you need help picking out the wallet, let me know," I said.

Shuman nodded and walked into the parking lot. I went into the store.

Late.

CHAPTER 22

I was late now and I had a vision of Rita in the break room beside the time clock, glaring and smiling at the same time. But Rita wasn't there. Ty was. He was fiddling with his BlackBerry, as if he'd been waiting for me.

He looked serious. Troubled. Something.

Ty glanced at the two employees seated at a table, eating and flipping through magazines.

"Could I speak with you for a moment?" he asked, sounding every bit the chain store owner.

Now what?

Jeez, he'd caught me on the Laura Ashley bed-in-a-bag sets, crying on duty, talking crap about the merchandise, giving an unauthorized discount to a customer. I'd told him to get screwed in front of his grandmother. What could he be upset about?

Jeanette.

She'd probably told him how I'd nearly gone over the desk after her when she'd tried to write me up for those bogus complaints against me. I guess Ty didn't appreciate my "spirit" the way his grandmother had.

I grabbed my time card and punched in. If I was about to get fired, I was getting paid for it.

I headed for my locker to put my purse away, but Ty stopped me.

"You'll want to keep that with you," he said.

Oh my God, he was going to fire me.

"Look," I said. "Those things Craig said were lies. All lies. I don't care what Jeanette says, I—"

"What things?" he asked, looking concerned.

Oh my God. He doesn't know. Jeanette didn't tell him.

"Nothing," I said and waved the air between us. "Never mind. What did you want to talk to me about?"

He kept frowning and for a few seconds I thought he might press for details, but he didn't.

"Actually, I'd like you to come somewhere with me," Ty said, then added hastily, "It's business. I'd like your opinion on something."

Is my life weird, or what?

"You mean now?" I asked. He nodded and I said, "I'm supposed to be working."

"I got someone to cover your shift."

"Somebody who knows the customer service booth?" I asked. "I don't want Grace stuck in there without good help."

"It's handled. Will you go?"

I had no idea where he wanted to take me. I hardly knew Ty, really. What if he was some psycho?

But this was the closest thing I'd had to a date lately—even if Ty had already told me it was business—so what the hell?

"Sure," I said.

Outside, he opened the door for me and I got into his car, a BMW 750i sedan—a plush ride—and we pulled out of the parking lot.

"So, where are we going?" I asked.

For a second I fantasized he would confess that he'd only said this was a business trip to get me away from the store. That we were headed up the coast to a quaint little B&B overlooking the ocean. That I was so hot he couldn't live without me another minute. That he was sick of women like stuffy, boring Sarah Covington who talked about nothing but—

"I wanted your opinion on the location of a new store." Ty glanced at me. "You live near here, right?"

My heart sank a little. I guess he'd gone through the employment records of everyone at Holt's looking for someone who lived in the area, and he'd come up with me.

Frankly, I couldn't have cared less that Holt's was opening another store. I didn't feel all that great about being here with Ty either. He had on jeans and a polo shirt, and I was in khakis and a red sweater. I figured he'd dressed down, knowing he'd be with me tonight.

Not a great feeling.

"Yeah, I live near here," I said. "And, really, I don't think there's any need for another store like Holt's."

I thought he might whip around and head back to the store, but he didn't. He kept driving. His cell phone rang. I turned my head to look out the window, pretending to be courteous and allow him privacy for his call, but I listened to every word. Some problem with an advertising agency. I figured he was talking to Sarah Covington and it irked me. I imagined her making notes in her Louis Vuitton organizer. Bitch.

Ty hung up as we drove past a mall I shopped at sometimes. It was a good mall, a nice mix of upscale and midrange stores. One end opened to an outside plaza with benches and flowers, surrounded by restaurants. The area continued for several blocks with office buildings, trendy shops, art galleries, boutiques, a travel agency, candy store, a bookstore, a movie theater, and more great places to eat. It had a small town feel. Narrow streets, wide sidewalks that urged shoppers to stroll, huge display windows inviting them inside.

Ty nosed the Beemer into a space at the curb. It was dark now, and the trees along the street glowed with tiny white lights. Music floated from speakers hidden in the shrubs. At some of the restaurants fire pits burned, warming the outdoor seating areas.

"Don't tell me you're going to knock down all these great stores and put in a Holt's," I said, getting out of the car.

I sounded kind of bitchy because that's how I felt.

"So you like this area?" Ty asked.

"For these specialty shops, yes," I said.

Ty stood there, gazing across the street for so long that I got annoyed.

"Are we done?" I asked.

Okay, now I'm sounding really bitchy.

He looked back at me, as if he'd forgotten I was standing there.

"Would you like to have dinner?" he asked, gesturing across the street. "I'd really like your opinion on this."

I'd already given my opinion, but apparently he hadn't been listening.

"I guess," I said.

This was hardly the romantic, first-date evening I'd envisioned with Ty. This was business.

We crossed the street to BJ's Restaurant. I'd been there a few times. The place had a real contemporary feel to it. We got a table on the patio. Candles flickered and heaters warmed the air. Ty ordered a beer and I got an iced tea since I was, technically, still on the clock.

I was afraid he might ask me about my make-believe puppy Pancake, or want to know about the confrontation I'd had with Jeanette that I'd mentioned at the store, and I was a little ticked off about being relegated to a "business" dinner with him, and twiddling my thumbs in the car while he spoke with Ms. Blondie, vice president of marketing, on the phone.

So I said, "Why am I here? Holt's has got marketing people by the dozen who can tell you where to build your store. Why do you care what I think?"

Ty looked slightly shocked by my outburst—I get that a lot—then he said, "Because you'll tell me the truth."

I wasn't prepared for that. It was true, but so few people appreciated it.

He rested his arm on the table and leaned forward a little.

"You're right. I've got corporate people telling me how great the stores are doing, our projected, record-breaking profit, but not one of them has ever said that the inventory sucks. Which it does." Ty sat back and shook his head. "I hadn't been in one of the stores for years, until last year. And when I walked in and looked around, I couldn't believe—"

"Hang on a second," I said. "Your family has owned the Holt's chain for five generations, but you hadn't been into one of the stores for years?"

"I always knew what was expected of me, but I didn't go down without a fight." Ty gave a rueful grin. "I did the dutiful son, dutiful heir thing. Gave up ice hockey at Minnesota State for Harvard and an MBA. Managed to get in almost two years' backpacking through Europe. Came home and went through the motions at the corporate office."

"If you didn't want to work for the company, why did you?" I asked.

He shrugged. "Five generations."

It was a lot of weight to carry. I'd had it bad enough growing up in the shadow of Miss California, third runner-up for Miss America. I'd have felt more pressure to continue with dance lessons and pageants to please my mom if my younger sister hadn't come along. She'd saved me too from Mom's alma mater. Guess Ty didn't have that luxury.

"About a year ago my dad had a triple bypass," Ty said.

I thought about my own dad and got scared.

"Is he okay?" I asked.

Ty nodded. "He had to retire from running the stores."

"And your fate was sealed."

He nodded again, but this time, in the candlelight, I saw a toughness in his expression, a grit I'd never seen before.

"Five generations," he said. "Holt's isn't going down. Not on my watch."

My belly tingled a little at seeing him, hearing the strength of his conviction. He hadn't wanted it, but appreciated everything those who'd come before him had accomplished. He'd stepped up. And he was going to win.

That's so sexy.

"You're right, most of the merchandise in the stores is awful," Ty said, then paused while the waiter brought our meals. "That's why I want to open a new chain of stores. Something smaller. Upscale, trendy. Clothes, shoes—"

"Designer handbags?" I asked, my heart racing.

Ty gestured toward the street. "I was looking at Pasadena for the flagship store, but I like this location better."

So that's why he was in Pasadena that night with Sarah. They were scouting locations. She really wasn't his girlfriend. My heart raced faster.

"Which place do you think would be better?" he asked.

I didn't even have to think about it.

"Pasadena is great, but it's crowded there. A lot of competition," I said. "Here, things are newer, they're growing."

Ty nodded. "The marketing people say the new store will work. You live near here. You know the people. What do you think?"

I thought I'd be perfect to run the store. My mind bloomed with visions of me buying the merchandise, deciding on the layout of the store. Negotiating the lease. Hiring, putting together benefit packages, supervising the clerks. Launching a terrific advertising campaign. Reporting to Ty on the astronomical profit I'd made.

Only . . . only I don't really know how to do any of that. A big knot landed in the pit of my stomach. Oh my

God, I really don't know how to do any of those things. Sarah Covington could do most of them. Detective Shuman's lawyer girlfriend could too. Even Rita—*Rita*— could do some of them. But not me.

What have I been doing with my life for the past five years?

Now I felt really sick.

Ty talked about his plans for the store, naming it Wallace, Inc.—some sort of family thing—and his intentions for the future. He didn't seem to notice that I was hardly listening.

When we got back to Holt's, I expected Ty to say that he appreciated my going with him, my info, my opinion— something—but his cell phone rang as we got out of the car and he took the call. Sarah Covington *again*.

It irritated me to no end that she'd called once more, and plain old made me mad that Ty seemed to hang on her every word, ignoring me.

He went to the offices in the back of the store with Sarah's voice and his cell phone stuck to his ear, and not even a glance at me.

I stowed my purse in my locker—Sarah Covington doesn't have a locker, she has a desk—in the break room. When I came out, Jack Bishop waited near the customer service booth.

Another failure.

That's what seeing Jack made me think of. My job at Pike Warner, the one thing I'd thought I'd succeeded at, was gone. Not just gone, but gone without even an investigation. They'd cast me aside, unimportant, worthless, expected to simply fade away.

I don't hate my life now.

I hate me.

"You shouldn't have waited around for me," I said to Jack, as I headed toward the customer service booth.

"I didn't wait," Jack said. "I saw you leave earlier, with Cameron."

"You followed me?" I asked.

I'd had no idea. Jack Bishop had tailed me from Holt's to the restaurant by the mall, then back again, and I'd not noticed him, not suspected anything.

I didn't know whether to think it was totally cool, or be annoyed.

"I found out what's going on at Pike Warner," Jack said.

My breath caught. Maybe tonight wouldn't be the worst night of my life, after all. Maybe everything had—somehow—been resolved at Pike Warner. Maybe I could go back to work there, an integral member of the vibrant accounts payable unit, at the greatest law firm in the history of civilization.

"Their audit showed you embezzled funds," Jack said.

"What?"

My thoughts scattered. Embezzlement? I wouldn't know how to do that—even if I wanted to. Then I knew what it must be.

"It was those tricky accounting codes," I realized. "I got them mixed up sometimes. Everybody did. Probably. Anyway, I'll just explain that to them."

"This isn't about accounting codes," Jack said.

"Okay, then," I said, "I'll pay back the missing money until it's all straightened out."

Jack shook his head.

"A hundred grand," he said. "They claim you stole a hundred grand."

Jack was in the parking lot when I got off from work. He followed me to my apartment and we went inside. He helped himself to a beer from my fridge, then brought one to me as I sat on my couch, frozen in a near trance.

I was sure Jack had not gotten this information from any official source at Pike Warner, but rather the friends in low places he'd spoken of before. But I knew, regardless of the source, that the info was accurate. Jack was good—very good—at what he did.

"Start at the beginning," I said. "Maybe it will make sense."

"Your job at Pike Warner was to pay their bills, right?" Jack asked. "How did that work?"

"All the accounts payable clerks were assigned specific companies to handle. Mine were mostly related to the up-keep of the firm. The janitor, carpet cleaners, the plant ser-vice, office furniture, supplies. Things like that," I said.

"And you paid whatever invoice those companies sent in?" Jack asked.

"No way," I said. "On my very first day of work, Mrs. Drexler showed me the files of vendors I was autho-rized to pay. All the companies I dealt with had been ap-proved by the firm, long before I got there. I made sure every invoice that came in fit the predetermined parame-ters for each account. Then I assigned an accounting code, entered it in the computer, and sent it to cashiering for the check to be cut. It wasn't a big deal."

On my first day of work there, I'd gotten the idea Mrs. Drexler didn't like me much. HR had assigned me to her department and she hadn't interviewed me, or any-thing, so I guess she was annoyed by that. The "orienta-tion" she'd provided was to pause by the desk I'd been assigned, point to the drawer with my account folders, and hand me a checklist I was supposed to follow when I authorized a payment.

"I followed all the procedures," I said. "How could those auditors possibly think I embezzled a hundred thou-sand dollars? I just don't get it."

"Some of the invoices you paid weren't for approved vendors," Jack said.

"Yes, they were," I insisted. "The folders were already in the cabinet when I went to work there."

"The firm says no, and the auditors didn't find any folders."

"Of course the folders were there," I said, coming to my feet. "Why else would I have written checks to those companies?"

"They were dummy companies," Jack said. "Bank accounts were opened under those names."

My heart jumped as I mentally saw a tiny ray of light beaming my way.

"Then find out who opened those accounts," I said. "Those are the people responsible for this, not me."

Jack hesitated for a moment, and the beam of light went out.

"You opened them," he said. "The firm contacted the Golden State Bank and Trust and confirmed that—"

"The GSB&T?" I asked. No wonder they'd sent me a preapproved credit card and a vice president had talked to me on the phone that day. They thought I had a hundred grand in their bank.

"It wasn't me," I said. "I never opened those accounts."

"No bank would open an account without seeing identification."

"My purse was stolen a few months ago," I suddenly remembered.

"Did you report it to the police?" Jack asked.

"I didn't think it was a big deal," I said, remembering how, at the time, I'd been more concerned about losing my D&G bag than my driver's license.

What an idiot I'd been.

"As far as Pike Warner is concerned, you opened bank accounts using company names that you fabricated, then cut checks from Pike Warner as if you were paying bills, and deposited them into those accounts," Jack said. "Fraud and embezzlement, plain and simple."

"Pike Warner needs to talk to someone at GSB&T," I said. "If they'll just look at everything carefully, they have to realize that someone else opened those accounts using my ID."

Jack drew a breath. I could tell he had more bad news.

"The bank isn't cooperating. It will take subpoenas, lawsuits—all kinds of legal actions—to get anything out of them. Their reputation is on the line. The last thing they want is for the public to know something like this occurred at their bank."

I shook my head. I couldn't believe this was happening.

"They'll let it go," Jack said, after a moment. "You can walk away from this, Haley, and never look back. Pike Warner isn't going to pursue you. They want you, and this situation, to disappear. They don't care that the money is gone."

"Pike Warner is okay with losing a hundred grand?" I asked, stunned.

"That's their bar tab for their spring retreat in Maui," Jack said. "It's nothing to them, compared to their reputation."

"Just like GSB&T," I realized.

"You can walk away from this, no harm, no foul. Get a job at another attorney firm—any company—and Pike Warner will give you a glowing reference."

I was sure this wasn't anything official he'd heard from Pike Warner, just more inside info from his source. But it made sense.

"They want this kept quiet," Jack said.

"But they still think I did it," I said.

He nodded. "Yes, they do."

Jack finished his beer and I walked with him to the door.

"I owe you big time," I said.

"I'll let you know what I want, and when I want it." He said it with a tiny grin and I knew he wouldn't want to collect on his debt any time soon, though it might be nice tonight. I could stand to be mindless for a while.

Jack left and I wandered through my apartment. Even

thoughts of my red Notorious bag and those purses Craig had given me at cost didn't cheer me up.

I wasn't surprised that Pike Warner was willing to write off that big chunk of money to save their reputation, or that GSB&T wouldn't cooperate for the same reason. Appearance was everything to firms like theirs. And it was good to know that, as Jack had said, I could get a good-paying job at another law firm, no problem.

I envisioned Mrs. Drexler on the phone, giving me a glowing recommendation, and that cheered me up a little. I could get another high-paying job, wear great clothes, buy designer handbags at retail without a thought or a care.

All I had to do was let it go.

But then I started to get mad. I'd let a lot of things go. The job at Pike Warner that I'd breezed through. My finances. College. A chance at a real career. My whole future, really.

And look where I'd ended up.

No more. No more letting things go. I felt that sickly knot in my stomach harden into something new, something I'd never experienced before. Determination bloomed inside me, filling me with a weird kind of rage.

I was clearing my name at Pike Warner. And I was clearing myself of murder charges too. I wasn't going to let those attorneys, or those homicide detectives, treat me this way. I was getting out from under all of this, and then I'd—I'd—

Well, I didn't know exactly what I'd do after that. I could figure that out later. Right now, I had two crimes to solve.

Chapter 23

"Do you have layaway?"

"No," I said to the customer across the counter from me at the customer service booth.

She huffed irritably. I didn't know what she was so upset about. *I'm* the one who had to answer that question a hundred times a day.

"Well, you should," she snapped.

"Would you like to complete a customer comment card?" I asked.

I love it when they complete a comment card.

"Yes, I would," she declared.

I shared a quick smirk with Grace at the inventory computer, as I handed the woman a card.

The next customer in line came forward, a woman in her forties with a unibrow.

"Those automatic faucets in your restrooms run too long," she said. "You're wasting water."

I just looked at her for a moment, then said, "Okay."

She left.

Another customer came forward, a young mom pushing a baby stroller. She held up a tiny bag, probably from the jewelry department.

"Can I get a gift box?" she asked.

For absolutely no reason that made good sense, the gift boxes were kept here at the customer service booth. That meant, after customers trudged through the store selecting gifts, then stood in our long lines, they had to walk all the way to the back of the store, stand in line yet again, and present their receipt. We were supposed to give them one box for each gift purchased, then stamp their receipt accordingly.

All this for boxes.

"How many do you need?" I asked.

She held up the bag. "Well, I only bought this one thing."

"Do you need boxes?" I asked. I'd been handing these things out like candy for days now.

Her eyes grew bigger—which was sort of sad—and she said, "Sure, if it's okay."

"No problem."

She told me what she needed and I slid them into a bag. She thanked me and left, a happy, satisfied Holt's shopper—and I didn't even have to give her an of-course-you-can smile.

The next customer in line came to the counter. "You should install hand dryers in your restrooms," she said, and walked away.

The woman who'd complained about our no-layaway policy pushed in front of the next customer and slapped her comment card down in front of me. With a triumphant head toss, she left.

I took it to Grace. "You want to process this one?"

She grinned, took the card, tore it in half, and dropped it in the trash.

The door to the customer service booth opened and in walked Rita, as I finished up with the next customer in line. She was really in the Christmas spirit today, wearing red stretch pants and a knit top with a goat in a Santa hat on the front.

"Are you offering credit?" she barked.

I hadn't done it once.

"Of course," I said. Grace nodded in agreement.

"You're supposed to be marking receipts when you give out boxes," Rita said. "You'd better be doing that."

"Yeah, Rita, that gift-box fraud ring is in full swing again this Christmas, but we're holding a lid on it," I said.

A woman approached the counter. "The water in your restroom sinks isn't hot enough."

"Okay," I said, and she walked away.

"What's with all the bathroom comments today?" Grace asked, and rolled her eyes.

"My suggestion," Rita announced. "When Mr. Cameron asked for suggestions, I said that we should post a sign in our restrooms advising customers to tell the customer service booth employees if there were any problems."

So now I'm the bathroom monitor?

"There's a sign in there?" Grace asked, pointing toward the restroom.

"Mr. Cameron thought it was a great idea," Rita informed us.

Bella came out of the break room. I guess she was feeling tropical today because her hair was styled like a pineapple.

"You got the goods?" she called.

"You bet," I said, and she continued toward the sales floor.

"Purses?" Grace asked.

I'd told Bella that I had knockoff handbags for sale, since she'd mentioned it to me on Thanksgiving Day. I didn't know word had gotten around.

"Do you have Chloe?" Grace asked, and her eyes got this faraway, dreamy look that I could totally appreciate. "I'd love to have a Chloe tote."

"What's this all about?" Rita demanded.

"Haley's selling faux designer bags," Grace said.

"That's illegal," Rita declared.

"There's no such thing as the purse police," I told her.

"You've never been to a purse party? They're so much fun. Women are crazy for those bags," Grace said, then turned to me. "I'd love to have a party, Haley. I know at least fifteen girls who'd come. You'll make a fortune—I promise."

"Yeah, that would be cool," I said. Wow, maybe Marcie was right. We could make a part-time business out of this.

Then I noticed Rita's eyes boring into me. I didn't think she was contemplating buying a purse from me. More like she intended to find out if the purse police really existed, and turn me in.

I hate her.

The phone rang. I answered it. A customer asked what time we closed. I hung up without telling her, and turned to Rita. "They need you at register four."

She hurried away.

I went into the bathroom and ripped down the sign.

When I came out I caught a glimpse of Ty going into the security office. No one was in line at the customer service booth, so I headed down the hallway.

As far as I knew, Holt's still hadn't hired a loss prevention person. Store management was taking turns watching the monitors. I'm not sure the store was all that anxious to catch shoplifters, for now anyway. After the publicity of Richard's murder, the last thing they probably wanted was cop cars out front with lights flashing and somebody being escorted from the store in handcuffs. Not a good way to lure Christmas shoppers.

I'd never been inside the security office and always wondered what went on in there, so I slipped through the doorway after Ty.

He closed the door, seemingly unconcerned that I was in there with him learning the dark secrets of the Holt's security system. Maybe because we already knew some of each other's secrets.

The room wasn't all that big, but it was packed with video monitors and racks of recorders; wires, cords, and cables ran everywhere. A shelving unit on the far wall held hundreds of carefully labeled videocassettes. Grainy, black-and-white views of the exterior and interior of the store glowed on the screens in the dimly lit room.

I didn't know if this was state-of-the-art equipment. I doubted it. The system had been set up to catch shoplifters, not a murderer.

"How's it going out there?" Ty asked.

"Busy," I said, then couldn't resist the opportunity. "Lots of complaints today about that sign in the restrooms. Customers said whoever came up with that idea must have been a complete moron. I took it down."

Ty shrugged. "It was worth a try."

"So, this is the security office," I said, looking over the monitors. Cameras covered most of the front of the store, plus the parking lot. There was a single camera on the loading dock, and the angle seemed off center, a little. Cameras over each checkout register and the customer service booth caught everything. Every department was surveilled, but I noticed a few blind spots. I saw Bella at register two, Sophia Garcia helping a woman in the shoe department, Grace in the customer service booth.

And there, big as life, were the monitors showing the entrance to the stockroom where I'd been sitting on the king-size Laura Ashley bed-in-a-bag sets just before Richard was murdered.

Weird, knowing that someone—anyone—who happened to be in this office could see most everything in and around the store. Then I realized this was how Ty had known I was crying in the stockroom the other night. He'd seen me on the video monitor.

It was kind of nice thinking he'd known I was upset and come to help, that he hadn't just happened into the stock room at the moment. But then, I couldn't help wondering who else had been in this room watching me, and that kind of creeped me out.

"Do you catch many shoplifters watching these things?" I asked.

Ty hit a couple of keys on the keyboard, then moved the joystick, changing the angle on one of the screens.

"We rely heavily on the sales personnel on the floor," he said. "When they see someone acting suspicious, they call and we can watch them from here. It's an important part of the job."

We were supposed to be watching for shoplifters? They probably covered that in orientation.

Ty studied the monitors, and I studied him—he looked way sexy in the dim light—then he pointed at one of the screens. "See that?"

I saw a teenage girl in the juniors department, flipping through the racks.

"She just put a top into her handbag," Ty said.

I gasped and leaned closer, and saw the big tote on her arm. She glanced around, slid another top off the hanger, and slipped it into her bag.

"Oh my God!" I exclaimed. "She's taking all kinds of stuff."

"We lose hundreds of thousands of dollars' worth of merchandise from theft every year," Ty said.

I figured it must have been more last year, with those high-priced game systems that had been shoplifted from Craig's department, but didn't think Ty would like to be reminded of it.

"I'm going out there, and tell her to put that stuff back." I was outraged. I couldn't believe this girl—no more than fourteen—was actually stealing.

Okay, I'd done a few bad things—well, yeah, more than a few—but I'd never, absolutely never, stolen anything.

"Hang on," Ty said, sounding way too reasonable, watching the other monitors now. "We have to be careful. That girl didn't get here by herself. She might have a mom here somewhere with hundreds of dollars of merchandise in her cart. We don't want to lose a big sale, and alienate a good customer, for the sake of a kid and a couple of tops."

"Screw that," I said. I was amped up, ready to roll, ready to get out there, yank those clothes out of that girl's bag, and toss her out the front door.

Ty turned to me, looking intrigued, or something. "Do you always get this excited about things?"

"Don't you *ever* get excited about things?" I countered, and flashed on the image of him atop me yelling, "Scream my name."

"I'll handle this," he said, and nodded toward the monitor.

He left the security office and I followed him through the store, from one black-and-white screen to the next, until he reached the juniors department. At the end of the rack where the teenage girl was flipping through jeans, he stopped, folded his hands in front of him, and stared at her. After a few seconds, she looked up. Even in black-and-white, I saw the startled look on her face. She ducked her head and moved away. Ty followed at a distance.

The girl tried to act cool, pretended to look at a couple of sweaters, but she left the department. I followed her on the monitors, thinking maybe she'd hit the door and make a run for it. I was wrong. In the men's department, I saw her pull the tops from her tote, drop them on a shelf of golf shirts, then hurry out the front door. On the parking lot camera, I saw her get into a car. It pulled away.

I looked at the shelves of videotapes. Hundreds of them. Thousands of hours. How many crimes had been recorded?

How many people had been caught, how many got away? One for every tape?

I scanned the labels and—oh my God—there were the tapes for the night of Richard's murder. What were they doing here? Didn't the police take them?

They were copies—had to be. Instead of the usual neatly typed label, all of them were scrawled with black ink. Maybe Holt's insurance carrier had required that all tapes be kept. Or maybe their legal team—the good ol' boys down at Pike Warner—had told Ty to make a copy before releasing the original.

But here they were. I'd been dying to see them, to find out exactly who had been in the stockroom that night. Even though the loading dock doors had been open during the time of the murder, I might find something here that would help.

I'd take them.

The idea hit me like a bolt of lightning. Yeah, okay, I'd just talked trash about that teenager who'd taken those tops, but this was different. Really.

My heart rate picked up. I might never get this chance again.

Where was Ty?

I checked the monitors. Oh God, he was at the customer service booth headed straight for the security office. Steps away.

I grabbed the two videocassettes marked STOCK ROOM and the one labeled LOADING DOCK, shoved them under my sweater, then yanked the door open. Ty loomed over me.

"Got to get back to work," I said, ducking around him.

He gave me an odd look. He probably expected me to say something about running off that shoplifter—men love it when you watch them do things—but I ignored him, punched in the code on the customer service booth keypad, and hurried inside. My heart hammered and my hands shook a bit. Whew! That was a close one. I was glad to be away from Ty.

Then I realized—jeez—I wasn't really away from him. He could see everything I did on the cameras, especially here in the booth. What was I going to do with these videocassettes? I couldn't work the rest of the night with them tucked under my sweater.

I really have to get better about thinking things through.

"I need to take a quick break," I said to Grace in a low voice. I raised one eyebrow in the universal my-period-started bob, and she nodded, understanding completely. I went to the break room, grabbed my purse from my locker, and dashed into the restroom. No security cameras there.

I barely got the cassettes into my Chanel satchel—wish I'd brought a tote like that girl in juniors—returned it to my locker, then went back to the customer service booth.

All this sleuthing had me buzzing pretty good, as I waited on customers. The night of Richard's murder raged in my mind—and I hadn't even had any chocolate lately. All I could think was that if that delivery truck hadn't been at the loading dock at that particular time, on that particular day, Detectives Shuman and Madison would have a complete list of suspects from the surveillance tape. Darn those truck drivers for screwing up everything.

Unless . . .

Maybe one of the truck drivers had murdered Richard. Yeah, that was possible—likely, even. Richard ticked off everyone. Surely that could include the truck driver.

I finished with the last customer in line and started sorting through the clothing heaped on the counter, shoving pieces into bins. I was on autopilot.

I wondered if the detectives knew which company's truck had made the delivery that night. From the weird camera angle at the loading dock I'd just seen on the video monitor, I didn't know if the field of view was wide enough to see the name on the side of the truck. They would probably have to slog through all sorts of red tape to determine which company it had been.

But I could find out. Right now.

Two customers were in line now but I ignored them—Grace would say something if she really needed help—and went to the inventory computer. The home office downloaded the info on all merchandise received into the store. All I had to do was find out what had been delivered that day.

Oh my God. This is great. I'm going to solve this murder. Me!

I scrolled through the entries looking for the date of Richard's death, mentally picturing the stunned expression on Detective Madison's face when I announce the identity of the murderer. He'll look like a complete idiot. They might even cancel his retirement ceremony. I can't wait.

Only . . . crap, this can't be right.

I scrolled through everything again, but there was no merchandise listed that had been received into the store on that date.

How can that be?

I gazed across the customer service booth, thinking, and noticed a woman in line glaring at me. I ignored her—my sales floor training always comes in handy—and thought about what that could mean.

Then I knew. The truck at the loading dock wasn't making a delivery. It was the returns truck, the one that picked up our defective and unsaleable merchandise and took it to our central warehouse.

Learning the identity of the driver would be simple. He was either a contractor or a Holt's employee. And that further explained why he'd killed Richard. He'd obviously known him at our other stores.

Maybe Richard was sleeping with the driver's wife too.

My heart raced. Yeah, I was on to something here. It all made perfect sense. All I had to do now was call Detective Shuman and tell him—what? That I knew who the murderer was? Hadn't I just told him that I thought Jeanette Avery was the murderer? And Glenna's husband? And Sophia Garcia?

Oh, crap.

He'd never believe me now—I wouldn't believe me either—unless I had more evidence. And I knew just how to get it.

"Grace, I really need a break," I said.

"Go for it," she said.

Grace is awesome to work with.

I left the customer service booth and headed toward the accessories department. I needed to talk to Craig. Yeah, I know he made up all those lies about me, trying to get me fired—I still don't know why he'd do that—but he knew everything there was to know about the returns truck. I'd seen him in the stockroom a million times getting the merchandise ready for pickup. He probably knew the driver. He'd know if there was a problem between him and Richard.

I picked up my pace through the children's department, anxious to get the info from Craig. He'd been involved with Richard's death right from the start. He'd been here that night, even though I didn't see his name on the work schedule that had disappeared, somehow. He'd taken over when the detectives arrived, showed them the body upstairs as if he already knew where . . . to find . . .

Oh my God.

My steps slowed and my mind raced back over that night. When I'd come out of the stockroom, seen Evelyn, and told her about Richard's murder, the first thing she'd asked was where Craig was. At the time I'd thought she was just worried that he would think she wasn't supervising the department adequately, but maybe there was more to it.

Evelyn had told me to stay away from Craig. No, she'd actually warned me to stay away, that time in the restroom. I'd thought she was just being weird, but now I was thinking maybe Evelyn knew more than she let on.

A lot more.

CHAPTER 24

I switched off my TV, ending the long, boring surveillance footage of the Holt's stockroom and loading dock.

I'd never have patience enough to be a detective. No wonder Madison was such a crank ass.

When I'd found those tapes in the security office this evening and rushed home to watch them, I was sure I'd discover something the homicide detectives had missed. But there was nothing. Just employees going in and out through the store entrances. A frail, gray-haired woman from Housewares, whose name I didn't know, who hardly looked strong enough to push a U-boat, let alone yank the bar off of one and hit Richard in the head with it. Craig was there too. Seeing Richard go into the stockroom, knowing he wouldn't come out, was kind of creepy. And there was me, of course, lounging on the king-size Laura Ashley bed-in-a-bag sets.

No image of Sophia Garcia, Glenna, Glenna's husband, or an unknown suspect on the tapes.

The loading dock surveillance tape showed nothing useful. A truck, backed in. A glimpse of the driver wearing Dickie pants and shirt, and a Raiders cap pulled down over his eyes. The camera angle limited the field of view to only one side of the loading dock; anyone could have entered or left from the opposite side and not been seen.

I hoped that Holt's would upgrade their security system soon.

Sitting back on my couch, I stared at the black TV screen, thinking. This afternoon I'd considered Craig a suspect, but nothing on the tape backed up my suspicion. Even something as simple as Craig following Richard into the stockroom might have been a crumb of evidence to go on, but it didn't happen that way.

Craig had entered the stockroom through the door near the intimates department. A few minutes later, according to the date and time stamp on the video, Richard had entered through the door beside the customer service booth. The two of them had entered from opposite sides of the huge stockroom. They probably hadn't even known that the other was in there. Just coincidence. Which was probably why Detective Shuman figured the murderer had slipped in through the open loading dock door.

But, still, I couldn't let it go. Something about Craig's behavior didn't seem quite right.

The stockroom was usually empty at night. No one went in there, unless they needed something specific. Like me, when I'd gone to look—sort of—for that customer's Wonderbra, or the woman from Housewares who'd come out carrying a stack of towels that she'd undoubtedly fetched at the request of a customer. Craig had probably gone in to handle the returns. But why was Richard in there? I wondered if it had something to do with whomever Evelyn had overheard him arguing with in the office earlier that evening.

Needing an energy boost, I got a Snickers bar from the kitchen and paced around until the sugar kicked in. Maybe if I thought like a detective I could come up with something. A clue. Some evidence. A connection.

I got another Snickers bar—just to heighten my awareness—and ran everything through my mind again. Nothing on the security tape connected. Just store employees going about their business. A routine night at a retail store—until Richard was murdered, of course.

So what was different about that night? What caused someone to murder Richard? And for what reason? Why would someone sneak into the stockroom through the loading dock, go upstairs, and kill him?

And could Craig really have been in the stockroom, near the loading dock, and not noticed anything? It seemed suspicious to me—really suspicious, not like with Jeanette, or Sophia, or Glenna's husband. It made me wonder about everything Craig had said and done.

I didn't trust him, that's for sure. Maybe I needed to find out more about him.

I found the Holt's store directory and looked up Craig's home phone number, then called Jack Bishop.

I can't do surveillance work. I haven't got the bladder for it.

I'd been sitting in my car for two hours, parked across the street and down the block from Craig's house. Jack got me his address last night—I still don't know how he does that so quickly—and I decided to check out the place first thing this morning, see if anything suspicious was going on. Like maybe Craig lived beyond his means in an expensive neighborhood, or drove a luxury car. But his place in Van Nuys was in an older, middle-class neighborhood that showed signs of age and slight neglect, and the car parked in his driveway was the Chevy Blazer I'd seen him in at the store.

So far, the only thing suspicious about Craig's place was me sitting in the car, watching his house.

I thought maybe I could catch Craig going somewhere and I could follow him. That would be way cool. I could tail him through the city, just like Jack had done when Ty and I were out the other night, and see where he went, what he did. Maybe I'd see him doing something illegal, find some evidence that he was involved with Richard's murder.

But, so far, nothing. All I'd done was sit here watching his house. He hadn't gone anywhere. The neighborhood had been busy for a while, with kids heading off for school and people going to work. Nothing now.

I'd brought magazines to entertain myself, and gone through the McDonald's drive-through for breakfast. My car reeked of fast food and I had to pee.

Somehow, this seemed more glamorous when Jack did it.

I glanced at my watch. Four more minutes had crawled by. I'd read the magazines cover to cover, so that left me nothing to do but think. Pike Warner bloomed in my mind. Since Jack had told me the whole situation there, I'd been so focused on clearing myself of murder charges I hadn't had time to think too much about it. I had called Kirk a couple of times, though, so I could update him on what happened, but hadn't heard back from him.

I dug through my purse—a Tory Burch T-tote seemed appropriate for a stakeout—came up with a pen and sales receipt to write on, and jotted some notes.

Somebody had stolen my identity and concocted an elaborate scheme to steal a huge chunk of Pike Warner's money. Who would do that? And why would they target me?

I put two big stars beside both of those questions because I had no answers for them, then moved on.

Those fraudulent vendor folders were already in the file cabinet at my desk on my first day, so someone had put them in there. Someone intended to defraud Pike Warner. Someone had set me up.

Mrs. Drexler hadn't liked me from the very start. That first day I'd gotten a sink-or-swim impression from her.

Had she tried to get rid of me?

A little tingle raced up my spine. Oh my God. What if I

could pin the fraud and embezzlement on Mrs. Drexler, and the murder on Rita? Wouldn't that be just the coolest thing?

I decided to call Kirk again. Perhaps he could give me some incriminating info, like maybe Mrs. Drexler had quit her job suddenly and moved to the Cayman Islands, or something.

I found my cell phone and called Kirk, but his voice mail came on again. I really needed to talk to him. According to my watch, another five minutes had somehow chugged by. After nine now. Pike Warner was open.

I hated calling the office. Wanda would answer the phone, then transfer me to Beth, Kirk's bitch-ass secretary. Both would want to know my name, and once I'd given it, they'd probably hang up on me, then talk about me to all the other secretaries in the break room.

But who said I had to give my own name?

I phoned the office, and when Wanda asked who was calling, I replied, "Sarah Covington from Holt's corporate office." She transferred me immediately.

Beth sounded a little more guarded, and I wondered if she had caller ID and knew it was really me. But she didn't sound suspicious when I gave Sarah's name again.

"Mr. Keegan is unavailable," Beth said, as if this were a normal, routine part of her daily work.

Unavailable? Kirk was unavailable? At a time like this?

Of course, in secretary-speak, "unavailable" could mean anything, from he was in court, to taking a leak. But how could Kirk be unavailable *now*? When I needed him?

"I'll have him phone you, Miss Covington," Beth said.

No, this can't be happening. It can't.

Beth said something else but I just hung up and threw my head back. I absolutely have to talk to Kirk. What am I going to do—

Oh my God.

I sat up straight in my seat. A car was in Craig's driveway alongside the Blazer. An old Toyota with the hatch-back up; grocery bags were piled inside. When did that get here? And, jeez, the garage door was open. Who opened it?

Craig walked out of the garage, looking a little frazzled. I ducked down in my seat. He loaded up his arms with the grocery bags and went into the garage again.

Craig was at the grocery store? I'd been sitting here for over two hours, watching his house, waiting for him to go somewhere, and all along he wasn't even here?

I'm really bad at this surveillance thing.

But I wasn't going to let this whole morning be wasted—plus, I couldn't bear to sit in this car another minute. I grabbed the disguise I'd assembled this morning—I don't think Jack wore a disguise, I'll have to ask him—and put it on: Nike cap and sunglasses, which nicely complemented the jogging attire I'd worn. I got out of the car.

My muscles screamed. I was stiff and sore, and I really had to pee now, so I started walking briskly down the street, as if I were readying myself for a jog. I kept my gaze glued to Craig's house. There were more bags of groceries in the back of the Toyota. He'd come for them any minute.

At the entrance to his driveway I dropped down near the back bumper of his Blazer, and retied my shoe while I got a good look inside his garage.

Nothing. No dead bodies wrapped in plastic, no marijuana plants growing under heat lamps, no bloody hacksaws hanging from the Peg-Board over his work bench. Just usual garage stuff. A bicycle with a missing wheel, shelves of dusty boxes, a toolbox, a fertilizer spreader, plastic bags of purses, gardening tools—

Purses?

I sprang to my feet, then remembered that I was on a covert operation, and ducked down again.

I craned my neck, looking into the garage, thinking

maybe I was mistaken. But no, those were handbags. Two big plastic bags of them sitting on the workbench. One of the bags had turned over and several had spilled out, each wrapped in cellophane. Gucci totes and satchels. Prada clutches.

Oh my God, Craig had stolen those purses from Holt's. He'd stolen them and he was going to—

No, wait. Something was wrong here. I squinted into the garage, homing in on the bags' detailing.

Knockoffs.

They were counterfeit bags, just like the ones Marcie and I had bought at the Fashion District for our purse party. I even recognized the black plastic bags with the self-adhesive handles attached to them. Why on earth would Craig have dozens of faux handbags in his garage?

Deep inside the garage I heard the connecting door to the house open. Craig was coming back. I took off down the street, away from my car so as not to draw attention, jogging slowly but thinking hard.

Then it hit me.

Oh, my God. He'd stolen my purse party idea. Craig had heard in Holt's that I was selling faux bags. That's why he'd made up those lies about me, told them to Jeanette, tried to get me fired. That rat-bastard had wanted to get rid of me so I wouldn't find out that he'd jacked my new business venture.

Livid, I jogged back to my car. This didn't prove Craig was a murderer, but I wasn't done investigating him. Not even close.

As if my day hadn't been bad enough, now I had to go to my mom's house. She'd asked me a couple of times to bring her the paperwork for the Edible Elegance food bouquets she donated at the fund-raiser, and I couldn't put it off any longer.

My cell phone rang as I was driving east on the 210 freeway. Jack Bishop's name popped up on the caller ID, which boosted my spirits a little.

"That Hasselhoff scumbag dropped his suit," Jack said when I answered.

I heard car noises in the background and realized he was driving too. I glanced in the rearview mirror, thinking maybe he was trailing me again. He wasn't. Darn it.

"So you owe me one," I told him.

"Ready to collect?" Jack asked, in that deep, mellow voice that always gave me a warm chill.

"I'll let you know," I said.

"What's up with Craig Matthews? You find the guy?"

A bolt of anger shot through me, as I remembered this morning. But I wasn't going into the details of my purse party business with Jack.

"It was nothing," I said, then realized there was something else I could ask him about. "Have you seen Kirk Keegan around the office? I really need to talk to him. I've called him a half dozen times, or something, and I haven't heard back."

Jack paused for a moment, then said, "I'll check into it."

"Guess that means I owe you again," I said.

"That's the way I like it," he said, then hung up.

I tossed my cell phone into the passenger seat and felt myself smile for the first time today. Jack always popped up at crazy times, just when I needed him. Like he knew, somehow. And no matter how things turned out with Pike Warner, I'd always have my friendship—or whatever it was—with Jack to thank for it, since that's where we met.

I changed lanes and realized I'd slowed down a little—I was barely doing ten miles an hour over the speed limit—thinking that, really, I had Kirk to thank for it too. I wouldn't have gotten my job at the firm if it hadn't been for that chance meeting with Kirk at the club that night, if he hadn't recommended me for the job, set things up with HR. Even though nothing romantic had ever happened between the two of us, we'd had some fun times together, meeting for drinks. I'd seen him at the office occasionally, even though he was usually too busy to talk. I guess it was fitting that I'd seen him outside the accounting department that last day, just before Mrs. Drexler called me into her office and told me—

Hang on.

I whipped around an SUV, driving faster as my thoughts sped up.

Maybe that chance meeting with Kirk at the club wasn't just chance, after all. What if he'd been looking for someone like me? Someone—

My stomach started to feel really icky as the scenario played out in my mind. Kirk had gotten me the job. He'd been in the accounting department the first morning I'd reported for work—I'd been so happy to see a friendly face that day—and he'd been there again on my last day.

Oh my God. Kirk set me up.

He'd gotten me hired, slipped those fraudulent vendor files into my cabinet, then taken them out when he learned—probably through his friend in HR—that I was about to be canned. He'd been with me at the club the night my purse was stolen. He could have set that up too, then used my ID—with the help of an accomplice who looked vaguely like my DMV photo—to open that account at the Golden State Bank and Trust.

But why me? Why had Kirk singled me out? What was it about me that made him think he could get away with it?

Because I was stupid.

The realization sickened me, but I knew it was true.

He'd seen me at the club—maybe he'd been watching me for a while, since I go there often, and I didn't realize it—and he'd figured out that I was smart enough to get the job at Pike Warner, but not smart enough to suspect him of any wrongdoing, or figure out that he'd embezzled funds from the firm, using me for cover. Too consumed with partying, clothes, handbags—not that there's anything wrong with them—to be aware of what was going on.

Sarah Covington flashed in my head. So did Detective Shuman's girlfriend. Kirk Keegan would *never* have targeted one of them.

I was feeling really sick now. What the hell was wrong with me? How could I let myself get into this fix?

Now I was doubly sick because I realized I was at my mom's house. I parked in the circular drive beside a Mercedes I didn't recognize, and dragged myself out of the car. Mom had company. But that was okay. I could drop off the papers for her accountant and get out before she even knew I was there.

As I crossed the driveway the front door opened and a young woman walked out. Wow, she was gorgeous. Not just pretty, or beautiful, but stunning. Tall, great shape, blond. Hair, makeup, nails, everything was perfect. She obviously spent every waking moment on her appearance.

And my hair was in a ponytail and I was wearing sweats.

My day just keeps getting better.

We exchanged a polite smile as we passed and I went into the house. Mom was in the living room, off to my right, standing at the window looking out.

Obviously, it wasn't me she'd been watching.

"I brought those papers from the fund-raiser," I said, and tossed them on the end table, thinking I could get away quick.

Mom didn't answer, just gazed outside, shaking her head with sadness.

"It's such a shame," she said and sighed deeply.

I didn't ask what she was talking about, but that never

stops my mom from telling me. She turned away from the window.

"That was Claudia Gray," Mom said with such gravity I thought maybe Claudia had cancer or something.

Her name finally registered. Claudia was a pageant contestant. Mom was in a group—or coven, as I like to think of it—of former beauty queens who mentored and sponsored rising stars of the pageant world. I'd known Claudia for years but rarely saw her.

"I was suspicious of Maxine," Mom said, arching one perfectly waxed brow, "so I did a little investigating on my own."

I wasn't in the mood for one of Mom's connect-the-dots conversations. Not that it mattered, of course.

"Claudia ended it." Mom was clearly awed by Claudia's courage, as if she'd taken down a terrorist cell knowing full well she might break a nail. "After months together, she called it off. Not that I blame her, of course."

Okay, here was a big chunk of gossip that, normally, I'd jump into with both feet. But my life was falling apart, I was questioning everything I'd done for the past four years, I was up to my eyeballs in two different criminal cases, I was flat broke, I didn't have a boyfriend, and I really didn't care about someone else's problem.

Mom, however, didn't pick up on that.

"He was consumed by his work," Mom said, completely baffled. "Constant interruptions, rushing off for meetings, always something *important* to handle."

"I have to go now, Mom."

"Claudia would always have been second in his life, and she knew it. So she broke it off."

"I put the papers for the accountant on the table," I said, easing toward the door.

"He was slumming." She narrowed her eyes. "Completely taken with some little . . . thing . . . some salesclerk."

That hit a nerve. I guess I was just ready for a fight, or something, because I said, "So, what's wrong with a salesclerk? They're hardworking people, and they put up with a lot of crap, for not much money, from customers who think they can treat them like dirt."

"But—"

"I know a lot of salesclerks, Mom, and most every one of them is honest, and friendly, and decent."

Stunned, Mom said, "But I only asked about Claudia because of you."

Now I had no clue what Mom was talking about.

"At the fund-raiser," she said. "You talked to him. You asked me if he had a girlfriend and I told you I would . . ."

A roaring noise in my brain blocked out Mom's words. My heart hammered in my chest, then beat its way up to my ears.

Ty. She was talking about Ty. And Claudia—gorgeous, beautiful, perfectly groomed, shapely, toned, tanned, blond Claudia—had been dating him.

And I'd been stupid enough to think he might be interested in *me*.

I couldn't take it. I headed for the door.

In a stunning turn of events, Mom followed me. I could see she was upset, but I didn't have it in me to say anything to try and make her feel better.

"Haley, please," Mom said. "I didn't mean to imply that this clerk, whoever she is, might not be of some consequence. Ada met her and, I heard, liked her very much. Claimed she had spirit, and—"

"I've got to go, Mom."

I hurried out of the door, jumped in my car, and raced down the driveway, feeling like the biggest idiot on the planet. Handsome, successful, wealthy Ty Cameron, who could have any woman he wanted—including Claudia Gray, apparently—might be interested in me. How stupid of me.

I hit the freeway entrance ramp and cut across two lanes of traffic. All I could see was the mental image of me, looking idiotic—again. Just like everything else that had gone on in the past couple of weeks. Just like—

Wait.

I cut back across to the slow lane as the rest of my conversation with Mom surfaced in my memory. Ty was completely taken by—translation: hot after—a salesclerk. Someone his grandmother Ada had met. Someone she thought had spirit.

Oh my God. *Oh my God.*

I swerved onto the shoulder and hit the brakes. My right fender scraped the retaining wall as I slid to a stop. I hopped up and down in the seat.

That's me.

Ty's hot after me.

CHAPTER 25

Screaming. Giggling. Whoops of delight. Chatter. A little pushing. Some grabbing. One quick tug-of-war. And—oh my God—this purse party was fabulous.

In the big conference room at Marcie's office building we'd filled the long table with our faux handbags and wallets for the lunch-hour party. These women had gone wild. They loved the bags! And Marcie and I were raking in the bucks.

It was over pretty quickly—the women still had to eat—and I was feeling like a real entrepreneur.

"We're doing this again," Marcie said, as we packed up the few bags that didn't sell.

"You bet," I said. "My friend Grace at the store, she wants to have a party. She knows about fifteen people who will come."

"Cool," Marcie said.

We hauled everything down to Marcie's mom's Pilot and she drove me to my apartment. I kept a few of the bags to show to Grace, then rushed inside to change; I was covering Bella's shift in Housewares this afternoon while she was at the hair show.

I felt sort of covert, coming in today at 2:00 p.m., instead of my usual evening shift. Technically, no one—except Bella and me—knew I was supposed to be working now. My name wasn't on the schedule. She'd mentioned to her department supervisor that she'd gotten someone to cover her shift, but the woman who ran housewares had been smelling fabric dye in the linens for a long time now, and I thought maybe she'd lost some crucial brain cells.

So, after I punched in, I saw no reason not to abuse the situation. I headed for the customer service booth.

"Are you ready to book a purse party?" I asked Grace, as she waited on a customer.

I expected her usual bright smile, but got a frown instead.

"Oh yeah, the purse party." Grace took a breath. "You should know, Haley, that your idea was taken. I heard in the break room that there's a party already set for tomorrow."

Craig. That rat-weasel. I *knew* he'd stolen my idea. And now he was stealing my customers—right here in Holt's.

I wanted to have it out with Craig, but not on the sales floor. The stockroom. I'd wait until he went into the stockroom. But I didn't want to take a chance that I'd miss him.

I could hang out in the security office. Yeah, I could do that. Nobody really knew I was here today. I could watch the monitors and see when he went in—

Wait a minute.

"Haley, are you okay?" Grace asked. "I don't blame you for being pissed."

I was plenty mad, all right, but something else had taken over my thoughts.

When I'd looked at the stock room surveillance tape at my apartment, desperate to pin this murder on Craig, I'd figured he couldn't have done it because the video showed Richard going into the stockroom after Craig was already in there. Craig hadn't followed him in.

But maybe I had it backward. Maybe Richard had followed Craig. Richard might have been in the security office spying on that whore-bitch Glenna Webb, seen Craig go in, and followed. That made sense if it had been

Richard and Craig whom Evelyn had overheard arguing earlier that evening.

"I'll still buy a purse from you, Haley," Grace said. "And I know some other people who will too."

What had they been arguing about? And why had they taken it into the stockroom? Was it something personal?

Probably not, since Craig's wife had cancer and wouldn't have been available for what was, apparently, Richard's favorite sport: screwing married women. So that left business, something to do with Holt's, and Richard's second-favorite sport: clawing his way up the corporate ladder.

"I'd like to buy a couple of purses," Grace said, forcing a smile. "And my mom might want to give some as Christmas gifts. Haley?"

So if it wasn't something personal the two of them had argued over, it had to have been something to do with the store. Was Richard trying to dig up dirt on Craig to make himself look valuable to the company? Craig didn't seem a likely candidate. The man worked constantly. If he wasn't on the sales floor he was in the stockroom. I'd seen him back there a number of times moving the luggage around, getting it ready for the returns truck to pick it up and—

What the . . . ?

For days now, I'd scrolled through merchandise on the inventory computer looking for info to either restock an item, or give a customer a refund. But never—not once—had I noticed a piece of luggage marked for return.

"Haley?" Grace called.

I ignored her, went to the inventory computer, and scrolled through everything. Not a single piece of luggage had been taken out of the inventory. Not one. But I'd seen Craig readying it to load onto the returns truck. Why would he do that? Unless—

Oh my God. Craig was stealing luggage.

Stealing luggage?

Why would anybody steal luggage? It's big, bulky, hard

to move around. It's hardly a high-demand item. It's Holt's house brand, not designer. I can't imagine there's some luggage black market out there. Even if you took it to a swap meet, or sold it on eBay, you wouldn't get enough money for it to risk your job. And certainly, if you were going to steal from a department store, there were bigger, more profitable items you could take.

Still, I needed to tell someone. I didn't want to talk to Jeanette, so I decided to see if Ty was here today.

"Haley, just don't be too mad," Grace said.

I realized that she'd been talking to me and I'd been so wrapped up in my own thoughts I hadn't been listening. But whatever she'd said must have been important. She looked worried.

"Look, I know you two have had your differences," Grace said, trying to sound calm. "But just because Rita is having a purse party doesn't mean you can't have one too."

I froze.

Rita? Did she say Rita was having a purse party?

"Yeah," Grace said, "she's a bitch for taking your idea, but—"

"Rita stole my idea?" I asked, feeling my blood pressure shoot up. "*Rita?*"

"Well, yeah," Grace said, and drew back a little.

Oh! That bitch! I hate her.

But I don't have time to deal with her now.

I stormed down the hallway looking for Ty. When I didn't find him in any of the offices, I went into the security office. He stood in front of the video monitors, looking as if he'd been expecting me—which I guess he had, since he'd been watching the screens.

"What's wrong?" he asked.

Note, he picked up on my *spirit* right away and had the courage to ask. I like that in a man.

I could have blathered on for a half hour about Rita and my purse party business, but instead I told him about Craig.

"I've seen him getting luggage ready for the returns truck," I said. "But none of it's been marked for return in the inventory computer."

"Maybe it's an oversight," Ty suggested. "Maybe Craig just hasn't entered it into the computer yet."

I shook my head. "The merchandise is supposed to be scanned as it's loaded into the truck, taking it out of the inventory."

Ty pressed his lips together, thinking for a few minutes. Then he said, "Do you think Craig is stealing luggage?"

"That's what it looks like."

He thought for another minute. "Why would anybody steal luggage?"

"Beats the hell out of me," I said. Then it hit me. "Unless—"

But I didn't get to finish my thought. Behind Ty, on the video monitor, I saw Julie, the credit greeter, blast through the stockroom doors near the intimates department. Her arms were up and, even without audio, I knew she was screaming.

Ty turned, saw it too, and we bolted out of the security office. We intercepted her near the children's clothing department.

She screamed incoherently. I was ready to bitch-slap her—just to get her attention, of course—when Ty grasped her arm.

"What happened?" he demanded, in that commanding voice men have.

Julie panted for a few seconds, then said, "Evelyn! It's Evelyn! I saw her in the stockroom! She's—she's dead!"

I shoved past Julie and raced into the stockroom. For some reason, I thought Evelyn would be upstairs, like

Richard had been, but I found her at the foot of the staircase. She lay on her side, one leg bent the wrong way, blood coursing down her face from a cut on her forehead.

My stomach heaved. My eyes welled.

Not Evelyn. No, not Evelyn.

Then she moaned. Oh, thank God. She wasn't dead.

Ty rushed past me and knelt beside her, feeling her pulse. I dropped to my knees and took Evelyn's hand.

"Looks like she took a hard fall," Ty said, glancing up at the tall, steep staircase. "Julie's calling 9-1-1."

"Hang in there, Evelyn," I said, talking kind of loud, for some reason. "Help will be here in a few minutes."

Evelyn roused a little, looking lost and bewildered. She mumbled something.

"You fell down the stairs. But it's okay," I told her. It was stupid, but people with absolutely no real knowledge of a situation always say it, so I said it. "You're going to be fine."

Her lips moved. I thought she was trying to tell me something, so I leaned down.

". . . locker," she whispered.

I guess she wanted me to get her purse from her locker to take to the hospital with her, so I said, "Okay. I'll get your purse. No problem."

She grimaced and shook her head. "Yours . . ."

"My purse?" I asked, trying to figure out what she meant. Then I realized. "You want me to come with you?"

Evelyn managed to shake her head, and I could see it caused her more pain, but she looked determined to speak. I leaned down until my ear was at her mouth.

"Your . . . locker," she mumbled. "Pushed . . ."

I sat up. My blood ran cold. I looked down at Evelyn and saw that her wild-eyed look wasn't from pain, but fear.

"She said she was pushed," I told Ty.

He lurched to his feet and started searching the area. I

stayed at Evelyn's side, watching, listening hard. A number of employees rushed in. Somebody ripped open a Candies comforter set and spread it over Evelyn. Someone else grabbed a couple of Egyptian cotton towels and eased them under her head. The loading dock door rolled up and I heard sirens approach.

The guys from the ambulance took over, but I didn't want to let go of Evelyn's hand. They were very gentle with her, attached some tubes, got her leg braced, and put her on a stretcher.

"I'll come to the hospital with you," I told her, as they started to wheel her away.

Evelyn shook her head frantically. "Your locker . . ."

I didn't know if she was delusional, or confused from the fall, but I stayed behind when the ambulance pulled away. Ty came up next to me and put his arm around my shoulder. It felt nice. I leaned against him. That felt nicer.

We walked into the store. Along the way, the employees asked about Evelyn. Everyone seemed concerned, as if they genuinely cared. Shannon was already taking up a collection for flowers.

Ty's cell phone rang—it was probably that Sarah Covington—and he went into the office and closed the door. I guess he was done comforting me; I wondered if his old girlfriend Claudia Gray had felt this way too.

I debated, for a minute, about what to do, then headed for the break room. That girl who'd lost thirty pounds was in there eating—finally!—a bag of chips. I guess news of Evelyn's fall had gotten to her. She deserved them, no doubt about it, but after my own failed improved-diet-and-exercise plan, I couldn't let her do it. An intervention was in order.

"Don't do this to yourself." I grabbed the chips off the table. She didn't fight me. I ate them myself as I went to my locker, just to remove her temptation, of course.

I couldn't imagine why Evelyn wanted me to come here,

but I needed to check it out. I opened my locker. Inside, atop my purse, were several folded sheets of paper that had been slipped through the slot in the door.

"Oh my God . . . ," I mumbled. It was the employee work schedules for the day of Richard's murder that had gone missing. Evelyn must have taken them. But why? Why would she want to cover for a murderer?

The other paper was an official Holt's form. An inventory request. I'd never seen it before and I didn't know exactly what it meant. But I knew who did.

I left the break room and went into the office. Ty was on the phone. I couldn't tell if he was talking to Sarah or not. I paced around, huffing irritably until he hung up.

"What's this?" I asked, shoving the form at him.

He read it over. "Where did you get this?"

"What is it?" I asked again. I was in no mood.

"We do inventory once a year, unless there's a problem, or a suspected problem," Ty said. He tapped the paper. "This is a special request for an inventory of this year's Christmas merchandise, the designer handbags, to take place in mid-December."

"And it was requested by Richard," I said. "On the day he was murdered."

Ty looked at the form again, but I knew he wasn't really seeing it. He was thinking—the same thing as me.

"Richard thought Craig might steal the designer bags. He was probably suspicious of all the game systems that were supposedly shoplifted last year," I said. "Richard was overheard arguing with someone the night of his murder. I'll bet it was Craig."

"Richard was arguing with someone? How do you know that?" he asked, surprised.

"On the surveillance tape, Richard went into the stockroom after Craig."

"When did you see the surveillance tape?"

"He must have seen him on the monitor, followed him

in, confronted him," I said, imagining the scene in my mind. "Craig's wife has cancer. He's desperate for money."

"Craig's wife has cancer?" Ty asked.

"That's probably why Evelyn didn't tell anybody what she knew," I realized.

"What's Evelyn got to do with this?"

Everything, I realized. On the night of Richard's murder, when I'd come out of the stockroom and told her I'd found Richard's body in there, the first thing she'd asked was where Craig was. I thought she was just worried because he was her supervisor, but as I'd suspected before, there was more to it than that.

"When I phoned the police and everybody to tell them about Richard, I caught Evelyn going through his desk," I said. "She must have been looking for the inventory request form. She probably thought it might incriminate Craig, and she felt sorry for him because of his wife. But she must have changed her mind about him, because she warned me to stay away from him, after he tried to get me fired."

"Craig tried to get you fired?" Ty asked.

I huffed. "Don't you know *anything* that goes on in your own store?"

I guess Ty didn't want to answer that because he said, "If you think Craig intended to steal the designer handbags, where's the proof?"

"In Craig's garage."

Now Ty was looking a little annoyed.

"You've been in Craig's garage?" he asked.

"He's got knockoff purses from the Fashion District in there. Dozens of them," I said. "Craig smuggled the real bags out of the store inside the luggage, with the help of the returns truck driver, of course. They probably have a store connection somewhere who bought them."

"And to balance the inventory, Craig substituted the fake bags," Ty added.

"He had to. He couldn't get away with that *shoplifting* excuse, like last year with the game systems," I said.

"Handbags would be easier. No serial numbers, and proving the purses were fakes wouldn't be easy."

"Only I nearly screwed that up," I realized, "when I rattled off my extensive knowledge of handbags, hoping I could work in that department. No wonder he'd told me to get my purses right away, he knew I'd recognize the fakes. And no wonder he'd tried to get rid of me by getting me fired."

It all made sense, perfect sense. Ty and I just stood there for a moment, digesting it. Then Ty said, "Where's Craig?"

Good question. I hadn't seen him in the stockroom, or out on the sales floor.

"I'm going to call the police," Ty said. "You stay here."

He picked up the phone and I headed out the door.

Craig must have known Evelyn suspected him of something. They worked closely together. She knew everything that went on in that department. Maybe he'd been waiting for just the right time to try and get rid of her. So why had he picked today?

Coincidence? Maybe. Or perhaps it was because he assumed that, as usual, I wasn't working. He had no way of knowing I was covering Bella's shift in Housewares—where I might actually have gone at some point this afternoon—so, for all he knew, I wouldn't be in the store until later in the day. Maybe he'd planned it that way. Maybe he'd taken a chance that I wouldn't have an alibi, and the police, already suspecting me in Richard's murder, might think I'd gone after Evelyn too.

It was a guess, speculation, on my part. But the one thing I was sure of was that Craig had intended to kill Evelyn when he'd pushed her down those steps.

I circled the store, but didn't see Craig. His Chevy Blazer was in the parking lot, when I peeked out the door, so he was here somewhere. The stockroom.

I went inside. It was quiet, just as it had been the night of Richard's murder. I guess none of the other employees wanted to come back here, after Evelyn's fall. Not that I blamed them.

Slowly, I made my way between the towering shelves of merchandise, looked in the janitor's closet, behind the pile of merchandise awaiting the returns truck. Nothing. At the foot of the stairs, I stopped. Evelyn's blood had left a dark spot on the concrete. I stepped around it and went up the steps.

I couldn't imagine that Craig would still be in the stockroom. If he had good sense, he'd have left. But I suppose that someone who steals from his employer, murders one person, and pushes another down the stairs can't be accused of having good sense.

At the top, I paused. Richard had been murdered up here. Evelyn had been pushed from here.

Why am I here? What am I doing? Am I crazy, or what?

Better to let the police handle it, I decided, and started back down the stairs. But then I heard a noise coming from the aisles of shelves off to my right. I scampered back up the steps. I just wanted to know if Craig was here. Just catch a glimpse of him. That way, I could tell the police where to find him when they showed up.

I crept forward and stole a quick glance around the corner of a big shelving unit. The aisle was long and the shelves were packed with merchandise. No Craig. I tiptoed to the next unit and did the same thing. Still no Craig. I went to the next one and—oh my God! Craig!

I jumped back. Did he see me? I don't know. I peeked again and—jeez, he's coming straight toward me.

I backtracked and ran down the next aisle. Craig was running too. I heard his shoes pounding on the concrete. He turned the corner and ran down the aisle after me.

He had murder in his eyes. But I wasn't going to be his next victim.

I yanked dozens of boxes of Christmas ornaments off the shelves to block his path. I had to fend him off. I couldn't run to the staircase. If he caught me there, he'd throw me down, just like he'd done Evelyn.

I heaved big boxes of pots and pans at him, personal massagers, foot baths—oh, jeez, those are nice, I could use one of them. He kept coming, jumping over, sidestepping everything I threw at him. I ran backward, grabbing everything off the shelves I could get my hands on. Picture frames, photo albums, candles. Craig batted them in midair and kept coming. Wreaths, Santa and snowmen door-hangers. I'm trying to fight off a murderer with Christmas decorations. Jeez, why can't Holt's carry guns?

Luggage—at last, something substantial. I heaved a nested set of four cases at him, then two duffel bags, then grabbed purses.

Wait. Oh my God, these are Prada totes. I can't throw Prada at a murderer.

Craig stops. Maybe he's overwhelmed by Prada too? No, he's looking past me. I glance back and see Ty. Suddenly, he looks taller, and broader, and meaner than I've ever seen him look.

Craig must have thought the same, because he turned and ran back down the aisle. Ty took off after him, sailing over the clutter of merchandise with ease. I didn't know he was athletic. Wow, that's so hot.

I went the other way, around the corner to the next aisle, and saw the two of them running. Craig was heading for the stairs. I followed and got there just as they clattered down the steps. Craig had a head start but Ty was younger, stronger, and faster.

He caught Craig at the bottom, yanked him around. Craig took a swing at Ty's head. I screamed as I ran down the stairs after them. Ty ducked, tackled Craig in the gut, and forced him backward into the jungle of mannequins.

Craig went down with a crash, taking a half dozen stiff,

naked women with him. I dashed to the panty hose, ripped open two packages, grabbed Craig's foot, and tied it to a headless torso. Ty jumped in and wrapped Craig's wrist to a detached arm. I ran back for more panty hose, but stopped. Detectives Shuman and Madison were coming through the loading dock door.

I'd been sitting on the stockroom steps for a while now, too exhausted to get up. The detectives handcuffed Craig and took him away a long time ago. They'd been asking questions, filling out forms, doing all the things homicide detectives do. Ty was on his feet, still, handling everything. He's so good at stuff like this. With Ty, you'd never have to worry he couldn't take care of something.

From the sound of things, I guessed this ordeal was over.

"So now you believe that I didn't kill Richard?" I called.

I flung the question at Detective Madison. It was totally unnecessary, since Craig had started blubbering and confessed everything as soon as Shuman snapped on the cuffs, but I wanted to hear Madison say the words.

He hitched up his pants and gave me a sour, begrudging look.

"Looks like you're not guilty," he grumbled, "of *this* crime anyway."

Bastard.

Detective Shuman shot me a little grin, and the two of them left.

Finally, Ty came over and sat by me on the stairs. He sat close. He smelled really good, like cologne and sweat. It made me want to get sweaty with him.

But I guess he had something else on his mind.

"You should have told me about everything that was going on in the store," Ty said, sounding a little hurt, a little annoyed.

I couldn't blame him. I'd have felt the same way.

"Okay, I'll keep you fully informed of every criminal plot I uncover from now on," I promised.

He grinned, just a little. Ty has the cutest grin ever.

"Is there anything else you want to tell me?" he asked.

I wanted to tell him that I was really hot for him, that he seemed like a great guy and I'd love to get to know him better, but I don't think that's exactly what he had in mind.

"I don't have a puppy named Pancake," I said.

"Really?" he asked, sounding all dramatic, like he'd known it all along.

"And I don't have an uncle with a body shop who was going to fix my fender," I said.

"No kidding," Ty declared. He'd known that all along too, obviously. "Anything else?"

There were about a million things Ty didn't know about me, but I wasn't in the mood to tell him. Now, or maybe never.

"That's it," I said, trying to sound light and breezy.

Ty looked serious for a moment. "Don't you want to tell me about your job at Pike Warner?"

I gasped.

"And how you got fired?" he asked.

"I was on administrative leave!"

"How about the fraud and embezzlement? And those accounts at the GSB&T?"

Stunned, I just stared at him. He knew everything.

Oh, crap.

CHAPTER 26

It was a Ferragamo day.

Fine leather satchel, minimal trim. Classy. Businesslike. Competent. In-charge.

Which was sort of the way I felt the next afternoon as I paused on the sidewalk outside the building that housed Pike Warner's offices. I had on a Christian Dior suit my mom had bought me for my second day of work here, and I'd put my hair in an updo. No pumps or sensible shoes for me, though. I wore Kenneth Cole stilettos.

Surprisingly, I hadn't lain awake half the night worrying about what I'd say to the two senior partners when I got up to sixteen. I hadn't called ahead for an appointment either. I knew they'd see me.

What had kept me tossing and turning last night was Ty. Right there on the stockroom steps he'd told me that he knew everything that was going on at Pike Warner and the GSB&T. I guess his lawyer and the vice president who'd handled the Holt's Department Store banking for decades had no problem with telling him everything he wanted to know; paying thousands in fees and services per year has that effect on people. And since I wasn't their client they saw no conflict of interest, just a concern that they'd lose Holt's business if they didn't cooperate.

It bugged me some that Ty had gone behind my back,

asking about me, but since he already knew so much, I filled him in on the details. Most of them anyway.

I'd told him I was coming here today to confront the Pike Warner senior partners about everything, and he'd wished me luck. No offer to help—which I wouldn't have taken—no suggestion of wild sex on the king-size Laura Ashley bed-in-a-bag sets, which I might have taken him up on. No nothing.

I guess he had a meeting to go to, or something.

But that was okay because I was going to handle things today all by myself. I was going to make my demands, thereby taking the first steps toward my new life. Then I was going to college. Really. Get a degree that would qualify me to do something important. And stop wasting my life.

I'd spent a little time last night wondering about Kirk's plan to embezzle money from the firm. He probably never counted on the audit uncovering the scheme, but even then, he knew Pike Warner wouldn't dig deep enough to discover he was behind it. He knew they'd let it go rather than damage their reputation.

What Kirk probably never counted on was that I would figure out what he'd done. Maybe that didn't matter to him either, since there was nothing I could do about it; I had no way to prove my innocence.

I could understand Kirk's impatience, not wanting to wait to earn the kind of money he craved. Maybe he'd gotten caught up in the atmosphere at Pike Warner. Expensive clothes, handbags, jewelry, cars, everywhere you looked. I'd gotten caught up in it too, and had the credit card bills to prove it.

But that was my old life. I was moving on from there.

I caught a glimpse of my reflection in the glass doors as I walked into the lobby. Wow, I looked great. Those two old geezers up on sixteen didn't stand a chance.

Chin up, gaze steady, I crossed the lobby with only a few butterflies tingling in my belly. The security guard who escorted me out of the building the last day I worked here gave me the evil eye, but I shot back my I'm-better-than-you eyebrow bob and he looked away. Wow, I was exuding confidence, self-assurance, and everybody better get out of my way because I was—

"Haley?"

I whirled around and saw Ty. And I fell completely apart. My knees shook, my hands trembled, my heart was pounding, and every intelligent thought flew out of my brain. I was so glad to see him my insides turned to mush.

Oh my God, I think that means I love him.

Ty gave me that little grin and he walked over looking devastatingly handsome in a gray Hugo Boss suit, and carrying a briefcase.

"I was afraid you'd changed your mind," he said.

He'd been here? Waiting? For me?

"I wouldn't miss this for anything," I said, surprised that the words came out in the right order.

"I just heard from the hospital," Ty said. "Evelyn is going to recover. Lots of rehab, but she'll be fine."

I was glad to hear that, and pleased that Ty cared enough about one of his employees to check; I'd go by the hospital and visit Evelyn later.

Ty looked me up and down, and his grin turned into a smile. "Ted and Gerald won't know what hit them."

Okay, I was guessing those were the senior partners. Maybe I'd pass on Ty's regards to Teddy and Jerry when I got up there.

"Do you want me to come with you?" he asked.

Yes, yes, yes. I wanted him to come with me. To stand next to me, to give me courage. But I couldn't let him.

"I have to do this myself," I said.

Ty nodded. "What are you asking for?"

"I want an investigation. I want my name cleared." And I wanted Pike Warner to know that I was *somebody.*

Ty opened his briefcase and handed me a videocassette.

"This might help convince them. I got it from the GSB&T. It's the surveillance tape showing Keegan and a female—not you, obviously—in the bank the day the accounts were opened."

I gasped. Oh my God. I'd intended to go up to sixteen and threaten to go public if Pike Warner didn't investigate the embezzlement charges and clear my name. I'd thought the prospect of all the negative publicity they'd receive would be enough to motivate them to get moving. But now I didn't need that. I had evidence.

"This should help too," Ty said. From his briefcase he pulled a Louis Vuitton organizer and handed it to me.

Oh my God. My Louis Vuitton organizer. The one I'd been dying for, willing to kill for.

I took it reverently between both hands.

"How did you know?" I whispered, unable to take my eyes off of it.

"You mentioned it a couple of times."

I did? And he remembered it? Jeez, I'd better pay more attention to what I tell him.

I slid the videocassette into my Ferragamo bag and tucked the organizer under my arm—so everyone could see it and be jealous.

"You look great," Ty said.

I felt great. My cheeks were a little warm, my outfit was hot, and my accessories were to die for. What more could I want?

Ty.

"One more thing," he said. "After your meeting, can I take you out to celebrate?"

And finally, *finally*, my first ever, genuine, heartfelt of-course-you-can smile bloomed on my face.

We walked through the front door of Ty's apartment. A single lamp burned in the living room. We had just finished a long dinner and I had way too much wine. My head was spinning a little.

This was so perfect. Ty's place was very contemporary, very modern. He looked so handsome in the dim light. Over dinner we'd talked for hours about everything. He told me that the only reason he asked his lawyer and banker about me was that he was worried, because he cared about me, because he wanted to help. He asked if I would work for him opening the new Wallace, Inc., stores he was so excited about. And I told him that, after I got my degree, maybe I'd open my own stores and put him out of business, and he laughed, like I was the smartest woman in the world.

It was all so perfect. I was going to get my life together, I was going to be someone important, and Ty would be my boyfriend. We'd have romantic evenings. We'd talk about business. I'd study while he made dinner; then we'd feed each other strawberries and sip champagne on the balcony as the sun went down, and then—

Oh, wait. Never mind.

Ty touched my shoulder, turned me in his arms. Wow, he's really warm. Deep, masculine heat is rolling off of him. He lowers his head and kisses me. Then kisses me harder. Then—

Oh my God, this is great. I'm kissing him back, and his hands are—jeez, that feels good—and he's touching my— oh no, which bra did I wear? I can't remember. Please, please, let it be the black demi-cups. Ty doesn't seem to care. My blouse is open and his hands are—

Something is ringing. Ty stops. Now he's groping him-self. No, he's looking for his cell phone. He yanks it out of his pocket and throws it across the room.

I fling my arms around his neck. He slides his hands down to my—oh, wow, that's terrific. I loop my leg around his and—jeez, that's really—

Something else rings. Over and over. Ty ignores it. He keeps kissing me and running his hands—

Then something starts pounding. Is it my heart? No, it's the front door. Somebody is banging on the front door. They won't stop. They keep at it.

Finally, Ty spins away, jerks open the door, and roars, "*What?*"

It's Sarah Covington. Oh my God, it's Sarah Covington. She rushes inside and starts blabbing about something. Then, suddenly, she stops midsentence and looks around.

I'm standing in the middle of the living room with my hair half down, my blouse is hanging open—the red lace push-up, even better—and Ty's tie is gone, his shirt is open, and his—well, it's obvious what's going on.

Only Sarah doesn't seem to care. No embarrassment, no apology, nothing. She just starts talking about some problem with an advertising agency.

Great. I wouldn't miss this for the world. I'm standing here, staring, tapping my stiletto against the hardwood floor, and he's going to toss her out of his apartment on her skinny ass. Then he'll run back to me and we'll—

Wait. He's not tossing her out. He's listening. Now he's talking. Low, quiet. Using his business voice.

This can't be happening. It can't. Ty is leaving me standing here, looking like a complete dork, while he takes care of some problem with the company.

Claudia Gray flashed in my mind. What had Mom said was the reason she'd broken up with Ty? Because she knew she'd be always second in his life.

Was I no different?

What about my perfect life?

I buttoned my blouse. Something started ringing again, and I realized it was my phone. Good, now I had something to do other than watch Ty and Sarah confer over some huge business problem.

Jack Bishop was on the line.

"Have you seen Kirk Keegan?" he asked.

Kirk had been the furthest thing from my mind.

"No, why should I?" I asked.

"He's disappeared," Jack said. "He was called to the senior partners right after your little visit with them. He took off. Nobody's seen him since."

"So?"

"They fired him. The accounts at GSB&T are frozen. He's lost everything," Jack said.

"Yeah? Well, serves him right," I said. So Kirk might be mad at me because I'd ratted him out. What did he expect? I couldn't care less about what happened to him. He was out of my life forever.

"I heard you had your way with the old guys up on sixteen," Jack said, with a little laugh.

"I steamrolled them pretty good," I said. "I think they liked it."

"Must have," Jack agreed. "I have it on good authority that they approved a settlement for you."

A settlement? I guess with the way Pike Warner threw money around I shouldn't be surprised. And having my back pay would be great. Except for the money I'd made at the purse party and my Holt's income, I was still close to broke. I doubted the Golden State Bank and Trust would send me that credit card now.

"How do you feel about a hundred grand?" Jack asked.

My eyes popped open wider. Wow, a hundred grand. Just like that. Now I could pay for my classes and my books. I could go to school full-time. Perfect!

"I also have it on good authority that they intend to make you a counteroffer," Jack said. "You impressed them, Haley, by figuring out what Keegan did. They're going to offer you a position on the start-up team for the new office the firm is opening in San Francisco. Double your salary."

"What?"

"Think about it," Jack said. "They're going to phone you with an official offer in the morning."

Jack hung up and I just stood there, staring at the cell phone.

Oh my God. This couldn't be happening. I'd figured out what I wanted to do with my life. College. A degree. An important career. Now I had the chance to move to San Francisco, be an integral part of a new operation, at double my pay?

What should I do?

I looked across the room, and Ty was still talking to Sarah. I'd thought he would be part of my plan. And he still could be. I was crazy about him. He felt the same about me. We could talk things out.

But not now. Not with Sarah here.

I grabbed my purse, pushed my way between them, and went out the door.

"Haley!"

I heard Ty's voice and his footsteps pounding down the hallway after me. I stopped.

"Where are you going?" he asked, looking genuinely confused.

"The moment is over," I told him.

He shook his head. "Look, Haley, if you're upset about Sarah coming over, well, I'm sorry but that's just the way it is. I have a business to run. There are things I have to take care of."

He gave me that little grin of his and I just melted. We could work things out. Sure we could.

"I'll call you tomorrow," he promised.

It was dark when I got to the parking garage in Ty's building. Security lights burned. I was glad I'd brought my car instead of riding with him.

Now I was as confused as I'd ever been. What should I do? Stay here, date Ty—along with Sarah Covington and the whole Holt's organization, apparently—and go to school? Or start a new life and a new career in San Francisco?

I chirped the lock on my Honda and opened the door. Tires squealed somewhere close by; then a black car skidded to a stop at my back bumper, blocking me in. The driver's-side door opened, and across the roof of the car, I saw a man get out. Light from the security lamps caught his face.

Oh my God. Kirk Keegan.

He extended his arm and pointed his finger and thumb at me, like a gun. Then he jerked his thumb, pulling the pretend trigger. He jumped back in the car and sped away.

Oh, crap.

DATE			